A Handful of Pearls

Mary Ann Noe

Black Rose Writing | Texas

ISBN: 978-1-68513-029-9
PUBLISHED BY BLACK ROSE WRITING
www.blackrosewriting.com

Printed in the United States of America
Suggested Retail Price (SRP) $21.95

A Handful of Pearls is printed in Sabon

*As a planet-friendly publisher, Black Rose Writing does its best to eliminate unnecessary waste to reduce paper usage and energy costs, while never compromising the reading experience. As a result, the final word count vs. page count may not meet common expectations.

For my mother, Dorothy Billmeyer Hentschel,
who fed me the first line, though the rest is fiction

A Handful of Pearls

A pearl is only a pearl once it's out of its shell.
— Nigerian Proverb

Does love always form, like a pearl, around the hardened bits of life?
— Andrew Sean Greer

Chapter 1
Betty

I learned to play golf so I could smoke. I remember that clearly. St. Ingrid's Women's College had its own golf course, stretching inland like a green cashmere scarf flung along the bluff above the Mississippi River. The first tee was perched safely back from the brink, not far from the wide stone gate that opened on the far side of the college quad. In the autumn, the trees, blazing red and yellow and that unique sugar maple orange, tumbled down to the river. Always, but especially at that time of the year, the trees provided a real distraction. Our drives down the fairway were never very long off that particular tee. My friends and I were too wrapped up with finishing conversations and admiring the trees. I never resented those distractions, though. Golf wasn't what drew me outdoors anyway.

From that first tee, the course wound away from the river and in through the trees, swooping out to the far reaches of our property and back again. The farthest fairway dipped out of sight of anything, including the Jesuits who ran the men's college next door, so that part of the golf course established itself as the only safe place to do anything even remotely illegal or immoral. Other than the social position and the opportunities it gave me, smoking didn't do much for me, and I gave it up once I graduated from college. I think that's right. Smoking was not one of the defining habits of my life.

•   •   •   •   •

I put down my old photos for a moment and mindlessly render a quick sketch along the margin of my little book as I consider where to go from here. The drawing is supposed to be the long-ago me, done in quick lines and swirls. My pen returns to the lines of the page. But a glance at my "high-class doodlings," as my husband, Earl, always called them, shows my granddaughter, Em, not a self-portrait. It doesn't really surprise me, as we do look a bit alike. My sweet Em—dear Lord, I almost called her Reggie. I certainly shouldn't mix up those two. My daughter, Reggie, doesn't resemble me much, not like her daughter, Em, does. Not in looks or in personality. Reggie is impulsive, like her father. Reggie decided long ago she doesn't like me much. I hoped over the years she would come to me, but it never really happened. I'm a good listener, but she doesn't confide in me. But I am still waiting, waiting and hoping.

I guess I understand, at least a little. I nearly destroyed her, or at least, through my silence or negligence, call it what you will, I aided and abetted her predisposition to self-destruct. Maybe I can make it up somehow, with this little book. Hopefully, it will contain at least a couple pearls of wisdom.

Anyway, when I saw my granddaughter, Em, yesterday, I really let her know how she looked with that fag—yes, I know the meaning's changed—hanging off her lip. She promised to quit for sure this time. I believe her, even though she's the only grandchild that resembles me in the slightest, and I'm not talking about just the red hair. Not that either one of us is a liar, saying yes, when we know in our hearts we don't necessarily mean yes, but I know how to make people hear what they want to hear. That's always been true for me. I suspect it's true for her too.

So. Back to St. Ingrid's.

My friends and I would put on our golf skirts and head for the links, or dress up for town and a movie. One photo shows us standing, like beauty queen contestants, on the dormitory steps, right arms around our buddies' shoulders, left arms hanging gracefully. Miss Hartwig, our housemother, must have been *in absentia* that day, or we never would have gotten out without hats and gloves. As it is, there we are, frozen in time, summer dresses shifting in the light breeze, although the ripples in those pastel lawn dresses have since stiffened into black and white ridges, locked in place forever.

Now when I look in the mirror, I no longer see a flaming redhead with Michelangelo marble skin, a complexion needing to be protected from freckling and burning in the sun. I am not the slender, straight-backed young girl in demure polka dots and lace, bracketed by best friends. No, by now all those lawn dresses have disappeared into some rag bag, if they're around anymore at all. Most likely, they disintegrated into colorless threads.

I was quite a beauty in those years, if I do say so myself. I didn't think so then, but hindsight has granted me the grace to see I really was quite attractive, even if my buddies called me Carrot-top. I had a shape, a real shape, and a slender face with lovely cheekbones. I always loved my eyes. Hazel, sort of, although tending more toward green than brown. When I look at those old photos, I see I had a lot more going for me than my eyes, but of course, who sees that at the time? We all criticized our too-long legs, even though now I can see they were shapely, or our too-full lower lips, even if our boyfriends at the time called them "attractively pouty." We thought everything we had was flawed.

I retained many of the freckles accumulated in spite of wide-brimmed hats and sheer makeup. If my freckles all merged, I'd have a lovely tan.

On top of the faded freckles, now I have liver spots, and white hair frizzing like a halo around my head. Maybe I'll be mistaken for an angel, who knows? My posture is not quite queen straight, unless you compare me to England's Queen Mother. But then, she's a hundred years old, or close to it, and I still have quite a few years to catch up with her. Twenty or so, I think. Well, since honesty prevails here, sixteen. I don't need to add any more years than necessary. Besides, I still stand straighter than she does.

I can't quite understand how I got this far. I'm slowing, but I'm holding my own quite well, thank you very much. No one wants to hear a complainer.

Well, never mind. That's not where I was going with this.

This journal is my gift. Lord knows it's taken me long enough to see clearly. It's taken even longer to be able to tell anyone what I've seen. At times, I shouldn't have kept my own counsel. I should've spoken out, told what I knew, given counsel instead of keeping it for once. Given consolation, perhaps. It's time to fix all that.

But I'm getting ahead of myself.

The lawn dresses in the photo are softening in my mind, moving slowly in the invisible breeze, picking up a bit of color. Rose on Dorothy, I think. Navy there, lavender and white there.

The gray concrete steps of the dorm are wide and welcoming. The quad they lead down into is broad, deep, green, and filled with sun and trees. Someone is singing "My Buddy," accompanied by one of the big bands on the radio, and the tones drift down from an upper floor, catching in the top branches of the trees and slipping down the trunks. My favorite tree is that big sugar maple on the far side of the quad, close to the gate leading to the golf course. The tree has finally turned brilliant orange, as if waiting until the less showy oaks and hickories flared and died out before making an entrance, like a grand duchess returning from a trip abroad.

Faintly, I hear my roommate, Margaret, like the whisper of the Delphic oracle, complex and mysterious. I can hear better if I just close my eyes...

1934

"Come on, Betty!" Margaret's voice was impatient this morning. "Can you not ever be prompt and ready, all at the same time?" Every word chosen for effect.

I was sitting on the dorm steps, still pulling on my golf shoes as she stood with the bags, one draped over each shoulder. Her fringed golf shoes shifted slightly, poised to be off across the quad. She had on her plaid skirt and cashmere sweater, and looked like one of those mannequins we saw in the windows at Daytons in Minneapolis. Stunning, as always. Dressed to the nines, even though it was only for a walk on the fairways.

"You know me." I kept my voice light. "If I'm late, you'll carry both bags. It saves my lily-white shoulders the strain."

"You lazy redhead," she said, then shifted gears. "Obviously, your mind is on other things. Distracted with Jack, I suspect. Sweet on him, aren't you?" An obvious attempt to catch me by surprise.

"Margaret." I heard the impatience in my voice. We went over this before. "I can't even turn around without him breathing down my neck. How can I make any kind of rational judgment when I have absolutely no elbow room with him?" I stood up, brushed down my skirt and started across the quad for the first tee.

"What do you care? He's gorgeous. And he's sweet on you. Isn't that enough?"

That didn't deserve an answer.

"Betty." She caught up with me and lowered her voice. "Bill and I are planning on getting engaged the night of graduation."

I looked at her. Actually stopped walking and turned in shock. She took her cigarette pack out, checking to see that she would have enough to share on the farthest fairway.

"Come on, keep walking," she cautioned. "If Sister Joan sees me with these cigarettes, I'll be stuck on campus all weekend."

I picked up my feet and took my golf bag from her.

"Caught you there, didn't I? Surprised?" She smiled. "Now, I'd never tell you this, but I know you know how to keep a secret. Bill refuses to talk to my dad about it yet. Says he wants it to be our sweet little secret until at least Valentine's Day. Then he'll ask my father's permission, and we can make the Grand Announcement—" I swore she could talk in capital letters "—at my graduation party."

She could go back to Chicago and her Graduation Party with Bill. Oh, yes, that was in capital letters too, though I didn't think she felt that way. She said she was just an ordinary college girl, not a rich society daughter whose clothes and parties were envied, if not copied, all over the city. And I? Well, I truly was just a regular college girl. Yes, money was there for my education, but not for the trips to Europe, or even New York, at that stage in my life. And there was no Bill for me on the horizon, although Margaret seemed to think Jack was perfect for me. He was handsome enough, that was true, and he was going home to his daddy to join him in the family business, the pride and joy of the two previous generations.

The family business. While being married to a mortician didn't really bother me, for the life of me, I couldn't picture myself with this particular one. I wondered if his daddy started him at the bottom; you know, the serf level, so he'd know what it was all about from the bottom up. What was the serf level for a mortician anyway? Washing the hearse? Dimming those awful pink lights over the casket? Fluffing up the pillow?

Suddenly, I began to giggle, and Margaret was offended. She thought I was responding to Bill. Naturally, she had no idea what was going through my head and I quickly said, "I was just picturing you at your graduation party in that lavender dress Daddy 'loves.'"

I managed to avoid the crater of that conversation quite nicely. She would press and press to find out my every thought about Jack the mortician. That and, of course, her secret engagement. However, I was not one to share my every thought.

"Elizabeth Evangelina! Are you listening to me?" she asked.

Lord, only my mother could come up with a name like that.

She continued. "You know what my father would say! That lavender dress sends him into fits. 'I can see your knees!' he hollers. 'A man would get Ideas from that dress!'" Margaret's hands flapped high and loose: Daddy trying to insinuate Male Ideas. "'You are not going out like that!' and on and on." She went off into a fit of giggles.

See? I said I could make people hear what they wanted to hear.

Margaret was the kind of young woman who attracted boys to her like butterflies to a flower. She was not really tall, although she was taller than I was, but she appeared statuesque because her posture was exquisite. Her brunette hair was impeccable, every marcelled curve in place, even after she took off those adorable hats. Being from Chicago, and being spoiled by Daddy, Margaret strode along with fashion panting at her heels, and self-confidence in her future just dripping off her ruby fingernails.

"That lavender dress—with white gloves and hat, of course," I added, and her laughter glittered across the sunny morning air.

We were past the blazing sugar maple and near the gate leading out from the quad to the high bluff. The old wooden bench that signaled the start of the golf course came into sight.

"My father," Margaret bubbled, "saw that particular fashion delight only once, and it certainly wasn't on purpose. Business trip, ha! Why did he have to show up just before Bill came to take me dancing?" She pirouetted away from me, golf bag and all.

"And you," she pointed dramatically, "of all people, you were the one who had to be on desk duty that night."

"You know I tried to warn you, Margaret. I would've run upstairs myself, but I couldn't leave my post. I did manage to send that little freshman up to warn you. It wasn't my fault she gave the wrong person the message."

"I know, I know." She forgave me long ago. Now, it was just one of those stories we kept coming back to. "I'm just glad Daddy didn't see how low I rolled my garters. He would've had a fit! But anyway," she continued as we stepped onto the first tee, "Daddy likes Bill, so we'll be all right." She started to laugh again. "That dress would be a picture, though, wouldn't it?"

I couldn't begin to imagine what Daddy would say if he knew the secrets Margaret and I shared.

Chapter 2
Reggie

1964

The voice was too loud. "Reg!"

A moment of doubt. Who was that?

"Reggie?"

I surfaced. My roommate. Her voice was insistent.

"Regina Marie!"

That name pulled me fully awake and upright.

The desk had flattened one cheek and my neck was stiff. "Oh, man, Sam, why'd you do that?" I hunched my shoulders. By swiveling slightly, I could see out the tall Gothic windows above our desks. It had gone from twilight to dark while I napped. I rolled my neck to take out the crick, scanning across the ugly brown cord bedspread and warped dresser past the door to the mirror image of the room, Samantha's side. A millionaire's penthouse? Hardly. Just cheap college housing.

Sam sat—no, draped—across her desk chair, waiting for my mind to re-inhabit my body. "So, Regina Marie, you've finally decided to rejoin the land of the living."

I couldn't suppress a groan. Only my mother called me by my full name, and only when she was beyond peeved. Which rarely happened. My mother left me pretty much to myself. Although I did phone once a week, I always pictured my mother only nodding on the other end while she stirred up some concoction in the kitchen, only half listening to my laundry list of the week's events. I called her The Great Stone Face.

I knew for a fact my mother was nowhere near. She was— where was she? My mind went blank for a moment before I remembered she was traveling in Europe with my father.

"God, Sam, I never should've told you my whole name," I groaned between neck rolls.

"A name only a mother could love," Sam baited.

"Yeah, well, I wonder." I pushed back my chair and slowly stood up. My back cracked. "Aw, man!" I cocked my arms, splayed my fingers across my hips and bent back, feeling every little bone settle into place again. "I really shouldn't sleep sitting at my desk."

"Ray Gee Na, Queen of the Ball," Sam teased.

"Leave it alone. You know I hate my name." I couldn't help snapping at her. "Why she had to come up with that..." My mutter trailed off into an incoherent grumble.

"No one knows you by anything but Reggie," Sam soothed, "and no one ever will." Then she baited again, "Remember where your mom came up with that name?"

"I told you before." I prickled with a dose of acid. "She read this novel in college and loved the name of some character or other. Said it sounded suitably regal for her 'baby queen.' Now quit asking."

"I know, I know. I just can't help it." Sam bent over in her chair, grasped her ankles and folded herself up like a rag doll thrown to rest in the corner of the toy closet. Her voice was muffled. "Come on, Reg, your mom is so cool. A name out of a novel. That's cool."

I gave a definite snort. While Samantha might see the charm of my mother, I really couldn't. She might listen to a few things I said, but she sure didn't talk much. Old Stone Face was definitely not cool.

"Cool," she repeated.

That merited another snort. "When we talk, she asks about *you*. She says to say hi. Big deal. We're roommates, what do you expect? She's not cool. She's just plain cold."

Sam shrugged. At least, she knew when to quit.

I walked a circuit of the room and stopped next to Sam's desk and did one slow deep kneebend. "Now that I'm awake, we need to get out of here."

Sam straightened up in her chair and stuffed her head back into her lit book. "No way, José. That's not why I woke you up. You need to get that work done. Besides, you were irritating me beyond belief."

"Was I snoring?" I leaned over the desk, stretching my hamstrings.

"Come on, Reg. You *told* me to wake you up if you fell asleep. I didn't wake you up so we could go out. So, now that you're fully awake, better leave me alone. I've got work to do."

"You can nap too, you know. Take a break, for Pete's sake."

"I can't." Samantha jammed her little fingernail between her teeth, a sure sign of nerves.

"What is it with you tonight, Sam?"

"Nothing."

The answer came far too quickly and I swung around to stare frankly at my best friend. "So, you've got tons of work to do. So do I. Shakespeare, remember?" I flung my hand toward the slab of a book open on my desk, a few words of Lady Macbeth's sleepwalking scene ironically glistening with drool. "So, I sleep at my desk occasionally. You're the one that falls asleep in bed with a book over your face. I've got news for you, my friend, osmosis does not work with books and brains." I stood hovering over Sam.

Sam pushed me aside and stood up, rising up on her tiptoes like a dancer and reaching toward the ceiling. Her long brown hair—what she called "beef bouillon brown"—fell neatly off her shoulders and down her back. She scrunched her big brown eyes into two little cartoon lines. In spite of her rumpled look, I couldn't help noticing how really pretty Sam was, no matter what she did to her face. Shiny hair, big brown eyes, great shape. I put in one last plug, hoping to draw Sam out of her rut, for a little while, at least.

"Sam, you know, life is just too short for this kind of nonsense. Come on. We need a beer." I squirmed past Sam, turned off her desk light, and shoved a bookmark flat on top of Christopher Marlowe, all in one deft move.

"Re-e-g-g." Sam dragged it out into a whine. "I've got to finish *The Jew of Malta* for tomorrow."

"He's dead. He ain't goin' nowhere."

Sam might as well fold. We both knew who was going to win. I clapped the book shut, and Sam let out what sounded like a reluctant sigh.

"All right, all right." Sam threw down her pen and fluffed up her hair. "I'm ready."

"Give me a sec, Sam. I don't have the luxury of straight hair."

When I stepped up to the mirror to fiddle with my hair, Sam peered over my shoulder like some little elf.

"You have the most gorgeous hair," Sam purred. "I am so envious."

"Well, take it then," I muttered as I forced a comb through the thicket. I knew it was not my mother's carrot-top red. It was a much deeper shade of red, more secretive somehow, almost brunette. My mother's hair shouted out to everyone in sight, "Hey! Look here! See me? Wow! Isn't this something?" My hair just sat and smiled, kind of like a cat in a sunny window. I actually liked my hair, unless it was all tangled, but my eyes were really my best feature. A great combination of green and brown. I read somewhere that Shakespeare had hazel eyes too, and everyone called him "Gentle Will." "Gentle" was not exactly one of my nicknames. More like—what? Impulsive perhaps? I was always sticking my foot in mouth. That must be an endearing quality anyway, because I could get along with almost everybody.

Everybody, that is, but my mother. Everyone else thought she was wonderful, but she never *talked* to me. Oh, she listened to me once in a while, but when I asked for her opinion, she always seemed to say something like, "Well, what do *you* think?" or "Uh-huh." Sometimes she just glued her eyes to me and didn't say a thing. When my lone decisions didn't work out, all I got was a frown, if that much. How come she never yelled? How come she never talked? How come she never tried to run my life? I guess I should be grateful for that part, but I wasn't. Finally, in junior high, I put aside thinking about it, and convinced myself it didn't really matter. I remained convinced.

I came out of my memories and saw Sam standing behind me with a look that said, "Okay, you got me into this. Now, let's go before I change my mind." My face in the mirror relaxed into a grin. We shared everything, from sweaters to swimming suits, from cocktail dresses to deepest secrets, and I did all I could to pull Sam into my schemes and plans. I knew Sam loved it when she was drawn into impulsivity and out of drudge work.

"Okay, let's go get us a beer." Sam turned to her own mirror. "If I can't finish reading *The Jew of Malta*, then let's go lift a glass to the memory of its author, ol' Kit Marlowe. He ended up dying in a tavern brawl, as I recall."

As I swept away from the mirror, laughing, Sam was gyrating to get a final look at her teeth.

"Stop it!" I demanded. "They're picture perfect. No spinach anywhere. C'mon, will you?"

"Okay! Okay!" She gave one last swipe at her teeth.

The two of us rattled down the stairs. We stepped out into the cool fall air and I closed the heavy front door behind us.

Our big Victorian house, university housing left over from earlier and grander days, was sandwiched between two other similar university residences situated on the fringes of campus. All of them had been slated several years before to be torn down to make room for an antiseptic jailblock dorm that wouldn't hold many more students than these three houses, considering the restrictions on the land. The Old Ladies, as the houses were affectionately known, were saved at the eleventh hour by an irate, and rich, group of alumni who had lived in them over the years. The houses were the maiden aunts of the student body and were highly prized by some for their peace and quiet and their Old World charm. In spite of being on the far end of the university's property, they were a priority on seniors' housing choices and the university resisted the temptation, at least so far, to give in to developers.

Sam and I stepped off our porch into the deep, cool darkness.

Nothing, truly nothing, could match the crispness of a Wisconsin autumn. Even the rustle of the oaks and maples, those that didn't lose their leaves already, was sharp and defined. The hunter's moon glowed low in the sky like some lost lamplighter wandering from street to street. We walked the first block without a word between us. It was that kind of night.

"Ya know," Sam began, and then stopped. Stopped talking and stopped walking.

"What?" I caught the hesitant tone. Sam sounded really distracted and was starting to look it too. "What?" I said again.

"Nothing." Sam moved out, scuffing her feet through the leaves, making them scrunch like potato chips.

Streetlights didn't wash the entire sidewalk with light, but only created little ponds, one after another along the concrete. We walked from circle of light to circle of light, in and out of the shadows scattered along the sidewalk, like Jimmy Durante closing out his show, walking out of one spotlight and into another as he made his way upstage and away. "Good night, Mrs. Calabash, wherever you are."

"I..." Sam began, then shut down once more.

This was not like Sam, and I was intrigued and perplexed. Usually it was me, not Sam, who went through the days swinging between placid and frantic.

"Hey, what's up? We've been friends for four years now…"

"Three," Sam interrupted. "Three. Remember, we met in the fall of freshmen year? This is only the fall of senior year. Three years."

"Okay, three. Anyway, what's up? Talk to Mama."

"Reg, I can't tell anybody else this, especially my mom, 'cause she'd kill me." She came to a complete halt, leaves settling noisily around her feet.

"Come on. Nothing can be that bad." I knew *my* mother wouldn't question me if I was beating around the bush the way Sam was right now. Of course, I didn't waste time beating around the bush with my mother. I usually stayed away completely. Who wanted to talk to a wall? My mother, the wall, didn't think deeply or often, didn't have opinions on much of anything. On the other hand, my dad seemed to be able to roll with almost anything. He'd have to, I felt, to be able to deal with my mother's lack of –lack of what? Enthusiasm? Interest? All of the above.

Sam's dad was "no longer with them," as Sam put it on the very first day I moved into our freshmen dorm. I didn't find out until months later that Sam's father abandoned them for parts unknown. For parts unknown, accompanied by a fresh young thing. It left Sam's mom as kind of a control freak about Sam.

"Nothing can be that bad, eh?" Sam echoed. Her bitterness wasn't deep, I knew, but it was always crouching on the edges of her voice when she talked about her mother. "Man, if only I had your mom. She really listens to you. You're like her—"

"I most definitely am not!" I reacted instantaneously. Concern with whatever was on Sam's mind was blown completely out of the conversation. "You, of all people, know my mom drives me nuts. It ain't all wine and roses. She knows how to push my buttons without even saying a word. Drives me crazy." I lowered my head, shoved my hands deeper into my pockets, and began heading into the next splash of light coming from someone's porch light.

"Okay, fine." Sam's voice was irritated and I could sense Sam's forehead scrunching up like it did when she was either mad or about to cry, even if I couldn't see her face as she moved back into the darkness.

"Sam," I tempered my voice to be apologetic, "you're my best friend. You can tell me anything. I'm sorry I let my mom get in the way. But you've got to tell me what's on your mind. If you're going to talk, talk. If you don't want to tell me, I'm going back in." I moved as if to turn back, and Sam stopped and grabbed my elbow.

"I'm married," she said.

A dead moment. Several of them.

"Reg? Say something. Anything. I'm married."

What am I supposed to say? I thought, but didn't utter a sound. For once, I became my mother, at a loss for words. Sam was the woman who knew every male on campus by first name. She was also the woman who said she wouldn't marry any one of them.

"Well. Okay," I finally spat out, then thought, *Now, there's something really intelligent to say.* "When?" I asked. And then louder, "And I thought *I* jumped into things." And then, "Why? For God's sake, why? You're not pregnant, are you?" It all came out at once.

"No. Just after school started." Sam answered in reverse order. "And why? Well, isn't that pretty clear? I love the guy."

My mind was finally racing, even if my mouth, for once, wasn't. It had to be Jim. Lord, I thought, I hope it's Jim, or I'm about to place the biggest foot in the biggest mouth. But Sam beat me to it.

"Jim. I married Jim. I've known him forever, Reg, and I really do love him. I just couldn't live without him any longer. He's been after me since we graduated from high school and, and…. I didn't want to wait any longer. Man, I sound like some kind of stupid romance novel." Her voice trailed off and I could tell she would break out in tears any moment if I went in the wrong direction with this piece of news.

I couldn't see Sam's face. We were in one of the doldrums between streetlights and all I could see, framed against the light up ahead, were the lines of her shoulders and few stray hairs coming out from beneath her hat. Neither gave me any help. I looked for Sam's shoulders to shrug or her head to come up, but she was cast in bronze. Sam was waiting and I was stuck. Finally, my lips started to move before my mind was entirely in gear.

"What's your mom going to say? Does she like him enough? What about school? You can't stay in university housing if you're married. Can you afford the tuition? Where will you go? Will you even be able to finish? What about him?" Everything tumbled out at once. And then, trailing after, "Congratulations."

Sam reacted only to the last. "Thanks."

My mind came to a screeching halt. But really, what *was* she going to do? If anyone found out she was married, she'd be kicked out of housing. So close to graduation. More than half this semester was gone and only one more to go. Now what?

Of course I'd keep my mouth shut and I told Sam that much. But not the rest. She'd get plenty of that from everyone else when it all hit the fan.

"Thanks, Reg. I knew you would keep this a secret. So now at least I have someone to share it with. Obviously, I can't tell anyone else."

Suddenly, the rest of my questions registered and Sam started to cry. "But I'm so happy, Reg. He's in Madison, so I don't get to see him very often, but he's so good to me. My mom knew him for a long time and seems to like him, but she doesn't want me getting out from under her control. I'm afraid if she finds out, she'll cut off my tuition payments and I can't afford to pay them myself. And she's going to be hopping mad she can't plan this huge wedding thing. I didn't want that anyway, so it doesn't make any difference to me. How am I going to do this? I can't leave school now, but I miss him so much."

Too many words to tumble out of someone sure of herself. I heard the rising panic. But I also heard the resolve under it all.

I got a firm grip on Sam's elbow and sailed her down the sidewalk before anyone started wondering why we were loitering so long outside their living room windows at night. We were past the last of the Old Ladies and the houses were smaller, though still Victorian, like the ladies-in-waiting for the old dowagers. Soon we would be into the neighborhood of the footmen and butlers, as Sam and I dubbed them, the houses of smaller stature that were newer, younger. But they would never have the grace and majesty of the big Victorians. They could only aspire, and cluster around, protecting the Old Ladies and their retinues from the shabby tavern and fast-food ring that had grown up around the skirts of the university.

I leaned and squinted, straining to see Sam's face clearly. "Is he staying in school? Does anybody in Madison know?" I met Jim several times over the past couple of years and, as I thought of it, quite often more recently. Questions arrived unsolicited: How did she manage to keep this from me? Should I be hurt or not? "Look," my better side took over, "no one has to know. You've got the weekends you can be with him, even if it can't be every single one. You've just got to be careful. Nobody's going to find out from me, and your mom will keep on paying tuition. Nothing's going to look different on the surface. We've only got a few months anyway and then you're home free."

We lapsed into walking normally again, out past the smaller ordinary homes, where I could finally see Sam's face under the brighter mercury streetlamps. Sam's eyebrows were pulled taut over her nose, typical when she was studying hard or worried about something. I realized how hard it must be to keep this secret, especially from me, her best friend. She stopped crying and peered at me sideways, as if waiting to see which direction my responses were going.

"No one else knows," Sam ventured the first words. "Jim's friends in the apartment could care less what goes on in anyone else's little lives, they're so wrapped up in their booze and broads." She sounded cynical. Then her tone lightened. "He graduates in December and has a job already lined up in Madison. When I'm out in May, I can just move right in. Provided I can get a job myself. But he's helping me out and, with his connections, I'll be okay."

Sam was talking about more than the job situation.

The cool air helped us regain some sense of calm. I dragged my feet through the fallen leaves—red, yellow, orange—all only shades of gray in the night light. The houses we passed allowed flashes of domestic life, like watching a stop-action film, never catching the whole picture.

Sam paced herself to me, slow as it was. I felt my mouth go dry, but I needed to answer her. Even without a voiced question, she needed some kind of an assurance. Impulsively, I put my arms around Sam and squeezed.

"We'll keep this little secret. Just don't get pregnant." I smiled at Sam. "Come on. We *really* need a beer."

Chapter 3
Betty

1934

I reached up to straighten the tassel hanging off my mortarboard. Through the silky threads, I saw two people in the near distance, gesturing at each other. Shifting my focus, I recognized Margaret and her father. I couldn't believe it. I absolutely could not believe this. Margaret stood with her father under the beautiful old sugar maple every one of us wanted to be under when our beaux asked for a first kiss. In contrast to that dreamy moment, today, neither one of them looked happy. I tried to get Margaret's attention because good ol' Sister Joan was up in arms about us not being in line yet.

"Come along, girls." Sister Joan came sweeping towards me, her veil billowing like a black sail. While Sister Joan still struck fear into freshmen hearts, we seniors figured out how to get around her. Even so, she could still threaten to ground us for the weekend if she found contraband of any kind, even though we'd be alumnae in about an hour and beyond her reach.

She flagged some little lambs, as she called us, into her flock, lining all of us up like so many animals ready for the sheep dip. The white academic gowns didn't help. We really did look like sheep.

I started to giggle.

Sister Joan came out from behind her veil, one eye at a time. My, but that woman could incinerate me where I stood, with that look.

"Betty," she intoned seriously, "this is graduation, a notable occasion in your life. St. Ingrid girls are always ladies. We have a reputation to uphold here. Show the appropriate decorum." She was about to launch into a full-blown sermon, but I waylaid it with a soft look.

"I'm sorry, Sister." I lowered my chin ever so slightly. "It's just nerves. My parents are watching from the stands."

"I know, dear," she whispered, matching my tone. "You'll do fine if you just keep in mind what we've taught you here at St. Ingrid." Through deceptively soft words delivered in a whisper, she could still cut me off at the knees if she chose. This time, however, she took me at face value. She heard what I wanted her to hear and clucked me back in line.

I couldn't catch Margaret's attention and it didn't look like anything good was happening over there under the maple. She stood with hands tucked up inside her gown's wide sleeves like a monk heading for prayers. Even her face looked like one of those saint's statues, gazing pensively up to heaven in the hopes God would drop some small miracle.

Now, though I could catch only glimpses of her and her father through the intervening crowd, I saw her turn sharply away. There was indeed something amiss. In spite of Sister Joan, I stepped quickly out of line to meet Margaret as she moved toward me over the lawn.

"Betty!"

I heard Sister's voice crackle to my right and instinctively slowed. But Margaret's face didn't allow me to come to a full stop.

"Betty!"

Margaret's hands emerged from the white sleeves. Our fingers almost touched before Sister Joan got to us. "Daddy..." was all she could manage before we were separated by a flutter and swoosh of black.

Margaret's eyes asked both forgiveness and support before settling into that stubborn, hooded look which pulled her away from all of us. With a sharp glance at Sister Joan, Margaret slid into line several girls ahead of me, too far to confer as we marched in.

I didn't want to step back in line, but Sister and the first few bars of "Pomp and Circumstance" told me otherwise. As slowly as I could, I slipped into place, watching Margaret's white mortarboard blend into everyone else's as she disappeared into the mass ahead of me.

We moved, whether I wanted to or not, and I would just have to wait to find out what Margaret's daddy put his foot down on this time. Over the past four years, I listened to her being dragged forward and backward. Not often, but often enough. And I saw Daddy in action. When she finally went out to dinner with her father after the fiasco on Valentine's Day, when Bill went down to Chicago to ask for her hand, Daddy made it perfectly clear that, while Bill was a nice young man, he certainly wasn't the great catch Daddy planned for Margaret. For weeks, Margaret refused to talk to her father, to take his calls, to answer the desk attendant when Daddy came through on business and stopped. In fact, she told Bill that Daddy, in spite of the apparent cold shoulder and rebuff when he asked permission to marry her, was thawing a bit and would surely come around by the time graduation was on the horizon.

Not a chance.

Today, spring gifted us with sunshine, stunning temperatures, and enough friction in the air over brunch alone to crackle like heat lightning. As we headed into afternoon, I perceived no love was lost between Margaret and Daddy. Actually, what I really saw, in spite of the sparks between them, were two people who loved each other, but just couldn't admit it. Her father blustered on, even in my presence, about how Daddy knew best and she chafed at the very mention of a bit or bridle. But it was very clear to me, in spite of this boulder in the road—Bill—the affection was still there between father and daughter.

For the graduation ceremony, thanks to fate or the providence of a kind God, I was seated directly behind Margaret and could whisper my concern as I pretended to brush an invisible dust mote off my white satin pump.

"Bill," she staccatoed back. "Daddy's not giving in."

"And?"

"Shouldn't have worn the ring today," she added, unnecessarily.

"He has to know sometime," I encouraged. "What are you going to do?"

"Hold on." A catch in her voice.

After Bill's visit with Daddy in Chicago, he came back to Margaret moving a bit more slowly than she anticipated. She feared the worst. Bill told her Daddy took him into the study and asked what he intended to do with his life. Bill looked around at the leather chairs, the big oak desk, the books lining the walls and scattered artistically on the end tables. It was apparent Daddy was an educated man, a man who appreciated learning. A man who would hold education and study in high regard. But when Bill waxed eloquent about a teaching career, Daddy frowned, stood up, and without a word, made it perfectly clear the interview was over. Bill asked for her hand as Daddy showed him out the door. The only thing Daddy gave Bill was a demeaning look. Bill came back from that trip and showed Margaret the ring perched in its small box, a perfectly beautiful little diamond smiling up at her from its pink satin bed. He'd not said a word after that, but when he started to close the lid, she impulsively plucked the ring from the box and said, "If Daddy won't hand me over, then I'll just have to take matters into my own hands, so to speak," and slid the ring onto her finger.

Now, over three months later, she was apparently still stuck in a holding pattern.

"I'm not letting go of this," she repeated over her shoulder.

I wondered if she was talking about Daddy or Bill.

Graduation slid decidedly into twilight and the sugar maple in the quad was full of shafts of light from the lowering sun. Clusters and clouds of bugs and spring dust gave the tree an ethereal look. Like the tree in the middle of Eden, I thought. I was going to miss the campus terribly. The physical beauty of the place alone was a considerable draw. Beyond the deep-pile green velvet lawns around the old buildings, the bluffs dropped down to the Mississippi River. The administrative and dining quad, the mainstay of campus, sat like a mother hen in the midst of a cluster of dormitories and classroom buildings. The two wide gates made eyes at each other from opposite sides of the quad. Beyond that wonderful maple, and beyond the far gate, was a breathtaking view of the top of the bluff and, of course, the beginning of the golf course. The sky seemed to burst from the trees, whose tops were just visible as they stretched to clamber over the edge of the bluff. Now the fingers of those trees were beginning to show true green against the mellowing twilight sky. The sky itself was still that kind of blue that dazzles after a long winter of gray and shades of white, but the promise of lavender and rose was there along the edges. In the middle of it all, and providing a filigree of green and brown, was that special maple tree.

Someday, I wanted to plant a sugar maple in the middle of my backyard just to remind me of that place.

I was brought back abruptly by the response of applause to the Dean's wish, "Congratulations to the new graduates of St. Ingrid's." The opening notes of the recessional washed over us and we simultaneously reached up to switch our tassels to the other side of our mortarboards and swiveled to march out of the graduation area. Even though I loved this place, I didn't hear another note of the music, I was so distracted. There were just too many things to think about.

The crowd around the quad's maple thinned somewhat and now might be the time for my father to take a photo of Margaret and me together. One last picture before we gathered up our lives at St. Ingrid's and stowed our memories in our hatboxes and bags.

With Margaret's arm slung around my waist, we sauntered up to the tree. We put our heads together, savoring those moments. I hoped we might get more than a few words in along the edges of everything else going on, and even opened my mouth close to her ear, beginning, "We—"

But no. A firm arm slipped around my shoulders and a white smile with a mustache above came into my peripheral sights. Jack.

"Hi, lovely," he said, then peered around at Margaret, still clutched to my side, "Congratulations. And the same to Bill too, when you see him. He couldn't make graduation, could he?"

"No," Margaret said. "He can't get away."

Little did Jack guess what import *those* words held.

Jack smiled down at me. Jack, the one Margaret was convinced was the man of my dreams, was not part of the world I devised for myself. He was not the one for me. It seemed I was the only one to realize that. Even today, people were asking me how he was, assuming somehow he managed to corner me and sweep me off my feet with his offer of marriage to a respectable man who would inherit the family funeral parlor. My mind immediately shot off to the picture of Jack having someday to choose which funeral home would handle his own father's body and finally deciding he would take care of it himself. He'd take care of his own. He'd be stoic and do it. I couldn't help myself. I started to giggle. Morbid, but I just couldn't help it.

"Are you willing to share the secret?" Jack pulled me aside, gently extricating me from my best friend's loose embrace. At the same time, his eyes begged Margaret's pardon for a stolen moment or two. Of all times for Jack to appear.

Margaret moved off discreetly, slipping her arm through my father's and drifting along with him and the rest of my family. Her own father followed, clearly anxious to get his daughter alone, but far too much the gentleman to pull her away now.

Jack and I came to a complete halt and I mentally fumbled for a moment. "Secret? No secret. I was just remembering all the good times that Margaret and I had last fall with you and Bill," I turned on my best smile. How did I manage to get people to hear what I wanted them to?

Jack didn't bat an eye. He was too gentle to be suspicious.

"I won't be far away. We could still have good times. I won't be working every single minute of the day." He repeated, "I won't be *that* far away."

He was as good looking as everyone said he was, but he was already a memory for me. I simply could not convince anyone that, as nice as he was, I was not in love with him.

"I won't be going back home and I won't be staying here." My mouth had a mind of its own and the words were out before I even realized they must've been tucked somewhere in my brain, hiding. They surprised even me. "I'm traveling with friends and then I'm moving. Actually, I'm moving first and then I'm traveling." Where was all of this coming from? It was true, I was offered a teaching job in the high school connected to St. Ingrid's and another at a school in Milwaukee, but I hadn't made a decision yet. At least, I didn't think I had. Now it seemed part of my mind was making itself up without consultation with the rest of me.

"Yes," I went on, getting more comfortable. "A few of us are renting a cottage up north before we have to step into the real world." None of us had to be anywhere until the first part of July. Dorothy and Joyce were both getting married in July and Margaret hoped to marry Bill as soon as she could. I myself was free until almost Labor Day.

"Oh," Jack said.

He sounded deflated, but he'd get over it. He needed to get on with his life without me. I thought he knew, deep down, it would never work for us. I was too restless and he wanted stability. I wasn't ready for stability.

"Jack," I was trying to be as gentle as he, "you deserve the very best, and I'm not the best for you. You know exactly what you want and I don't. Go home and be happy." My giggles, deep inside of me in spite of my sincerity, almost surfaced. The best mortician. If I said it out loud, he would never believe I truly meant it, because I'd start smiling, at the very least, and it would ruin everything. I didn't want him going away angry. Only a little regretful it was not going to work out the way he hoped—hoped since last fall.

"Betty." He took my hand, almost shaking it. He clearly came to some kind of decision and I could only hope it was the one I wanted to hear. "I hope you find everything you want." He looked carefully at me, then turned away and moved off. He never even looked back.

I realized I was holding my breath, and I exhaled evenly with clean relief. In spite of that, I felt a wash of unanticipated emotion. He was simply walking away? No begging, no fighting? In spite of my relief, I was surprised at my disappointment and, yes, resentment. Was I not worth fighting for? I pressed my lips together, but my thoughts were interrupted.

"Finally!" Margaret's familiar voice chimed behind me. "What were you two so *intime* about? Did he ask you?"

"I told him to go back home. I'm not available."

"I had a feeling. Well, I guess that's that." She frowned. "You are so cold!" But then she shifted her hips and smiled. "To be honest, I can't picture you as a mortician's wife. But can you, despite your pain and anguish, find it in your heart to join us at the cottage, or are you going back home to pine away your years alone, Dickenson-like?"

She was being sarcastic and we both knew it. "I would not miss this little junket for anything and you know that perfectly well, you vixen. I'm spending a week at home, during which, my dear, I shall trip to the city and find myself a place to stay. I shall pack up my steamer trunk, deposit it at said new address, and traverse, quick like a bunny, the distance between there and the lake, thereupon fulfilling my prior obligation to appear at the cottage in due course."

"Aha! You decided on the big move! Good for you. Before that, you can soak away your troubles at the lake and return, phoenix-like, to begin yet another new life."

I did not forget the desperate look on her face as we lined up before the ceremony, and it was still there under the bantering. "And you? Can you soak away your troubles too? What about your father? I'm sorry Sister Joan came steaming over just at the wrong time. What exactly did Daddy say this time?"

"The usual." Her face lost luster suddenly and she took my arm to lead me away, even though my father gestured for us to come over to the big maple tree, where a momentary break gave us a chance for a photo. Margaret's father was deep in conversation with one of the nuns. "He is so sure this is a bad match," she said. "Just what is wrong with teaching? You are going to be a teacher. Bill will be a college professor someday. Isn't that good enough for Daddy? In fact, Bill just heard yesterday he's been accepted at Wisconsin's graduate school. That place is nothing to sneeze at. Not only that, they've offered him a teaching assistant position, so he can make some money. He's got a good job for the summer too, working in construction, but Daddy says that's no place for a man with a college education." She actually sniffed. "Bill's been working that job for the past five summers and they really want him back, he's such a hard worker. Sure, we'll struggle for a while, but I can get a job now too, at least for the summer."

She looked at me. We didn't even need to say out loud what Daddy would say about that.

"What are you planning?" I asked. It was clear she had a plan. I saw that look in her eyes before, but it was never about anything this serious. This could mean estrangement from her family and, perhaps, even from Bill's family, a casting out into the wasteland. Was she really aware of what she was doing?

She breathed twice before answering and didn't risk a look in my direction, not even a twitch. "We're running away. We're eloping. To Las Vegas."

"Las Vegas?" The den of sin for those who just couldn't hold out long enough for a church wedding and wanted to leap into bed as soon as possible. I'm sure that all washed over my face, but she didn't turn my way.

Now she did. "Yes, Las Vegas. They don't require a waiting period and we can get a blood test out there, if they need it. I heard they don't. Once it's done, it's done, and Daddy can't do a thing about it. Bill already has housing all set up for us at the University and the train tickets purchased." She pursed her lips tightly. "Daddy doesn't know," she added.

I was sure he didn't! I tried to stay calm as she laid this plan out, as if simply setting the table for a family meal. This was not ordinary. "When do you propose to carry out this little scheme?" I couldn't believe my voice was so calm.

"That's the easy part," she said. "We leave the day all of us go up to the lake. Bill arranged to meet me at the train station and we'll go out to Las Vegas from there. By the time Daddy finds out, we'll be out and back. Bill can go back to Madison and I'll come up to the lake and join all of you for a few days. Daddy thinks I'll be at the cottage the whole time." Here came that anguished look again. "Do you think he'll find out? I can't have him finding out."

"Who's going to tell? Certainly not I," I reassured lamely. She already knew that. "No one else knows, do they?"

"No."

"Well then, not to worry." I had to find out what that argument under the tree in the quad was all about. Out of the corner of my eye, I saw my father relinquish the tree and head in our direction. "What did Daddy say to you before the ceremony? You were more than upset."

Margaret saw me watching my father come toward us. "I was trying one last time. I warned him if he couldn't accept Bill, he might lose me. I wouldn't speak to him again. His comeback was, 'Well, if I let you marry Bill, I'd lose you forever too. That will *not* happen.' I just can't deal with that man anymore. I saw you and knew if I could just talk to you for a minute, I could make a decision I could live with."

"Too bad Sister Joan cut us off," I told her.

"Well, Bill already arranged everything, but I wasn't positive I could go through with it. Even when I was talking to Daddy, I couldn't quite picture myself pinning on my hat and getting on a train for Las Vegas. But I saw you move out of line toward me and I knew. I knew this was the right thing to do. Daddy or no Daddy, I want Bill. It won't kill Daddy to have me belong to another man, especially when he sees how well Bill has planned for us. So, thank you. Thank you for giving me strength."

That meant, if anything went wrong, it would be my fault. I spoke not a word. Nothing could be said that would be the right thing. If I opened my mouth now, I risked losing everything. Her friendship, her trust, my own sense of security. This time, I couldn't make her hear what I wanted her to hear. I couldn't say it out loud. I couldn't say everything would be fine.

My father drew closer, camera at the ready. He called, "Ladies, the tree is available for photos now."

Maybe it wasn't the worst step Margaret could take either. Bill was a good man and I knew her father loved her, in spite of everything, but I found I had no words to tell her that.

"We'll have a few days at the lake, at least," I said. That sounded so inadequate, but it would have to do.

"Yes, we'll have the lake," she agreed.

"Always," I promised, as we linked arms and turned toward my father.

Chapter 4
Reggie

1964

Off-campus college housing never claimed to be the Ritz. Our old gray Victorian was filled to the brim, with four bedrooms, a bath and kitchen upstairs, and house parents not much older than we were living downstairs. It was never totally quiet; someone was always working away in the kitchen, having moved the typewriter out of her shared bedroom for humanitarian reasons. The bathroom had one of those old claw-footed tubs, almost big enough to hold President Taft, although, unlike him in his White House tub, no one got stuck in this one. None of the beds matched and neither did the dressers. Everything else was brought from home or jerry-rigged. On the surface, it was a sorry place, but it *was* clean. We all saw to that, divvying up the chores and posting everything on a neat little chart in the kitchen. The best part was none of us had to badger the others about fulfilling household duties. We were more than family. We were friends.

Today, all seven housemates were crammed into our flat's tiny kitchen, everyone trying to make breakfast. We looked like one of those intricate Renaissance dances where everyone appears to be whirling along on their own and then, suddenly, pattern emerges. Somehow, over the past two years, all of us, who hardly knew each other at the start, found an amiable groove. Who stayed up late and studied? Who got up early to run? Who couldn't stand to have the light turned on when she was sleeping? Who was out for the night so we could go ahead and lock the door? We knew each other's important secrets.

But tonight, our happy little group would be breaking up. The girls of the old Victorian would graduate.

I headed out of the kitchen and down the hall to finish packing. Sam's and my bedroom looked like a tenement, at this point. In contrast, outside, it was one of those wonderful Monet days when everything was slightly out of focus and the colors were jewels. As the day closed in on lunchtime, the slanted lines of the sun through the window over my desk were butter yellow. The prism in the window turned the floor into fractured pieces of red and orange, with a bit of purple on the side. Everything, even the piles of boxes, glowed ever so slightly. God in Heaven, I sounded like my mother, all artsy-crap! I discarded *that* thought. It was May, it was almost time for graduation, and I reveled in it.

The flat was full of boxes and bags, suitcases and stacks of everything needing to be carted away in one direction or another. Our belongings, most of them packed already, were piled high on the beds. Between the beds, brown cardboard boxes begged from the downtown liquor store filled the gap, leaving hardly room to walk. An obstacle course of striped and patterned bags filled to overflowing stretched out along the pathway to the bathroom door. It all looked like a maze laid out by crazed goblins. The bookcases were stripped of anything that made the place homey. The varnished shelves sat forlorn, scratched and dull without their books and knickknacks. Our posters were off the walls, leaving the faintest trace of dust where the edges had been, or maybe it was faded paint, it was hard to tell which. The matching bedspreads, folded neatly, sat at the end of the bed, ready for laundering before next year's tenants claimed them. The only thing I couldn't bear to pack yet was the photo of Sam and me, sweatshirts tied around our waists, standing with one arm thrown across each other's shoulders and the other elbow cocked, hand on hip. The photo made it look like these glorious days of hard work and hard play, this friendship, was going to go on forever. So confident.

I stared at the photo, thinking, well, they will last forever, won't they? I didn't want to think about it.

Sam strode into the room, the same sweatshirt as in the photo coincidentally flung across her shoulders. A small shock rippled up my back as I pictured Sam for a moment as another still photo, preserved for all time in the album in my head. Jeans. Pink shirt untucked on one side. Hair tied back loose over her ears. Every detail was registering and it was suddenly too much. Ten minutes before, I told everyone who would listen I couldn't wait to get that degree in my hands and get out and away.

But I didn't really want to go. Now the time had come, I couldn't bear to let Sam move down to Madison without me and begin a whole new life with Jim.

"This isn't fair," I muttered. "It *won't* go on this way forever." The end of the year, the end of four years, rose up abruptly in front of me. "Sam," I started, trying to talk about something else to get this out of my head. University life was over. In August, I'd be starting a real job, with real art students and a real paycheck. I was ready. I was already on my own since the previous year. My work/study job paid enough to buy books and food. My parents still picked up tuition, but I was capable of managing my own money. It felt good.

Who was I kidding? In spite of that, I didn't want to give up any of this.

All right. That's enough. I closed my mind to all of that. It was too powerful right now.

"Sam," I tried again, "one last party tonight? I'm not leaving until tomorrow anyway. Can't you spare one last fling with your best friend?"

"Come on. Stop being such a whiner. Jim is all set to whisk me away to his castle in Madison." She perched on the edge of my bed and all the boxes and bags threatened to slide off.

I thrust out my arms to catch the teetering piles. When all the junk stopped shifting, I looked up. "You rat!" I said. I recognized the devious glimmer in her eyes. "You've arranged something sneaky, haven't you? Did you talk to Jim already or what?"

Sam leaped up and threw her arms around me. "Are you crazy? Of course I have!" she said. "I called him two days ago. I want that last fling too. You didn't guess before this?"

I didn't suspect a thing. We never kept secrets from one another and Sam was surely hard-pressed to keep this one. She probably knew it would be worth it, just to see the look on my face.

At this moment, above all the other comings and goings, we both heard a familiar step on the hardwood floor. Sam's mother.

The look on Sam's face told me everything I needed to know. Actually, I didn't want to know any of what I saw on her face. Both of us had trouble with Sam's mother. If my mother was The Great Stone Face, her mother more than made up the difference. Mrs. Schuster wanted to run her daughter's life, along with everyone else's even remotely connected.

I couldn't see any clean way out of the room and I was afraid I was going to get caught in the middle again. "You haven't told her, have you." It was not even close to a question. "You haven't told her you and Jim are married. Now what?" I hissed. That was all the time I had before Sam's mother materialized in all her glory in the doorway.

Mrs. Schuster was not at all a large woman. Seeing her walk down the street, no one would give her a second glance, she was that ordinary. Today, she was just as ordinary as ever. With sensible shoes, muted plaid skirt smooth below a perfectly starched and tucked white shirt, she fit the image of a British headmistress at a girls' school or a sorority housemother at some hoity-toity Eastern school. But when her eyes drilled us, I thought more of Oliver Twist and watery gruel than of a refined girls' school.

"Reggie, how nice to see you again. My, but don't you look good."

She always trotted out the same greeting. I couldn't stand her and I was pretty sure she knew it. "Hello, Mrs. Schuster." I could never figure out what else to say. Especially since it should be something pleasant. Usually, it didn't matter anyway, because I was never the center of Mrs. Schuster's world or even of her attention. That, of course, suited me just fine.

Mrs. Schuster turned to Sam and said, "You'll never guess who I ran into this morning. Remember that nice young…"

I tuned out. I was too busy looking for an escape hatch. Over the bed? The bed was full of far too many piles. Under the bed then. No reason to panic. Not yet. But I knew there wasn't enough room to crawl under the bed.

I was trapped for the duration unless I could figure out some humane way of saying, "Excuse me, but I hate your guts and I need to get out of the room before I puke." As the Dragon Lady gave the room the once-over, I caught Sam's eye and mouthed, "Tell her now!", then went for the over-the-bed route, upsetting a box or two as I stood on the pillow. Luckily, it was my pillow, not Sam's, or the Dragon Lady would never let me out alive.

"I've got to get some books back to the library or they won't sign my diploma." I sounded like an idiot, but I really shouldn't be around when Sam dropped the bomb on her own mother. If the shrapnel didn't kill me, the radiation would.

"Oh, no, dear, I'm taking you both out to lunch."

Dear? I was mentally brought up short, for once. Since when did she call anyone "dear"? Who was she trying to impress? "Sorry," I said. "I've got to get those books back. I really have to go. 'Scuse me, but I'm outta here." *Lame, lame, lame*, I added to myself.

"Mom." Sam moved behind her mother and closed the door. "I want Reggie to be here."

Now, I really was stuck. Sam was determined to have me around to absorb the flying objects after she told her mother about marrying Jim. I could see it in her eyes. Sam was getting ready to drop the bomb and it was too late to turn back now.

I sat down on the pillow.

"Mom..."

I willed Sam to say it all in a rush. If all the military did was push one little button to open those bomb bay doors, all she had to do was spit it out. Go for it, I thought.

"What, dear? What is it? You're not pregnant, are you?"

I couldn't help it. I laughed. And not just a little giggle. No, this was the real thing, right down to my hipbones and then some. As usual, I picked the worst time to laugh.

Sam looked at me. Her face softened from that hard I-gotta-get-through-this look. Neither one of us could hold it in. Suddenly, we were both hysterical.

"Well, if that's the way it is..." Mrs. Schuster turned to push past her daughter, but Sam stopped laughing and put her hands out.

"Mom, Jim and I are married. We got married last summer. He's here for my graduation and then we're moving into an apartment in Madison." An abrupt flood. Her words poured across the gap, came up against the wall of Mom, and spilled and spiraled out of control every which way. "That's all," she stopped.

"What in...?"

I knew how my own mother would react. She wouldn't.

Sam's mother ran on about being kept out of the loop, and got more worked up as she talked. Old Stone Face, I was sure, would only look at me placidly and murmur a soft, "Mm-hm. That's nice." Even if I were a pot-smoking, swearing lesbian—I was positive there too—there'd be no response. Nothing reached my mother. Not any of the new hairstyles, not any of the new moralities. Old Stone Face never faced anything worthy of getting rattled about. Or never recognized anything worthy of getting rattled about.

I snorted softly. I was sitting on a pillow on my last day of college. My mother's dull face, dull voice, and dull response receded abruptly.

I was no longer laughing. No longer breathing either. Which one of us will need artificial respiration first, I wondered, as Sam's mother ran down like an old music box.

"Mom," Sam broke in, "it's fine. I'm not pregnant. I'm not crazy. In a couple of hours, I'll have my degree and I even have a job, if you remember."

I fumed inside. I hoped her mother did remember. It was a darn good job too, with a small firm in Madison. It was perfect. She'd be making a ton more money than I would. I was lucky to get four figures; she'd make five. I doubted I'd ever see that.

All of this flashed in a moment, of course, and I wondered what would happen next. I was getting desperate to get out of the room. From my perch on the pillow, there was only one narrow possibility. I reached over for the doorknob in the hopes of sneaking out behind both of them.

"Don't you move a muscle, young lady," Mrs. Schuster said, very clearly meant for me, though she didn't shift her eyes, or much of her attention, in my direction.

Sam shot me a level, but pleading, look.

We were roommates and friends too long now. I settled back, albeit precariously. Somehow, I figured the blame for all of this hanky-panky was about to fall on me, but for once, I kept my mouth shut. I refused to stick my own foot in my mouth willingly. This time, Mrs. Schuster would have to stuff it in for me, if she could.

"Was this your doing?" Mrs. Schuster turned on me.

I was better off not saying a single word. But I couldn't help it. So much for good intentions. "I try to avoid confrontations with witchy mothers." I actually said that out loud.

Apparently, she didn't hear me, because she was already turned back to Sam.

"How could you do this? How could you up and marry that man"—she did call him a man after all—"without telling me? I am your mother! Well, I guess that goes without saying, doesn't it? Are you pregnant?"

As usual, she didn't really hear what Sam told her.

"I told you, I'm not. And I love him. We didn't want a big wedding planned..."

Intelligent to trail off right there, Sam.

Her mother picked up. "By me? Is that it? You wanted your own little plans? Who do you think weddings are for, young lady? It's not just the bride and groom, you know. It's the family, it's the whole family."

"Come on, Mom," Sam began.

I could tell from her tone, Sam was about to slide the dagger in. They were never really a family. Dad ran off. Mom was a bitter dictator.

"So." I literally sidestepped in, moving off the bed and right between the two of them. There was nowhere for either Sam or her mother to go, and I deliberately came down off the bed facing Sam, turning my back on the Dragon Lady. "Your mom can plan a big huge reception and you can all attend and everyone will be happy." I gave Sam a look direct from God Himself. She got the message.

"All right," Sam conceded after a small, deep pause. She looked over my shoulder, easy enough to do at her height. "We didn't do this to hurt anyone. We just didn't want a big blowup— a big, extravagant party."

"What about his parents? Do his parents know?"

I was startled. Was the Dragon Lady coming around? Or was she just looking for ammunition, having run a bit short at the moment? I managed to turn around, protecting Sam behind my back.

Mrs. Schuster glanced ever so briefly over my shoulder. She didn't look any softer around the edges. Her hawk eyes were still trained on the prey.

"Jim and I told them last Sunday. They invited us for dinner and we decided it was time. I didn't want to tell you over the phone. I wanted to tell you in person. Besides—" this rather lamely— "I know you really like Jim."

Silence for more than a moment. Hang on, Sam. I clenched my mental fists. Sit tight and let her have the last word.

"You are very lucky I do like him."

Silence. Hang on, hang on, I willed.

"My dear, I just don't want you to get hurt."

A definite move toward victory. I stepped to the side and squashed myself against the empty dresser, tipping it back against the wall. "I'm going," I said, but neither of them heard me.

Mrs. Schuster went on. "I eloped too. I should've listened to my parents. My mother told me it would never work out. He was a deadbeat. A charming deadbeat. But no, I had to go off on my own. It was the worst mistake of my life. I couldn't bear…"

At this point, I couldn't bear to keep my mouth shut. Admittedly, I did not like this woman, but I conceded the Dragon Lady managed to raise a great daughter. I stepped back in.

"Look," I said directly to the Dragon Lady, "I never would have such a great friend if you listened to your parents. You've got Sam. And so have I." With that, I squeezed past them and managed to get out into the hall before anyone had a chance to say another word. I closed the door tightly and quietly, and began to breathe again.

"From here on, they're on their own," I whispered. "And I'm afraid, I am too." Gone were the days when all of us would sit up until all hours playing cards and talking over our current loves. Gone were the evenings at The Library—the bar, not the book collection. Gone were days of folding laundry together and sharing clothes and running out impulsively for ice cream. But then again, gone were the tedious classes and jumping to someone else's rules. No more curfews or "Sorry, you're underage" or heartbreak from watching someone else kissing the man you were grooming to phone *you*, not her. All the petty squabbles, done. Done! Finally, I'd be out on my own, earning my own money and able to buy what I wanted, more or less. I'd only have to see Old Stone Face once in a while, not every other weekend. I had an excuse—I was working. Of course, that last one would bite the dust early, because I wasn't about to let Dad suffer through weekend after weekend with Mother when I could drive on up and relieve the tedium.

I was out from under now and, though I wasn't sure exactly what I'd be facing out there in the Real World, I sure as hell was ready to give it my best shot.

Chapter 5
Betty

1934

When my mouth stopped talking about moving after college, I did just what I said I'd do. I went home for a week and broke it to the family that I was, indeed, leaving the nest. I traveled to Milwaukee to find a place to hang my hat, then returned home to pack my worldly belongings. My college steamer trunk made its way alone to Downer Avenue, Milwaukee, Wisconsin where it waited patiently until I could join it.

As for myself, I went up to the lake and proceeded to have a marvelous time for one last fling with my college buddies. The pine trees sighed just like in the storybooks, the lake was warm enough for skinny-dipping after dark, and the cabin, though pretty basic, had electricity and indoor plumbing. What more could we want? We had each other; that was first and foremost. I swam every morning, walked in the woods, wrote poetry on the dock, sketched, and talked non-stop with the others about our futures.

We grew nostalgic. We vowed to stay in touch. I was the only one heading down to the city to work and, though I made sure they all knew they must come and visit, I knew even then it was unlikely. Margaret, on the contrary, was full of hope once she joined us. She told us all about her elopement to Las Vegas and the Little Chapel in the Palms. Everyone saw a radiant new bride, eager to get on with her life. She *was* radiant. But when I caught glances from her, I could see she was also certain the door to her past was swinging slowly, but inexorably, shut behind her. She couldn't bear to think of it, I could tell. Her smiles didn't make those little crinkles around her eyes when we talked about our futures. It was a sure sign she saw what I saw: most of us would never see each other again. Living in Madison would put her out of touch. Almost everyone else was farther north and I would be the only one near enough, a couple hours away, to maintain any kind of connection, tenuous though it might turn out to be. Many of the others were getting married over the course of the summer and I appeared to be the "lonely only," as they insisted on calling me. The nickname didn't bother me much. I was independent, not alone.

I was one of the few in our circle who didn't insist upon finding a man to marry. Everyone else was searching diligently for "Mr. Right."

My original plan was to remain single. That plan, however, seemed to be a matter of public concern. "It's too late for her," my mother's friends would sigh. "Looks like she'll never marry. Such a lovely girl too."

But then, Earl Quinn came along. At the lake, on the last evening when we went across to the big lodge to treat ourselves to a dinner out, I met the man I'd marry. Of course, I didn't know it at the time. Earl tells me over and over he knew it, but I was totally oblivious. The more I find out about men, the more I see how hard they fall when they succumb to love. Tunnel vision, in fact.

Earl was a big man, taller than I was by a head and more. He had the beginnings of a small paunch, which might go on to develop into a somewhat substantial pillow in his later years. At first glance, his head seemed large for his body, but it was easily balanced by his broad shoulders. His hands were what drew me to him from the first. His fingers were large and plump, but from the moment he began to talk, they came alive, supplementing and enlarging his conversations. They reminded me of attentive translators that would jump to life to clarify and refine points made by the head diplomat. He intrigued me. At first, it was only intrigue. After that evening at the lake, he quietly pursued me.

Starting in the fall, he made special trips to the city, bought me roses, even hired a violinist one night to serenade me. Most important, he talked to me. Not like a child, but like a functioning adult. People treated me that way at the college, but most people everywhere else treated me as fragile. I even looked fragile with my red hair and alabaster complexion. After all, I was a woman, wasn't I? I deserved to be taken care of. Earl was an astute and farsighted man; he didn't take care *of* me. I could do that myself, and he knew it. He took care *for* me. You see the difference?

He cornered me in Milwaukee one windy winter day, three years after he began the siege, and proposed. I had no plans to fall in love with anybody, but by the time Earl proposed, I surprised even myself and fell head over heels in love with him. He was a good man and the intrigue I felt at first grew into a fierce love. I discovered I didn't want to go on in life without him. He knelt down in the snow—in the *snow,* can you imagine!—under the streetlight at the corner of my block and asked for my hand. I had all I could do to nod, my throat closed up tight, just like that. When he stood up and put his arms around me, I buried my face in his camelhair overcoat and cried like a baby. Isn't that strange? I was so happy, I just fell apart. The best part was, Earl cried too when I said yes.

Over the years, there were plenty of things to cry about, but we laughed more. Right from the beginning, we had things to laugh at. Like the china fiasco. When I first moved to Milwaukee to work, I purchased a lovely set of china and crystal, figuring the investment was worth it. In my little rooming house, I entertained friends and colleagues, and my luncheon plates served up elegant repasts. No dinner parties for me. I was going to remain single and serve only elegant little brunches and luncheons. Once Earl and I married, he and the other husbands complained about how small the plates were. These were meat and potatoes men, and there just was not enough room on those little luncheon plates. I went out and bought larger plates.

So much for my elegant little plans of an elegant little single life with elegant little luncheons.

We married the September following that wintry proposal. On Labor Day, in fact, because it was the only day Earl could get off work. We liked to joke we were married on Labor Day and never stopped laboring. I, of course, quit my job in Milwaukee and moved back to my hometown right after school was out, in order to help my mother organize everything for the wedding.

Earl worked in sales in Milwaukee. Margaret and Bill weren't far away. After they eloped to Las Vegas, Daddy eventually came to terms with the fact they didn't want to live near him in Chicago. It was a good piece of luck that landed Bill a good teaching position in Madison after grad school. I was ecstatic we were all so close.

Earl and I had a grand first two years, none of which is worthy of mention. All in all, he was a marvelous husband, and I grew to love him more and more as we merged our lives. He took care for me and I took care for him. Within two years, I was pregnant.

I was twenty-six years old when I married; twenty-eight, pregnant.

Reggie waited even longer than I did. By the age she married, people in my day would have given her up as a spinster school teacher, doomed, as it were, to walk life's road alone. But I kept my mouth shut. I watched Margaret's father handing out advice—dictums, really—on how she should live her life. Up until college, he ruled the roost. When she met me, things changed. She rebelled. I ruined her, according to her father, or at least damaged her. I'll admit to unwittingly showing her another way. She watched me and saw possibilities. I wasn't out to change her at all. In time, I realized, for Margaret, it turned out to be liberation, but for others, it might be something more sour. My advice wasn't always welcome, nor necessary. I was better off keeping my own counsel than taking the chance of ruining someone's life course. It turned out, silence caused more damage than I could imagine. Or desire, certainly.

Chapter 6
Reggie

1966

I checked over my shoulder for cars emerging from the school driveway, then pulled out, putting the day's storms and triumphs behind me. February was extra cold and the sun didn't burn off all the frost on the windshield. I could see my breath, even inside the car. The snow crunched and squeaked beneath the tires as I pulled out of the parking lot. The sun was out, but the clear skies meant uncommon cold.

I muttered out loud. I'm cold. I'm tired. I'm hungry. I cannot for the life of me figure out why in the world I chose the teaching profession. I could make a lot more money going into the editing business. Heck, I could make a lot more money going into the book selling business. I allowed myself a moment of reverie about the charm of flitting here and there, peddling textbooks or maybe even novels. But having no idea how booksellers actually sold, I abandoned that train of thought to concentrate on driving.

The thought of a career change lasted only as long as it took for the light to change from red to green. After two years on the job, I realized I really did want to plant myself on the couch in the evenings, surrounded by piles of papers, a red pen stuck behind my ear, with the rumblings of a benevolent dishwasher, like a Parisian maid, coming from my tiny kitchen.

My nights were full of homework and housework. My weekends didn't end up with much free time either, what with preparing writing or literature lessons, correcting more papers and trying to squeeze in a social life besides. Every once in a while, I called Sam, or she called me. We spent a long hour on the phone, laughing and catching up. Most times, it felt like we could pick up where we left off. Other times, when Sam brought up the cute little neighbor kids or the redecorating she was doing, my mind slipped slightly. I realized the same thing probably happened when I waxed eloquent about the student who finally started turning in homework, or complained about the latest difference of opinion with an administrator. It was easier when we could actually get together, but that didn't happen as often as we liked. Jim certainly didn't resent our friendship. He was right there, encouraging us to keep in touch. We did, as much as we could, but we branched out too. We made friends in our own circles. Considering we weren't living in the same town and she was married to boot, we obviously couldn't share an apartment anymore. I kept my eyes peeled for someone to move in with me and share expenses.

Laurie and I met at the first inservice for new teachers to the district. She was a third-grade teacher and I was set to teach high school. We were both new to the area. After a full morning of meetings, when we were all in the buffet line for lunch, she and I grabbed for the same plate, then let go of it at the same time, creating quite a commotion when it shattered on the tile floor. We both burst out laughing and it was downhill from there. Sitting together for lunch, we discovered we had a lot of interests and tastes in common.

We got together regularly, often on Fridays right after school at the local watering hole to lament about the aches and pains of the week. Eventually, after we both taught a year in the same district, we decided to save some bucks and share an apartment. We wished we could afford a place on a lake, but that was hopeless. Even the summer cottages were too expensive. Lake property prices rocketed into the stratosphere, especially since the villages stopped dumping sewage into the lakes and insisted on bringing in city water and sewer. Now, everything up for sale or rent was gone before it even went on the market. For years, owners created charming little flats over their garages or boathouses, but even those were being phased out in favor of swimming cabanas or studios of one sort or another. So, we were stuck in a tiny upstairs apartment whose kitchen had been, we were convinced, a walk-in closet. We shared everything. In spite of our lack of storage space and elbow room, we didn't complain. With our own place, we were delighted.

I was twenty-four and free of the burdens I knew I'd face sooner or later. For now, all I had to do was show up for my job—which I made no bones about loving—and decide how I'd spend my paycheck.

•   •   •   •

Once home after the cold drive, I struggled in the door with the usual stack of books and papers, able to keep it balanced just long enough to drop it, like from a front-end loader, on the miniscule kitchen table.

"I've found a wonderful place!" Laurie met me in the living room. "A truly wonderful place!"

It took me a moment to realize Laurie wasn't talking about new living quarters. Our conversations more recently were concerned with travel. Travel was our consolation prize for having survived a year in the classroom. I thought Laurie deserved more of a respite than I did. Even though I often came home complaining about the low pay, the long hours, and the myriad other things that pecked away at me during the day, she had it much tougher. Laurie taught elementary school and that meant constantly going in at least forty different directions at once. Though I had my work cut out for me with one subject, Laurie had math, science, writing, reading, and all the other "fringe benefits," as Laurie put it. Things like penmanship and milk detail.

"Sure," I said, "you get to color those cute bulletin boards, but, then again, you *have* to color those cute bulletin boards." I added in admiration, "I honestly don't know how you do it."

Laurie reminded me about all the other joys: grubby little hands around knee-level pulling and tugging, and little nasally voices begging attention—"Miss Palmer! Miss Palmer!"—right now! This didn't even take into account the kids who forgot their lunches, or worse, threw up their lunches right on her shoes.

Laurie loved it. Well, not the throwing up part. And as for me? No, none of that was my style. I'd take high school thugs anytime.

"Wonderful!" Laurie repeated as I backflopped onto the couch, allowing tired muscles to turn to jello.

"So? Where is this Nirvana?" My tone was pathetic. Fading interest would be a generous description. Every spare minute, Laurie searched for the perfect vacation getaway spot, so by this time, my enthusiasm was beginning to wane. Not for the travel part. Just for the listening to yet another pitch for the "most wonderful place" part.

"Okay. Are you ready? This is really big."

"I was born ready," I said, waving my hand like a diva in her direction. "Shoot."

"Okay. This is a whole summer of opportunity. We set our own itinerary and just wander all over Europe. We are committed to only the flight part with a group, and then we can take off on our own, if we don't want the whole tour bit. There are several groups coming and going, so we could be gone the entire summer, if we want."

This time, I perked up my ears. The whole summer? Impossible, the rational side of me said. Where would I get the money? But it wasn't even a real question. I didn't care. By the time Laurie was halfway through her explanation, I was sold. So far, my quick decisions resulted only in a little foot-in-mouth infection, not even a full-blown attack of pedodontitis. Now, there was no chance of saying the wrong thing. It didn't take much to say yes. I was primed to go already. How long could it be from February to June? This would give me a reason to make it through second semester.

"Where do I sign?" I asked. "Let's make the Grand Tour."

"Doncha wanna talk to your folks?" Laurie asked. "I'm gonna call mine tonight, just to check in, ya know. I don't need permission or anything."

"Check in, huh?" I spat out a laugh and propped myself up on my elbow. "My dad—I love him dearly—won't discourage me. He loves to travel. Says it's like a course in human behavior, political science and geography, all wrapped up in one."

"I gotta agree with him on all counts," Laurie said, sitting down in our one big chair and curling her feet under her.

She knew better than to ask about my mom. But I went on about her anyway. "And my mother..." Laurie shot me a look that said you-really-wanna-go-there? I ignored it. "She could care less about me, period. I know why she and Dad didn't have any more kids. She had one for him, then said, 'Forget it, buddy. One's plenty.'" I stuffed a little decorative pillow under my head and dropped back onto it. "Not that she did much in raising me, anyway. Dad did all the work. Hell, when I fell off my bike, she just covered her mouth and ran to get him. Couldn't even take care of me herself. How's that for maternal love?" I stopped. Why did I let my mother, who wasn't even around, get me so mad? It's not like she beat me or anything like that, but maybe that would've been better. At least I would know she felt *something* for me, even if it was loathing. The way it was, she didn't care at all. I felt the start of a headache.

"Well," Laurie said, "don't worry about it. I'm sure..." She trailed off, knowing anything she said to try and rationalize things would only upset me more. "So, anyway," she started again, "doesn't this sound like a dream deal? All summer! Can you imagine?"

She was giving me a way out and I took it. "All summer. Yes, I think I can imagine it."

"I'll get all the paperwork tomorrow," she said.

"This'll take some planning," I said. "For sure it'll take our minds off lousy arithmetic charts and asinine essays."

"Second semester will fly," she said. "Are we ready?"

"Bring it on," I answered, closing my eyes to let my mind wander through ancient town squares and forested hills.

Chapter 7
Betty

1940

Earl and I finally moved out of our first tiny upstairs flat and into our own home, small, but wonderfully adequate. Just like one of those needlepoint pictures with flowers leading up to the front door and a morning glory vine on the mailbox and the scent of hidden roses in the backyard. Everything seemed perfect.

"Earl!" I couldn't quite keep the excitement and, yes, a bit of panic, out of my voice. "I think we'd better go. I think Teddy's ready to be born." We were so sure the baby would be a boy that we called him by name for several weeks now. All of the girls' names we picked out just folded into each other. None seemed adequate. We stayed with Teddy and hoped our intuition worked.

We ran this pre-hospital scene by each other so many times that Earl knew I meant it this time. I kept the early contractions to myself, not wanting to worry him. Or myself, for that matter. So, we went on through dinner as though it were just another ordinary day. When he noticed that I wasn't eating much, I told him about the twinges. He jumped up and was ready to leave right that moment. I convinced him the contractions were still too far apart and didn't seem to be regular enough.

Though he was sitting in his favorite easy chair, pretending to read the newspaper, I knew he was on alert for any signal I might send. I was trying to read too, but without much success. I kept watching the clock, sneaking looks like a schoolgirl waiting for the bell and not wanting the teacher to catch her. The contractions were a steady rhythm now, and getting stronger. "I think we'd better go now."

Without even looking up from the newspaper, Earl flung it away like a bullfighter's cape and ran upstairs for my overnight bag. I heard his feet come banging back down the stairs. He was always so organized and, as he swept by, I knew he had everything under control. He loaded up the car, came back in and took my arm, helping me across the kitchen and out the back door. He even remembered to lock the door. While I seemed to be in this heightened state of seeing and feeling everything, I never even thought about the doors.

I slid gingerly into the front seat, trying not to dislodge the towels Earl spread, "just in case." I looked out the window and up at the old trees arched over the driveway. I sat, heavy and full, waiting as Earl ran around and clambered into the driver's seat.

Another contraction struck and I saw, silhouetted against the early evening sky, the oak leaves' outlines. Not just the tree, but every single leaf, it seemed. They trembled ever so slightly, sounding like silk moving, as if waiting to see if the wash of pain would pass quickly. It did, and I receded into myself. My hands smoothed over the baby within me, tracing the tight, smooth skin and the bump that was my bellybutton. I was aware of how rock hard my abdomen was, gathering strength for another assault. I cradled my belly, fingers sprawled across and under the tightness, the tension. The baby, packed in tight, must've felt my caresses. I lifted, as if the baby were already in my arms.

In spite of my shape, or lack of it, I suddenly felt sexy—no, beyond sexy, erotic—then blushed at the thought. There was nothing sexy about sitting with legs braced for the next contraction.

"You are glowing." Earl glanced over and smiled. He was nervous. He didn't really understand what I was feeling, and it was beyond me to try and explain. The only glow he saw was the rise of perspiration along my hairline and my upper lip. But it didn't matter. Again, there was that feeling of sexuality, of desire. Again, a blush.

I smiled back and urged, "Please hurry." I shifted my hands to hold onto the edges of the towels spread under me, hoping that my water didn't break before we reached the hospital. Blue towels, I noticed, wondering if that meant we'd have a boy. I mentally saw Earl cleaning up the water and probably blood, and immediately rejected that vision. The pain came in waves rather than washes now, and I was concerned that things were going just too fast.

"Please hurry," I added needlessly as a few minutes later, we pulled up to the emergency entrance.

•   •   •   •   •

Seven hours. I was lying there seven hours, hovered over by too many people. I barely saw my surroundings, fuzzy and dim, and the pain that went from washes to waves now escalated to thunderous wrenches, in spite of the medication. "It's taking too long," I heard float into my ear as another wrench struck. The squeeze on my body was the squeeze on a toothpaste tube. But someone left the cap on. Nothing could push out. Nothing would push out.

I was floating away from this. I couldn't seem to stop myself, to squeeze and push some more. Or even offer any help. I was floating away.

When I was jerked back, it was to ever tightening wrenches, and my abdomen that I thought so turgid before was screwed down tighter than a drum cover. My hands went instinctively to cradle and lift, but that did not help, and I couldn't even feel the bumps and angles I could before. My skin was stretched smooth, like a marble Madonna.

It started, and everything was lower, and harder, and tighter. The feeling of erotic sexiness was gone, replaced with sweat and hard, hard yearnings. And I was alone. Earl was banished. I was traveling this road alone.

"Lie flat now." I was helped without request, my legs pulled up and open as another wrench struck, taking me farther and farther from control. I was ecstatic and angry, beyond comprehension angry, all at the same time. What was happening to me?

"She's crowning." A nurse to a doctor. My nurse. My doctor. Yet no one consulted me.

As another wrench gathered me together, squeezing me open—I could feel it!—I felt suddenly the rhythm within me. The power was too great and I rose to meet it, bearing down with all my might. The rhythm was right and it overpowered me. I could ride with it now. I rose, ready.

"Yes!" I cried as the black rubber mask moved over my open mouth and nose, and suddenly I was gone.

• • •

"Betty?" The voice was familiar, but I couldn't seem to place it. The touch too was familiar. My hand was lifted, but I was powerless to protest or return the grasp. Did I really inhabit this body? There was a sense of emptiness.

"Betty." The voice was more insistent this time and I squeezed my eyes tight before I allowed them to open.

The sunlight was subdued into bars and shafts across the white blanket. My blue and white hospital gown lay flat against me, flat clear down to my knees under the white blanket and sheets. Everything was smoothed down, tucked in, disciplined.

"The baby." Earl. It was Earl, of course. Suddenly, with mention of the baby, I fully possessed my body, forcing it to attention. The voice was wrong. That was not Earl's voice. Was it?

He engulfed my hand and our eyes locked.

"The baby." I could only repeat, and I knew better than to make it a question. I could see it in his shoulders, in his eyes. I knew.

For the first time, he turned from me. Walked to the window. Put his hands through his hair. Turned. His white shirt was flat against his body, his gray pants were creased flat and smooth, disciplined. Even from here, I caught the scent of his Old Spice.

"What..." I could not—would not—say what might, or perhaps may not, lay between us there on the floor, on the gray and green tiles on the floor. There they were, all the words that need to be picked up and said. I could almost see them on the checkerboard of gray and green linoleum tiles. Black characters in loops and lines of his handwriting. He wouldn't bend, and I could not. Even though he looked at me, somehow, I couldn't see clearly.

He moved as if he was looking down into a fishpond, a fishpond I inhabited. He was no longer smooth, but distorted, undulating slightly against the ceiling as I looked up from my watery depths. Then he stepped across and out of my field of vision and away from my pond.

Almost immediately, he was behind the nurse, but he stood on the tile walk above my pond, refraining from touching the water. Not standing aloof, exactly, but somehow protecting the upper air where I couldn't go yet.

"Teddy?" I said. "Give me our baby. Earl?"

I heard the almost silent answer through the thick water that I inhabited. "Gone," I heard them say. "Gone," and then the beginnings of an apology. There seemed to be more that they were saying, but I couldn't hear anything. I needed to know. I had to know.

"How?" I whispered, and the nurse explained how the umbilical cord cut off our little boy's life as he struggled to be born.

If I had known. If only I had known. If I had been in any way in control, I would have taken a knife and cut him out myself.

Pulled him by foot or hand or anything I could lay my hands on. I would have saved him. If I'd known. If only.

"They didn't know. They didn't know until it was too late. That Teddy was strangled. Our baby was strangled." Earl's voice reached into the fishpond and lifted me out into the air which I could no longer breathe. I was suffocating, dying on the green and gray tile walkway above the fishpond to which I could no longer return. Dying without breath. Like my baby. Choking and gasping without water to soothe. Dying of the very stuff that should give me life.

The pain in Earl's eyes was clear, seen this directly, without benefit of anything between us. He leaned away from my screaming. Just a tremor, hardly a movement. I saw it, though. How could he know, how could he ever know what I knew?

I was suddenly angry again, clawing and hitting, fists hard, hard as my belly was. I hated him. I loved him. This pain was unbearable, with no rhythm, nothing to push against, nothing to rise to. Earl couldn't help me. If he could not help me before, how could he possibly help me now? No one could help me. Through my own tears, I watched the tears move down his cheeks too, small brooks finding their ways over and around the terrain of his face. His pain, so helpless and visible, streamed into my ocean, now overflowing continents and swallowing cities.

"My baby!" Came out in washes and waves and wrenches, crashing and booming off the walls, like a Bach fugue in an empty cathedral, until a nurse came with a needle.

As my reverberations faded, I cried, and wondered if Earl would get anything to take away the pain.

* * * * *

They let me hold him. Just for a moment. Long enough to count his toes and fingers and look at every little crease. They buried him in a small cardboard coffin at the back of my parents' cemetery plot. "He'll rest peaceful there," they said, "and will be gone long before any other family member needs that end plot." There was not a marker, not even a name. It was as if he never came into being.

After a week in the hospital, I was home. We were home. Just the two of us, when there should have been three. I couldn't look at Earl. He was tender, surely, but as we drove away from the hospital, I sat tight against the car door, trying not to think about the last time I rode with him, fertile and full. Now I had trouble breathing. It would be easier to breathe underwater than to consume the thick air that was supposed to be a source of life.

"Darlin'?" Earl said as he opened the car door for me when we reached home, and held out his hand.

I really didn't want to answer. In the hospital, he turned away from me just when I needed him the most. Of course, I was sure he hurt too, but couldn't he at least have plunged in and reached out to me then? I didn't need help getting out of the car nearly as much as I needed help when he turned away from me. Why couldn't he grab my hand then?

I looked up at him and he pulled back his hand.

"I'll get your bag," he said, stepping back. His eyes clouded for a moment. I wasn't sure if it was tears or confusion. Either way, I couldn't touch him.

"Thank you," I forced myself to say, then stepped out of the car, leaving the door open behind me. I heard him close the trunk, and then the car door, as I went into the house and stopped in the middle of the kitchen.

"I...I'll just take this upstairs," he said, coming in and continuing past me. He ducked his head and ran his hand across my shoulders as he passed.

"Thank you," I repeated. It seemed to be the only thing I could come up with, that simple automatic civility. The only thing I wanted right then was a bath. One of those that steamed up the bathroom mirrors and would plunge me into a physical fog that matched my mental state.

Earl returned to the kitchen. He turned his big hands palms out and shrugged slightly. "What can I do for you, darlin'?"

Get my baby back, I wanted to scream. But, of course, he couldn't do that. Neither of us could. Still, though we were together, there was a gap. How could we go through that and now feel so alienated? I was so cold and maybe he could make me warm again. Maybe not. "Nothing," is what I said. "I just want a bath."

That seemed to make sense to him. The furrows in his brow cleared and he smiled slightly. "Then that's what I'll do. I can draw a bath for you." He moved as if to come to me, then instead turned to the stairs. "Why don't you make yourself a nice cup of tea and I'll put some of that pink stuff in the tub for you. That always smells so good." He stopped and looked over his shoulder at me. "Are you okay?" He caught my eye, but only for a moment. "I'll go fill the tub." And he was gone.

A cup of tea. Yes, that did sound all right. I put the kettle on and set everything out on the wooden tray my mother always used when I was sick. She served me tea with toast cut into long strips— three, if I remembered correctly—and would sit on my bed with me while I ate. Sometimes there would be a small flower tucked in a miniature vase.

I went to the windowsill and plucked a small purple blossom from my best African violet plant. I set it next to my teacup, the one my father bought my mother in Canada on their honeymoon. Just then, the kettle shrieked and, taking it off the stove, I finished my rituals, using my favorite old teapot, the one with the cabbage roses on the front and the fine gold line running up the back of the handle. The tea could steep in the bathroom.

Earl's voice came drifting down the steps. "Okay, it's all ready! Nice and hot, just like you like it."

He deserved an answer, I guess. "Thank you." Picking up the tray, I headed upstairs.

"I left the door closed so it would stay nice and warm in there." He looked like a little boy at his grandmother's garden party, uncomfortable, but determined to stick it out. He took the tray from me. "You go get ready. I'll put this in there for you."

I heard him move into the bathroom, settle the tray down with a small clink, then come out and close the door behind him. I heard him start down the stairs, calling back as he went, "Holler if you need anything. I'll just be downstairs."

Our bedroom was almost as we left it. Earl even tried to make the bed while I was in the hospital, but the spread was crooked and the pillows weren't covered. I closed the door behind me. I needed to be alone, without noise, without interruption. I unbuttoned my housedress, loose now, let it fall to the floor and stepped out of it. I pried off my shoes, leaving them where they were. I slid my slip easily over my head and tossed it onto the bed. I was stiff from holding everything in—my tears, my rage. My shoulders hurt. Leaving my clothes melted on the floor and bed, I grabbed my robe and turned to go to the bathroom.

My image in the full-length mirror mounted on the back of the bedroom door froze me in place. There stood a woman, bathrobe in one hand, ready to be swung around her shoulders. She was not tall, but her proportions were good for her size. Her red hair shone in a short bob, backlit by the morning sunlight streaking in through the far window. I couldn't see her facial details clearly through the sudden tears that blurred my eyes. Her panties fit too well over her flaccid belly.

I dropped my robe and faced myself in the mirror, even took a step closer. Everything shimmered. I rubbed the heels of my hands savagely across my eyes, angry at my inability to control this reaction, dislodging the tears and clearing my vision. Like a surgeon, I looked myself over. I wasn't interested in my face. I already knew all about that and didn't want to see anything more.

Although my feet and legs didn't interest me either, I started there, then moved my examination upward, hoping for—what was I hoping for? Perhaps to see that protruding belly again, a chance to do it over, to do it right this time. But no. By the time my gaze reached my belly, all I saw was silk and skin without any hint of life beneath. I swiveled into profile. But nothing changed. Still no sign of fertility, of hope. How could my body have already gone back to its original shape? How could it forget the contours of that little boy who'd resided so long within? I was deprived of everything. My body didn't even remember, or remind me. I was supposed to be back to normal. Even my physical self was telling me that.

Turning back to face the mirror, I spread my fingers across my belly. The fingers intertwined, no longer stretching for each other across a dome of skin that moved beneath, communicating with me, telling me, "I'm coming! I'm coming!"

I forced the tears inside and unhooked my bra, letting it fall to the floor. I moved my hands up under my breasts, cupping them. Here there was memory. Though there was no milk after the drug they gave me, my breasts were still large, heavy, fleshy. I rubbed my thumbs across the nipples, around the large areolas, but they didn't stir. No milk, no arousal. They stayed soft and flat as vanilla pudding. I doubted they would ever stiffen again. Not even Earl would be able to do that anymore.

I couldn't hold the tears back. They spilled over silently and ran down to my chin. I grabbed my robe from the floor and, gripping it close, flung open the bedroom door, escaping to the enveloping steam in the bathroom.

＊　　　　＊　　　　＊

That was my routine for the next six weeks. The days became static. Get up, make breakfast, though I could hardly bear to eat, get dressed and carry on with the necessary drudgery of each day, the cooking and cleaning and all that. Earl took over grocery shopping because I couldn't make myself leave the house. He stayed on the fringes of my life, watching. I didn't know what to do myself. All I could see was the moment when he had turned from me when I needed him the most. Why didn't he wade into my pain and hold me? I was unable to touch him, my reach wasn't long enough. I could see pain on his face, so why couldn't he see mine? I knew he did. But he turned away in the hospital just at the moment I was drowning. And now, now he was doing it again.

Six weeks. I was reconciled to the way I was living. Each evening, I bathed, though I surely didn't need it. Earl continued with a tray of tea, adding toast with sugar and cinnamon or scones from the corner bakery in what I'm sure he saw as an attempt to draw me out. I was having none of it. I couldn't let him touch me in bed. When he left the house, he only gave me a peck on the cheek. At meals, he carried on one-sided conversations that petered out long before they reached resolutions.

I was frozen, unable to move forward.

Chapter 8
Reggie

1966

"Hey," Laurie whispered, "take a look at *that* stranger of the male persuasion!" She whistled low, but not loud enough for anyone else to hear. She elbowed me, tipped her head to the left and mouthed, "What a *looker*!"

The open market of this small Spanish town wasn't very crowded, so it took me a few moments of seeming nonchalance to arrange my view so I could look where she indicated. The red, green and yellow awnings and umbrellas stood well above the stands piled high with brilliant summer flowers gathered in armloads and pails. The stands with eggplants, beans and too many types of peppers to count were brimming to overflowing. Shafts of sunlight provided brief moments of glare and heat for the shoppers drifting along with string bags, strollers or wagons. Everywhere I looked, color exploded.

I returned to rummaging in the produce before taking a second look. I didn't want to be too obvious. When I did turn to scan the area directly to my left, toward which Laurie was pointing, a bit more frantically by now, I had to stop myself from doing a double-take. "Wow! He is *gorgeous*!" Dark hair under a khaki hiking hat, expressive hands gesturing to this and that bundle of flowers, a loud and sincere-sounding laugh as he talked to the flower-seller while she wrapped up a large cluster of daisies. I tore my gaze away before I crossed some cultural boundary. "Carrots look pretty mild after that," I said to Laurie.

She chuckled. "We still have to eat, ya know. Eye candy isn't enough."

"Too bad," I said, picking up a plump bunch of carrots.

"You don't want those," a voice broke in and I turned to see Laurie's *looker*. "Try these. They were pulled just this morning. Look, you can tell if you examine the tops. Still crisp."

His accent slid like caramel sauce across a Spanish flan, melting as it went. Pure Castilian, easy on the ear. I mentally took myself by the collar and shook, hard.

Automatically, the way a child would respond to an adult's suggestion to think about that impulse purchase, I looked down at the bunch of carrots in my hand. Sure enough, wilted tops. "Thanks," I said, then reconsidered. It was such a mechanical answer. "I wish—I mean, I don't garden— Well. Thanks." I took his offering of fresh carrots, grasping them by their tops.

He laughed. "I don't harm helpless shoppers, you know. I just didn't want you to get home and discover they weren't as sweet as they looked. My mother says I put my nose in where I don't need to, but I can't seem to help myself."

I took my time answering. I convinced myself I didn't need a pickup line; I only wanted carrots. I wasn't ready for more Mediterranean male assistance, which usually involved admiration and wandering hands. "Thanks for the help," I told him.

"Enjoy your carrots," he said, turning away with his bunch of daisies grasped in one hand.

"*Gracias*," I said, my voice weaker than usual, and he tossed a quick wave back as he left.

A bit distracted, we continued shopping for some other gifts we could take to dinner that night. We met a wonderful couple touring an ancient monastery a couple of weeks before. All of us were on vacation, all of us in unfamiliar territory and, as it goes when strangers are thrown together, we struck up a conversation. While my Spanish wasn't perfect, it was better than adequate and gave me the advantage to travel the way I wanted, blending in among native speakers.

We all had dinner together that night because we found each other pleasant company. The next morning, when the couple headed toward home, they gave Laurie and me directions to their home, and an invitation to visit if our roamings brought us close enough. The more we thought about it, the better it sounded to bunk down for a homecooked meal and a little tender loving care, so we arranged our meanderings to visit them a few days before we were due to fly home.

When we got to their apartment with our bundle of fresh market carrots and potatoes and eggplant, the *looker* from the market was standing at the door with the armload of daisies. I couldn't believe it. Funny how things happen.

"Hello!" he called, clearly happy to see us. "How lucky am I to see you again? What brings you to my aunt and uncle's house?"

My Spanish—and my English—suddenly deserted me.

Laurie launched into the explanation in her high school Spanish.

"I knew it, I knew it," Laurie said a few days later when I explained I arranged to take a later plane home. "The way you look at Carlos—"

"Hold it!" I protested. "Well, all right, he's a big piece of why I want to stay longer."

"You don't have to explain a thing to me. And don't worry about it. I'm a big girl. I'll find my way back to London."

Two days later, I saw Laurie off to connect with the group going back to the States. I was free as a bird for another two weeks.

• • •

"Yeah," I said to Sam. "Yeah, Europe. I'm calling from Spain."

Although I would never say it to her, I wished Sam were with me. When Laurie and I took off weeks before, Sam wished us the best, but by the look on her face when she dropped us at the airport, she wanted to go along. We both knew that wasn't possible. She was married, and pregnant to boot. Now I was in Spain, I wasn't about to rub in my good fortune. Back home, I managed to see quite a bit of her. Sixty minutes wasn't all that far to drive, and the countryside between Madison and Milwaukee was so gorgeous, especially in the fall. Summer was best, by far my first choice because I could stay overnight with Sam, even during the week. Then, both of us could get up and hover over a cup of coffee before she headed out to work. Jim, bless his heart, was always affable about me hanging around. I never stayed long enough, or came often enough, to wear out my welcome. I was no fool. I remembered Ben Franklin's comments about how fish and guests stank after three days. Of course, Sam was always sorry to see me go, and even Jim, to my surprise, often urged me to stay.

But now I was standing in a small Spanish post office, phone pressed tight against one ear, a finger stuffed in my other ear, feeling like an idiot. Behind me, Carlos couldn't seem to resist breathing on my hair, which was both annoying and distracting, although not at all unpleasant.

Carlos. Ah, yes. He was all one would expect in an exotic, foreign lover. Tall, but not too tall; unusual brown eyes, but not too brown; romance-novel attentive. I easily fell into him without considering if he was also viewing me as an exotic.

Sam's hollow voice pulled me back. "Are you still in Spain? I thought you'd be heading back to London by now."

"I know. Did you get my postcards yet?" I asked. This phone call was taking entirely too much time. Overseas phone calls weren't very reliable in the first place, and weren't cheap either. After her Yes, I moved along. "Look, I've only got another minute. I just wanted you to know I'm not coming home with Laurie. The group has another flight going back later in August and I've managed to finagle a change on my ticket to go home then instead of now... What?"

"I said, what on earth would keep you over there longer? You've been gone almost all summer."

I could picture Sam screwing up her nose on the other end. Just because she was settled and starting a family, I had a feeling she felt I should be too. Settled, if nothing else. "I just decided to hang around a bit longer. There're some things I haven't had time to see yet, and I want to see them." Carlos turned closer next to me, careful in a public place. His hand barely touched my forehead as he moved a wisp of hair away from my eyes. Through the distraction, I continued, "Listen, Sam, will you call my mother? I can't get a hold of her. She's taking a couple of courses at that new art and design studio, and is gone every time I call. Either that, or she doesn't want to talk to me." I laughed, but it wasn't meant to be funny.

"It's gotta be expensive, calling from Europe and all. You do realize, don't you," she added, "she'd love to talk to you? But you know how demanding those studio courses are. She's probably spending tons of time down there, trying to get everything done."

I reached up and touched Carlos's fingertips, drawing my own along the back of his hand. "She's got to come home sometime. I can't reach her, and trying is getting too time-consuming. So just call her, will you?"

"Of course, silly," she said before I finished the question. "I'll get right on it."

I knew Sam would keep calling until she reached my mother. Truth was, I didn't want to keep trying. The news I was staying extra weeks would probably not affect her. Nothing seemed to take my mother by surprise. Nothing disturbed her. She'd say, "Oh, that's nice," and that would be it. I gave up long ago searching for something running deep underneath. There wasn't anything. She was as shallow as a drainage ditch. No use going down that road. I was here, Mother was there, who cared? I shrugged my mental shoulders. Sam agreed again to tell my mother and I finished with, "Thanks, Sam. I'll talk to you when I get back. Bye."

In the narrow cubicle, I couldn't help but snuggle against Carlos. Not that I wanted to avoid him. When he brushed his hand across the top of my head and down across my ear, I shivered pleasantly. I rationalized I really didn't see everything I wanted to see and, luckily, it was all in Spain. How convenient. It was more than just Carlos. Carlos was the frosting. Pretty sweet frosting.

As I hung up the phone, paid for my call to Sam, and headed out the door, I knew I'd be home in plenty of time to get organized for classes in the fall. Now that Laurie was gone and later flight arrangements were final, I could admit that Carlos had everything to do with me hanging around for a bit longer. This was just so strange. I figured I was set. Teaching, the apartment, my friends, my car, my bank account. Everything was set. Were things really any different now? Yes, they were. I just didn't know where it was all going from here.

Carlos drew his arm back from across my shoulder and I could feel his fingertips, each one separately and lightly drawing tracks across my neck. I was aware of his touch, pressing lightly, like children leaving footprints in damp sand, and my mind spiraled away from Laurie and job and home. My breathing revved up. Why was I doing this? We were in a Spanish parking lot and I was feeling—I didn't even know what. A shiver ran along my arms and I couldn't control it.

"Carlos?"

"Mmm?" He tucked my arm under his, drawing me in toward his summer warmth. He smelled of musk and spices, and lemon for some reason, and I would recognize it anywhere, even in a crowd of strangers. His nose brushed the top of my ear and again I was swept away.

"What?" he asked. "What did you want to know?" When I didn't answer, he said, "Listen, let's go get some strawberries. No," he adjusted, "let's walk the woods trail to that small café. They have strawberries and cream, and that wonderful wine you like. We have the whole day. Let's enjoy it." His eyes combed my face, as if memorizing details. The sun glittered through his hair as he stepped back and led me around the car. I couldn't see his face clearly because the sun created a halo behind him.

"Don't you work for a living?" I teased.

"This is more than a vacation, you know. This is my retreat. My aunt and uncle's gift to me. I get to forget about work; they get to use me for whatever they need. We both win. This time, you win too." His look was soft. "I win more."

My mind careened off. What was I supposed to do with this? We knew each other for what? Four days? Why was his man-smell already recognizable? Why could I close my eyes and reproduce his laugh? Hearing footsteps on the stairs, why could I pick out his tread, knowing when he stopped, adjusted his step, began again? Without meaning to, without thinking, I leaned into him, breathing in. He fit into me, our angles and slopes somehow meeting with little gaps of light, breathing spaces, in all the right places. The rest, like soft cogs on some human machine, rested against and worked with their counterparts. We fit, and I loved the feel of it.

Carlos maneuvered us out of town.

"Why don't you come to the States sometime?" I was hoping for subtle, but it came out blatant, unpolished. I immediately wished I could rewind and come up with something else, but I didn't know what. Where did this all come from, anyway? Yeah, his good looks knocked me off my feet at first. Yeah, I fired up whenever he touched me. But what was it, really? Did I want to make love to him all day long, or only take him home and parade him around all my friends like a souvenir? Lord, I hoped that wasn't it! He wasn't a charm to hang on a charm bracelet. The making love part—well, that didn't sound so bad. I wasn't sure what I wanted, a short, flaming affair or a long-term relationship. For right now, I shoved it in a back closet in my mind and focused on him. How would he respond?

He was negotiating the narrow roads and runs that led to the forest, but spared me a glance. "Come to the States? I'd like that. But I don't know the language. What about that?" His eyes were back on the road.

"What about it? I'd be around to negotiate for you." I wondered if, in his very Spanish heart, he knew how that would feel. To be led. I added, "English isn't that hard. You could learn."

"Here we are." He parked, and turned toward me, one arm draped on the steering wheel. He was evading my words. "Let's walk. We can worry about America tomorrow. Right now, we're here."

Right now, we were here. Everything else stretched out ahead of us, so I slipped that idea into a side pocket and decided to concentrate on the here and now. I wasn't ready to think too deeply about it anyway. We started into the woods.

Halfway down the trail, we crossed a stream. There was no bridge, but there were plenty of rocks worn smooth by the water and earlier feet. Carlos stepped to the middle and, straddling two flat boulders, stretched out his hand. I was concentrating on my feet so much, when he pulled me to him, I could do nothing but slide into his arms, cocooned before I knew what was happening.

"I can make it," I said, then turned my face up to meet his.

"Can you?" With an enveloping smile, he held me. "You are my prisoner now."

"I'm no one's prisoner." That came out without thinking, and I cringed inwardly. "I mean, I choose not to be trapped by anyone."

"You are free to go," he said, but his arms wrapped themselves around me and my own hands, of their own volition, pressed against his back, bringing him in tighter.

There was absolutely nothing I wanted to, or could, say. My mind left me adrift. That happened too frequently lately.

"Well?" It was not so much a question from him as an announcement as he leaned over me.

I could feel his breath once again, stronger on my hair than before, as he hovered over me. Breath on my hair. Breath at my temple. Breath at my lips. "Yes." The moment my lips moved, breath in my mouth. I felt frozen in time. I heard distinctly the sound of his breath pulled suddenly into his nose, a soft pulse. I felt the brush of sunlight and his whiskers, not quite smooth-shaven. His fingertips mapped my jawline, and suddenly there was again daylight between our lips, a feather of light and breathing.

I was never kissed like that before. No thunder and lightning. No earth moving. All light. All light and breath.

Voices coming down the trail pulled me out of the captured moment and put us right back into the middle of the stream, balanced on boulders, suddenly precarious.

"More hikers," he explained without taking his eyes from mine. "Come on. I'll help you across."

I began to giggle as he shifted his weight to move across. Like heat waves, the moment shimmered and was gone. In a heartbeat, we were on the bank, hand in hand, laughing. I didn't want anyone to slip into our moment, but the voices arrived ahead of their attendant bodies by only a fraction of a minute. A short greeting, good manners between strangers. Soon the voices were trailing off after their owners, hurrying to catch up as the hikers splashed the creek and moved on ahead of the two of us.

I could barely get my head around what just happened, but I knew I wanted it to happen again.

"Come on," he whispered. "I know a private spot. Hidden away, lots of soft grass." He leaned down and kissed my ear.

Maybe I'd stay in Spain.

Chapter 9
Betty

1941

"Earl?" I was afraid to ask, but I simply had to. I was still, in a way, drowning from the loss of Teddy. I needed to get away by myself for a bit. Maybe it was just to lick my wounds, but maybe I could really deal with the melancholy. Earl was so good to me, after. In spite of that—or maybe because of that—well, I simply had to go.

"Hm?" I knew he was attentive behind the newspaper. I'd have his full attention as soon as he found a natural break. That first response told me that he was shifting gears.

With a flutter, the paper went down and we were eye to eye. I really couldn't let go of the doorjamb, but I mentally moved into his lap.

"Okay, darlin', what's up?"

Now that I came to this, I didn't think I could go any further. But I had to. "Earl, I love you." What an inane beginning. This was not anywhere near where I wanted to go.

He smiled. "I know that. I love you too, darlin'. Is something bothering you?"

I could almost hear the cringe, as he knew perfectly well what was bothering me. And him too. We just couldn't get past the baby. The loss of the baby. Because *I* couldn't get past it. "Earl, I really need to get away a bit. Not a long time, you know. Certainly not for a long time. But I turn every corner and see..." I trailed off, and he came to me.

His arms were around me and I was suddenly warm. But somehow not warm enough.

"I know, darlin', I know." And he did. He knew. His chin trembled too as I pressed myself deeper into him. We were both suffering. "I know I can't get to that piece of you that still belongs to the—our little boy."

How did I find so good a man? It was eight months now, and I was still as empty as I was when I walked out of the hospital, having to go home and look at all of those darling little blankets and booties. So many things, and all needing to be packed away. I still couldn't do it. I wouldn't let him do it either. So, through my own choice and my own frozen self, I was surrounded by beautiful baby things. But no beautiful baby.

Now I simply had to release Teddy. Never from my heart, never. But from my everyday comings and goings. We still desperately wanted babies—I cried at even the word—but we couldn't. Not as long as I was clutching him so. The doctors said I was perfectly fit and would have more babies. But there would never be another first. Never. "Earl, I want to spend a little time alone."

He didn't even flinch, just took my chin in his big hand, nodded, and hugged me tight once again. "And where will my darlin' be? Not too far, I hope."

"I thought maybe the lake." The lake up north gave me wonderful memories of the summer after college, and it gave me Earl. Maybe if I went back, I could conjure up some white magic to help me. Maybe I could get beyond it all.

"Let me take care of everything," he whispered. "I'd like to do that for you."

"I'd like that too," I found myself answering. I never let others do for me when I was perfectly capable, but this just felt so good.

It felt right to let Earl handle all the arrangements. I relaxed on his shoulder and started to cry.

The late April air was still quite cold as I clumped up onto the porch. Earl chose well. The cabin was far down the lake, the last in a line of widely spaced, snug little bungalows. Ordinarily, nothing was open at this early time of year, but Earl pulled some strings. I didn't even want to know what he told the owners, but apparently, it wasn't about—wasn't the whole truth. At least that was what I thought, because I got no sympathetic long faces from the owners at the lodge. I couldn't handle anyone else trying to embrace me when it was clear it wouldn't work, or saying they understood when they had no idea at all what I went through.

Overnight, it snowed. How appropriate. I had a week to hibernate, if I wished, and I did wish. I had my pastels and my charcoals to keep me occupied, though I was not taking anything home with me. At the end of this retreat, I'd make a bonfire and burn them all. I wanted to end this somehow, and fire seemed most fitting. I picked up my tablet and watched to see what appeared on that pristine surface. I went from page to page, drawing out my pain, pulling it out of me somehow, some way. I was convinced this was going to work. It had to.

• • •

It was Thursday. Each morning, I stuffed my box of charcoal into the bottom of my jacket pocket, pulled on Earl's old hunting boots, even though they were far too big—he insisted I bring them, bless him, anticipating a late snowfall—and every other piece of gear I needed as I got ready to move out of the cabin's warm cocoon.

Every morning, I walked into town, small as it was. I took my cloth bag and stocked up for the day. This was part of the ritual. All I wanted was a perfect regimen, something to follow, like a farmer following the plow that followed the horse. The horse knew what business it was about, and turned at just the right spot at the end of the field to begin a new furrow. My mind was doing the same. Telling me to get up early, put the coffee on, move through all the routines signifying beginning again. Part of my mind didn't quite believe routine would help, but the part that was automatic, in place even before the baby, cautioned patience, time, and, above all, following the horse which knew the way down the field.

So, I walked into town. The small general store, so bustling in the summer, was open, as it always was, no matter the season or the weather. Real People lived here too, and took no heed of the comings and goings of an early stranger in their midst. I was just one migrating duck lost from the flyway, or perhaps a stray who was convinced spring was truly right behind. No matter. They were friendly enough and I, although not convivial, was at least conversant.

"Morning." Succinct greeting from John, who was busy stocking shelves.

"Morning," I answered. This was part of the comfortable ritual. His voice too was comforting, but I doubted he was aware of that. It was just all so normal. Of course, he didn't know why I was there, so everything was simple. We quickly reached a nice level of ease over a few days. John always had a story to tell, usually about the goings on at the lake the previous summer with the tourists. We both found the Lake Lunkers, as he dubbed them, amusing, even though I was once a Lake Lunker myself. Now, it was different. His stories brought me into his inner circle. Yesterday, he breached the barrier. He told me about his mother.

"Died young," he said, "of a burst appendix. The doc was a family friend and sent her down to the hospital in Green Bay.

Didn't want to operate on her himself. Never should have done that." He turned and began moving the crates. I could no longer see his face.

This was family, landscapes we didn't touch before. Family and death. Dangerous territories. I turned to the door, made some bland comment about seeing him tomorrow and escaped. I was shaking.

The next morning when I walked in, John was bringing in eggs from the back where one of the local farmers delivered them.

"Fresh eggs?" he asked, turning my way. "Just came in."

"Yes, I can see. Your face is pink from the cold." Today, maybe I could do more than say hello and run away. "I'll take four, please," I said.

"Four." He reached for a small egg box. "You must be eating hearty this morning." Chuckled. "Or ya got company coming."

He knew I was at the cabin. Everyone here knew. It was far too small a place to have a lost duck wander in early and not know. I took a deep breath. I owed him. "No, no company. I just want to add them to the potatoes and ham from last night." I went hurriedly on. "I—I owe you an apology. You were telling me about your mother. How you—how you lost her. I wanted to say—" My stomach tightened clear up to my throat.

He stopped and leaned on the crates of canned goods stacked next to the counter, looked down at his hands.

"I'm so sorry. I know how you feel. That kind of hurt." I spoke before I knew what words were forming.

He swung his eyes up to meet mine. "Lost someone too."

It was not a question at all, and yet I answered, "Yes, a—" and could go no further.

I found myself outside the store suddenly, with no idea at all of how I got there. I was hurrying away, back to the lake, even as part of my mind begged me to return, to slow down, to think.

No. That was the last thing I wanted to do, think. I just wanted to get away as quickly as possible. I couldn't talk to John. This was impossible. I could barely talk to myself.

That afternoon, as every afternoon, I started on the same path down to the lake. By then, the snow that fell earlier in the week was gone and the way was partly frozen, partly soggy. Still, it was an easy enough path to follow, covered in pine needles and last year's leaves. Though the dock was pulled in for the winter, the old wooden bench on the beach was still there, and the mid-April sun created a promise of warmth. On the sturdy table back in the cabin, charcoal drawings were scattered like autumn leaves, lying willy-nilly this way and that. Most were vague trees and clouds, formless pictures with harsh Xs slashed in finality across their faces. Not satisfactory at all. I didn't have the energy to move any of them, so they remained on the tabletop, waiting for an errant wind to sweep them away. I refused to think about Saturday, when I had to do something about them before I left.

But this day, this day, maybe I could do other things. I wanted to draw the lake again. I couldn't quite seem to get it right. I didn't know if I could with only charcoal, but I was not ready for color yet. How metaphorical my life became! There remained the inkling that something might be warming inside, however. Hardly enough to put even the finest dry moss on yet, so fragile it was, and so prone to be extinguished. I could only watch my own mind and body without participating in what was going on.

The afternoon sun beat directly on my bench as I perched on the blanket spread to keep the residue of cold from seeping up. Spring's promise was heavy in the air and soon I slipped off my gloves to feel the charcoal directly in my fingers. The sun was actually hot, without a breeze to blow the warmth away. I quickened and the portions of the page started to fill with bits and pieces, images of the water, trees, stumps, anything I could see.

"Hey-ho!" I heard behind me. I groaned audibly, not welcoming any disruption in my rhythm. But I was not a hewn-off stump and simple courtesy demanded some kind of response. I turned rather reluctantly, I had to admit, but was surprised to see John. Actually, I was pleasantly surprised. "Hey-ho, yourself." He tramped his way down the slope to the lake to my secluded corner. His black and red wool mackinaw was open at the throat. My heightened attention to the details of the lake transferred to this new subject. "What brings you here?"

He laughed. "Needed the exercise." Then suddenly, "I—you left your eggs."

Eggs? Oh, Lord. I saw myself running out of the store and there, in my mind's eye, was the small carton of eggs left sitting on the counter. The rest came back too and I turned away. "You didn't have to come all the way over here. It's not a life or death matter." I managed a smile.

He reached the bottom of the path and swung around to cross in front of me. "I—uh—I know. But I brought them anyway." Almost as if he didn't want it heard, he added, "Seemed like life or death."

I pretended not to hear. "How did you find me, anyway?" I knew the bench was screened from view. Even from across the lake, no one would spot me, so far away.

"Path's been trampled. Seemed obvious."

I looked at his hands and they were empty. "So," I turned the conversation, "where are the eggs? I hope you don't carry them in your pockets?"

Again, a laugh, a relief. "Naw. Left them on the porch of your cabin."

"You could have gone in. I don't lock the door. There's no one around to lock out—or in, I guess." When I looked up, he was smiling and I couldn't help but answer with the same. "Won't they freeze?"

"Not that cold today. Your porch is a perfect refrigerator." He looked upside down at the drawing on my lap. "May I...?" And sat down next to me.

"Sure." There was room and my rhythm was broken anyway. "They're just…"

"Don't start apologizing. Doesn't look like you've got very far. Looks like just a start." He bent over my sketch. "Nice," he continued. "I like the way you've got that pine there, leaning over the water. Catches the spirit of the place."

An art critic. A gentle art critic besides. I couldn't help but smile again. "Well," I lied, "I was about to quit. I got these few things down and sort of lost interest." I packaged up my charcoals and shoved them into my pocket.

"No, you didn't. I just came along at a bad time. Just when you were getting rolling. Sorry." He moved as if to get up.

"Wait." I actually put my hand on his arm and he glanced back. "How do you know that—"

"Only got one page there that I can see. Not enough to have been down here long. I didn't mean to interrupt you. Better be going."

"I'll walk back up with you." The desire was gone and I might as well pack it in, for a while at least. "I should get those eggs off the porch before I forget about them. The raccoons would have a feast, wouldn't they?"

"Sure would."

I hugged my tablet, slid off the bench and started up the path. He grabbed the blanket off the bench, slung it over his arm and followed.

The package of eggs sat forlornly in front of the door. Here in the shade of the trees and porch, it was chilly and I shivered.

"You're cold," John said and I noticed he buttoned up his mackinaw.

"Would you like a cup of coffee before you head back? It looks like you're cold too." Impulse reaction. My hostess instincts kicked in. There was no immediate response and I turned from the door to look at him.

"You sure it's okay?"

He was worried about my reputation. Sensitive and gentle. How many of those were around? I looked around. "Don't worry. You won't tarnish my honor. Even though everyone knows I'm here, I get no visitors." I realized what I just said. "Oh! I..."

A smile. "That's all right. I'm just a delivery boy."

"Come on in. I'll get us some coffee." I stepped in, walked out of my boots and into house slippers.

"Want a fire? Won't take but a minute." He followed, moved past me and began to lay a fire without waiting for an answer. "Little bit of extra warmth as the sun goes low feels good."

We still had our coats on, busying ourselves with mundane things. John's fire caught immediately and the flames began to energize. The coffee was on. The room warmed. I moved toward the fireplace and stretched out my hands in that prehistoric gesture. I heard something in the back caverns of my brain. Something like the faint humming in high wire lines.

"Here," he said, walking over to face me, "let me get your coat." His was already flung across the rocker.

I grasped my lapels, then shrugged the coat off my shoulders. He moved in close, reached over my shoulder to take the collar in one large hand. His other hand swept up along my back and stayed there, as if waiting to see if I'd allow him to draw me closer.

My arms dropped down and back, and he let my coat slide to the floor with a whisper. Immediately and inadvertently, I rose to meet him. Without thought, almost without movement, I was enveloped by him. I felt his breathing, heavier and deeper now. His head dropped and his ear was on my cheek, his breath on my neck as his hand, freed of the coat, pulled me to him. He stood very still, breathing quickly. Breaths became forms, not words exactly, but full of heat and understanding. A soft "Ah!" escaped from both of us at the same moment. A world of meaning there. Neither of us moved or changed. He still stood with his hands cradling me, warm and large and gentle. I still stood pressed to him, arms flung back, breathing hard against his chest and hair.

I reached around him and clutched him tighter to me, feeling every pocket of warmth and every fine detail of him. His hair rising and falling under my breath, his crush on my chest, his arm cradling my shoulder and back, his thighs, each and every finger he slid along me. It lasted but a moment. I shifted and he felt it. I stepped back and he allowed it.

We stood only inches apart and the humming receded somewhat. I recognized the tension, but somehow, it warmed me. John looked directly at me, no embarrassment or shame. I met his eyes equally. What just happened? Without words, John gestured to the couch in front of the fire. We sat, not touching. He fit himself into one corner, leaning toward the fire. I sat in the other, legs pulled up and feet curled beneath me.

I shifted my eyes tentatively from the fire to his face. "You could have taken me right there." I wondered at that, and it came through in my voice.

He clasped his hands on his knees and turned to look sideways at me. "Don't think I didn't want to. I watched you all week. Kind of consumed me at times." He laughed. "Good of you to leave your eggs this morning. Gave me an opening." He checked to see how I was taking all of this.

I couldn't take my eyes off of him. Why didn't any of this register when I went to the store?

"I know," he continued, now leaning toward me intently, "you didn't notice much. You didn't notice me. In that way, I mean. But something brought you up here, I figured. I just had to stay out of the way, I guess. That's why I couldn't. Couldn't…rush things. Not until you worked it out, whatever it was." He eased back again into the corner.

"I'm s—" No, that was not where I was going. I was not sorry. "Yes, I did come up here to work something out. I never dreamed anyone would see that."

"Pretty clear," John said. "Wrong time of year, for one. Your face told a lot too. Pretty bare pain there. Knew for certain when you ran out. So, bringing the eggs out was kind of a matter of life and death."

In spite of myself, I smiled at him. John, quiet but friendly grocery man, spotted my secret.

"Want to talk?" His voice was so soft, I could barely hear him and I turned toward the fire, now curling and dancing. The light of the afternoon was fading and shadows inhabited the corners of the room. John slid off the couch, squatted in front of the fire and set another log gently on top. His back was to me and I knew I could choose not to hear him, if I wished. He would honor that.

I reached out and touched his shoulder. At that, he moved up again, sitting on the edge of the couch, hands out to the fire, allowing me the privilege of telling it in my own way, in my own time, without eyes on me. I knew he was listening.

"A baby." My voice, like his, was but a murmur, but he heard me. He clasped his hands and his head lowered ever so slightly. "A baby boy," I went on. "Our first."

"I'm sorry." He turned to me. "I'm sorry."

The look from this man who heard my confession released me and I felt the tears spill over. His fingertips touched my knee, but it was enough.

I didn't know how long we sat there as I cried myself empty while he held me. I told him nothing more. There was no need. He didn't ask, perhaps sensing somehow that those details were for other ears. He felt my need right then and filled it. It was a simple gesture, but it meant the world to me.

Finally, I found my voice. "Thank you, John," I managed to get out. "Thank you."

"Just listened." He looked over at me. "Guess that has to be enough sometimes." He smiled quietly and pulled away to put another log on the fire.

"Enough, Lord, yes, more than enough. I wasn't ready before this. I just couldn't seem to talk about him, about the baby." The words still didn't come easily, but I knew I'd be able to put words together, at least, from then on. "You've been my saving angel."

John laughed outright. "No one's ever called me that before. Plenty of other stuff, I'd say, but not angel."

He stood, looked down at me and then checked the window. It wasn't late, but the day was leaning into dark when he slipped his coat on. "Should I...could I...stay?" The collar of his coat caressed his neck, but his hands were positioned to shuck off his coat.

All I had to do was say the word. But he already did all he could for me. For my part, I could give him no more. In a way, I was sorry I couldn't return the favor. At my small hesitation, his eyes brightened, but settled into dusk when I shook my head.

"Don't walk me to the door." He stopped me with a small gesture and smiled. I hoped he was memorizing the moment, storing it away for some time when he might need to remember he was a good man. Then he was gone.

I was suddenly exhausted.

I made sure the firescreen was in place, picked up the Hudson Bay blanket on the couch, and stretched out to watch the flames and let my mind drain.

Hours and hours later, I woke up to a dead fire and sunlight again.

I couldn't waste a minute, it seemed, and I was up and turning on the cabin's heater. Today, I wouldn't go to the store. Sometime this day, I would be hungry, but at that moment, I couldn't clear the drawings off the table fast enough. I heaped them on a new fire and watched them all crinkle and burn.

I retrieved the charcoal from my coat pocket and, tucking my feet under me, began a final odyssey, sketching abstract lines and shadings, elements of the lake, perhaps, but not that either. I didn't really know where I was going with all of this.

Bars of light created new quilt patterns on the loose papers on the table as the sun moved up into the sky. The sketches piled up, almost as many as I'd done throughout all the days before.

They were changing, the drawings—trees, water, the bench on the beach, boats. Lake movement. Abstract, concrete, abstract again. On top, finally, softer drawings with more form. Globes and circles, some with auras of fine lines and swirls. Angels' faces. Babies' faces. A baby's face. The best one, the one I cried over when it was done, I slid into the back of my sketch book. The rest I fed to the fire, an offering of love rising up to our little boy.

I was ready to go home.

The trip back took a half-hour less than the trip up to the lake. It was just barely dusk when I pulled in the driveway. I jumped out of the car and slammed the door. Earl materialized at the back door.

"Hey, darlin', I didn't expect you back until way after dark."

His face was brilliant with happiness. However, his eyes clouded over and I could see the wheels turning. He was probably wondering if I came back thawed or still frozen. I walked up to him and ran my hand along the side of his face. His shoulders dropped and his face muscles relaxed. The glow came back into his eyes.

"Can you draw me a bath?" I asked. "I could use a good soak." I gave him a good, honest smile. He grasped my hand, kissed the palm and tucked my hand securely in the crook of his arm. We turned for the house. "Wait," I said, "all my things are still in the car."

As we reached the back door, he said, "You go on in and get ready and I'll bring everything in."

"You've got yourself a deal," I said, handing off the car keys.

Earl ushered me in the back door and, with a flourish of his hand, headed back toward the car.

It didn't take long to shuck off my clothes and slide into the tub. The warmth of the water and the steam loosened my mind, letting me relax without thoughts intervening. In the midst of my drifting, I heard a soft knock on the door. The door opened a crack before I even thought of responding.

"Hey, darlin'." Earl, in his pajamas, padded in with bare feet. "I thought I'd bring you some tea. You want company?" He set the tray on the floor and sat down on the toilet seat without waiting for an answer.

A return to the old routine. I felt the hot steam rise around my face, depositing pearls of moisture along my hairline and across my upper lip.

"Betty?"

I didn't answer, but rolled my head slightly in his direction.

"Oh, Betty, don't cry." He leaned over, arms resting on his legs, clasping and unclasping his hands.

He didn't see my tears as relief, as ice melting and flowing away. But I could feel the heat of the bath, and of him, finally melting the pain, the ball of cold I finally acknowledged at the lake.

"Oh, ba—darlin'." Earl stood up and stepped right into the tub, pajamas and all. "Come here." He knelt down, slipped his arms around me and gathered me to him. "I don't know what to say to you. I felt like I was on the outside of everything. You were the one who carried the baby. You were so close to it all. I didn't know what to do."

I felt my face tight against his chest, the rise and fall of his short breaths, the beat of his heart. He was crying. I loosened my arms and spread my hands against his chest, then slid them around to press the full, strong muscles of his back—I could feel them shifting as he stroked my hair. The dam broke and I sobbed against his wet pajamas.

"It's all right," he said, bending close to my ear. "It's all right."

"Oh, Earl!" I said, my voice muffled against his chest. "We lost our baby and I wasn't sure I could ever breathe again." I felt his arms tighten around me. The steam rose around us and I smelled the scent of roses from the bath salts. Earl's arms wouldn't let me go. He held me and stroked me. Slowly, ever so slowly, our tears receded a bit.

"Come on, darlin'," he said. Still holding me against him, he pulled me upright and water sheeted off his soaked pajamas. "Look at us! What a sorry sight." I could hear the smile in his voice.

"We're going to catch a dandy of a cold," I said, trying to match him. But even in the warmth of the bathroom, I started to shiver.

"Nah," he said. "We've got plenty of towels. And hot tea besides," he added, pointing at the forgotten tray. He pulled the drain plug with his toes and the water began to recede around us. He took me in his arms and lifted both of us out of the water and back onto dry land.

Chapter 10
Reggie

1966

I was soaking up the atmosphere, and the heat, of the town square when Carlos blindsided me.

"Why don't you stay here in Spain?" he said.

My mind immediately went into overdrive. Oh, Carlos! I groaned mentally, though my face betrayed nothing. What are you asking me? This is ridiculous. I know exactly what you're asking. Time slowed so that voices slurred and became round, like heavy masses of raw bread dough. Cars in the town square of this small Spanish town no longer whizzed, but dragged. The sun, usually indifferent to anyone else's needs, actually seemed to stop in the blue sky in order to give me more time. More time for what? I wondered. To fall even farther? No, not exactly. To decide if I wanted to fall even farther.

Three weeks ago, I hardly knew this man. Now, I did. He dressed in solid shoes and shirts that spoke of a man who loved the woods and was comfortable in it. He had served in the army. He loved daisies and violets. He could outwork any man in the neighborhood, and did so willingly, with a kind of joy in his ability to build something, dig something, lift something. His hands were large and rough, and I loved their contradiction. Hard tough fingers that lifted a splinter out of my palm without producing so much as a drop of blood. Rough dirty hands that would draw a clean glass of water for a friend before he would think of serving himself. Firm hands that held me with a most gentle touch.

The sounds of his voice hovered in the air and I realized I still had time to think and decide. But very little of it.

•　　　•　　　•　　　•

A few days before, some nasty bug grabbed my stomach and wouldn't let go. Montezuma's revenge, translated to Europe. Of course, I had no idea how long I would be laid low, but travelers' illnesses seemed, from what I heard, to last only a day or two at the most. I hoped it was only a twenty-four-hour bug.

As I lay motionless on the couch, waiting for the next internal attack, Carlos's aunt hovered over me, dousing me with some strong Spanish home remedy which did seem to work, however slowly. Still, at that point, I was a ways from normal.

"Come on, Reg," Carlos crooned from near my ear. He sat on the floor, obviously feeling fine, which was a lot better than I felt. "Come on, rouse yourself. Let's go down to the square. There's a concert this afternoon."

I turned what I hoped was a jaundiced eye on him. My stomach still had a residual ache. I am going nowhere, I thought, and hoped he could read it in my eyes. I felt rotten enough not to want to talk.

"It'll only last an hour. It'll do you good. A little fresh air?"

"Come on, Carlos, have a heart," I finally said. My voice was low and scratchy and I hoped it conveyed how tired I was. I didn't have the energy to add more.

"Hey." He knelt now, hands gently resting on my ribs. "You are looking so much better. Come on; let's get out. Uncle and I are going down and I want you to come along." His fingers unexpectedly tickled me. This was a side of Carlos I hadn't experienced. How could he be so cruel?

This awakened the remnants of my former self. "Don't 'hey' me," I snapped. "And don't tickle me. My stomach still hurts." That should have been clear enough.

Carlos laughed, delighted in any response. "She's alive! Come on. I really want you to come with us. So does Uncle." He tickled me again, broadening the scope, pinning down both of my hands in the process.

I was powerless, caught unawares. My stomach still hurt and I had no strength to fight him. I flushed, angry at my weakness. Even angrier at his unusual lack of empathy. Perhaps he thought I was about to laugh. Instead, I was about to cry.

"Stop it! Please, please, please! Stop!" In spite of my aching body, I had to put up some kind of defense. I managed to snap one hand free and clawed at him before he could stop me. "Can't you understand your own language? My stomach hurts and I'm going nowhere with you." I amended it. "I am going nowhere."

Carlos laughed and trapped my loose hand again, pulling me to his chest.

I was raging. "What is this? My Spanish isn't that bad. I want you to stop!" This was turning into more than just a small struggle.

"You just don't like me," Carlos retorted, finally backing off. He still held onto my hands, but was crouched quietly, without tickling me.

I didn't even have the strength to wrench my hands away, but I made them go limp in his and the message was clear.

He pulled my hands to his lips. "All right. We'll go without you. But I won't stop thinking about you." He stood up, stepped away, and moved off to meet his uncle in the kitchen. Until the door closed behind them, I couldn't take a full breath.

"Is he always like this?" I asked his aunt.

She smiled and kept on with her needlework. "He's a good nephew. And a good man." She looked up at me. "But he should listen to you. You haven't recovered yet."

This sounded like a conspiracy. Maybe I should just go back home to recover.

But I didn't want to go home. At least, not just yet. In spite of the flash of harshness from Carlos, he was still the best kisser I ever met. And there was much more to this man than either kisses or insensitive teasing revealed. I couldn't go home until I learned more about this wondrous find. What else was hidden under his smile?

• • • • •

"Stay." The last sounds emerged in a small bubble from Carlos's mouth, just like in the cartoons, floating off into the hot air of the town square, taking the margins and boundaries of speech with it.

"Car—"

"No, please don't say anything yet. I just need to look at you. Wait. Don't answer. Just let me look."

Again, his fingers were in my hair, moving down to trace the angle of my jaw. His breath was close. His eyes were mapping my face. I watched him watching me.

"I love you." This was no small collection of words to him. Nor was it meaningless. We talked enough to know this did not come easily to him, that he really meant it. He did not say it often. We both knew the truth of that.

"And I—" I began, but couldn't go beyond that. My eyes didn't waver. I didn't dare move, not even my eyes. I knew the answer must be clear the first time around. There could be no missteps, no need for explanations. It had to be truth, as sharp and as clear as finely cut crystal.

His eyebrows went down. He was waiting for an answer.

"I—" I tried to force more out of my throat. I wanted to say it.

The heat rose off the cobblestones of the square behind him and, over his shoulder, I saw the cars begin to move again, the sun to move again. They at least already knew my real answer.

"I can't," I choked out. My mind was made up and my lips took over, without warning. I could no more stop the words than I could stop time.

The heat rose and all I could see around me was yellow. That sunbaked, adobe kind of yellow. The train station behind me, the cobblestones, the light. All appeared yellow to me. No glow from within, but a rich hue imposed by the sun. With no pause, I continued. "I made promises. I promised to help start a new program at school. I can't back out. School starts in a week." The color deepened further around me, and I thought I would never be able to explain this sense of duty. But I hoped Carlos would understand.

"Carlos, you know—" Again I could go no further. My hands went up to his face. His fingertips still rested on my hair. His arm dropped and pulled me close to him. The other hand touched my face. I went on without allowing raw emotion to creep in. "If this is meant to be, it will be. I'll be back. I just need this one year to get my bearings. This last year." I was afraid to say I needed time to see if this was more than just a summer fling.

His eyes didn't change. They were locked on me. His fingers traced each line, each cove, each wisp of hair, measuring and mapping, mapping and measuring. Slowly, every moment heightened, every movement noted, he bent even closer and his familiarity rolled into me, like a wave come from faraway Africa, first covering and then pulling at a Mediterranean swimmer.

"I love you," he breathed into my ear.

"I know," I said. I couldn't stop looking at him. I saw his face close up, every detail through my haze of lashes, and he took on an ethereal quality. Then it was his breath again. Along my nose. Along my hairline, as he lightly kissed my neck. He pressed his lips to mine with more breath and passion than ever before.

Then he was gone.

I saw him withdraw, felt him slip from my hands, but I was powerless to react. It was not that I didn't want to. I couldn't.

The pressure of his hand against the small of my back was still there, but the hand was not. The light in the town square became thick as he paused in the median, an island among the cars, turned and raised his arm in the air. Even at such a distance, I could see his face, although it was hazy and shimmered in the heat. He was smiling, but I knew his eyes glistened. I saw that much before he pulled away. He thrust his hand into the air, a gladiator's gesture, strong, triumphant. Doomed? I thought. Maybe I was the one doomed.

In a split second, Carlos moved out, threading his way through the slow, thick traffic. I saw him reach the far side and he disappeared into the crowds, water spent on the beach, withdrawing itself to surge again. I felt spent too, and left adrift.

The square lay hot and yellow, golden almost. The railroad station behind me, its arched openings looking like carved butter, beckoned. Cool recesses looked so welcoming, stretching inward and drawing me forward into the gloom. I was supposed to be heading home, but I couldn't get my feet to move.

Finally, I hefted my backpack and turned away from the heat. I felt caught in a moment in which I could go neither forward nor back. I willed myself not to turn and look for him. The thought of that barren square, so busy now in the midday sun, could not be tolerated, not then. I knew I would see emptiness. Of course he was no longer there. I couldn't bear to see that. What I wanted in my memory was his small figure, arm raised, and his quick turn and run across the heat. What I really wanted in my memory was he never said goodbye. I was afraid if I turned around, I would hear goodbye. I wanted him back. If he hadn't disappeared in the crowd, I would run to him yet. Perhaps.

My mind commanded and I moved into the cool shadows of the station, deserting the square. I moved into another world entirely. My heart cried out to stop and my body did, in fact, stop. In front of happy, busy strangers, I started to cry. Not for going. Not for not staying. This was far deeper than that.

The previous three weeks scrolled across my mind. The hikes, the day trips, the dinners, the discussions, the singing, the sharing, my first successful joke in Spanish. And that was only the beginning. The feel of my hands roaming the map of his body. His lips on mine. The height and arch of his back. The smells of him, of us. All to be reread at any time I chose. My cherished private book to be burned on the day I died, and not before. My own storybook.

I thought that was why I cried, although it wasn't at all clear. I wondered, Am I crying for Carlos, or for me? Or am I crying for the loss of a summer romance, like a book, somehow not real. I spent the last few weeks in a Spanish household, speaking Spanish, eating Spanish, dreaming Spanish. I was living out a romance novel. Was any of it real? Is it easier to say "I love you" in another language? Does that make it somehow less real? I didn't have any answers. This wasn't like me. I always had answers. Not today.

I stood crying in the dark arcades of a foreign place. I left the sunlight of the square and fervently hoped it wasn't a sign. But I knew somehow it was all behind me already. I couldn't admit this to myself, but I could feel it there nonetheless, under the surface. Someday, I would take it out again and decide if it really happened.

At that point, there was no backward, only forward. I made sure of that when I couldn't answer him.

I sniffed loudly, ran my fingers through my hair and, without allowing myself even a sideways glance, headed for the platforms.

I was homeward bound.

Chapter 11
Betty

1942

I would have more babies. The doctor was right. Nothing was wrong with me inside. The umbilical cord around Teddy's neck was a fluke, an accident. But we could try again.

Finally, I did get pregnant again and though it felt wonderful again, fear was very close to the surface this time. I couldn't help it. With every twinge, every ache in the most remote spot, every small touch of nausea, I choked back tears. I tried to be normal, but I knew anything could happen. Even at the last minute, anything could happen. I felt like my soul held its breath for the full nine months.

I grew bigger and bigger, just as before. Life was within me, life I could see bumping and kicking my clothes. This new child jumped for joy, reassuring me that life was far too strong to let go. My belly grew more and more turgid. Again. In spite of that exuberant life within me, Earl and I couldn't bring ourselves to name this baby. Neither could we play with whether this baby would be a boy or girl. We were both afraid we'd jinx the whole pregnancy. With each month that proceeded, most women became more and more confident. We became more and more afraid. I stroked my belly, as if I could feel with my fingertips where the umbilical cord coiled. I willed it to be where it needed to be, where it would not harm. When the contractions started, we didn't wait. We left early this time. I took it as a good sign that the scent of early apple blossoms greeted us as we entered the hospital.

• • • • •

Our daughter, our angel, was born on a fine spring morning in April, a year after the lake. She came into our life whole and pink and crying. We cried too.

"Earl," I couldn't keep the tears out of my voice, "she doesn't even have a name yet." Then we were laughing.

"Marie's a nice name." His mother's name.

I loved the woman a lot, but somehow it just didn't fit. It was too—well, maybe too soft. This baby was our survivor. She needed a stronger name. "I love the name," I hedged, "but it would make a better middle name, don't you think? It really gives melody to the whole thing if it's in the middle."

"So, what did you have in mind, darlin'?"

I suddenly had it. "How about Regina." More affirmation than question. "I love the idea of our little queen."

His eyes softened and I knew the name was approved. He chuckled, "Our little queen. Done and done."

Reggie thought the name came out of a book, which, in a way, I suppose it did. In the brief moment of choosing, I really wanted a name fitting the active baby within me, born properly, a name inviting joy and celebration. I remembered an art book of portraits.

Of all the portraits I studied, Queen Elizabeth I of England intrigued me the most. Studying the paintings done over the course of the years of her reign, I could see her growing from a regal young princess into an extraordinary ruler. It was all right there on the canvas. Even in old age, her face was intriguing. She lost none of her power as she aged. On the contrary, the face became more and more interesting, more and more commanding, more and more astute. She was the kind of woman I hoped our little baby girl would become, strong, self-willed, independent, and above all, wise. But Elizabeth wasn't a strong enough name. That was really why I named her Regina Marie.

She grew in wisdom and stature, just like it says about Jesus. We both loved her dearly, and Earl spent more time than other men I knew catering to Reggie. Like a skittish colt, she took to his attention, drawing closer and closer until, eventually, all he had to do was smile at her, and she would giggle and toddle over to kiss his knees. I could smile at her and she would turn to him for affirmation. I guess I just didn't have his touch. Daddy's little girl. At the time, I didn't think a thing of it, so grateful was I to have her at all.

• • • • •

That wasn't the end, of course. I wanted more babies, now I knew I could do it, and so did Earl. Two years after Reggie was born, I was pregnant again. This time, we picked names and talked about baby clothes, moving along like any other normal couple expecting a baby. She was to be born in August. I always thought of her as a she.

"Can you believe this cold, darlin'?" Earl asked, peering out the kitchen window at the temperature gauge hanging on the garage. "They say it's the coldest snap in twenty years. It's fifteen below zero out there. Ol' Jack Frost has painted these windows up really nice. Look, Reggie," he lifted her up to see the whorls and ferns and clouds of frost on the window, "isn't it pretty?"

They were such a pair. Big Earl and little Reggie. He adored her and she knew it. She had her daddy wrapped around her little finger. That was just the way he wanted it.

I was smiling at them when the first pain lanced. This was not supposed to be happening and the old fear returned, but the pain subsided. I breathed. I took one step toward the bathroom and was stricken again. This time, I sat down on the closest chair, like a stone dropped into water, plop. Earl heard me and turned from the window. There was an immediate reaction.

"What's wrong?" His voice sounded strained. This was a check, a hopeful check that he only imagined trouble.

"Call Carrie."

He was on the phone to our neighbor in a moment, Reggie hanging on his shoulder. "Can you come over and get Reggie? Betty's got a little pain, and I—"

She obviously cut him off and, before I could think about the tightness in my belly and the third strike of pain, our neighbor was there, taking Reggie and some of her toys.

"I'll call an ambulance from my house, Earl. You just take care of Betty. Unless you want me to stay here?"

I cut Earl's response off. "No, thanks, Carrie." I waved her off. I felt better. The pain was gone and I was praying it would stay gone. "Thanks for taking Reggie." As Earl walked her to the door, I stood up carefully. Everything seemed to have settled down.

I started for the bathroom once again, and knew there was something wrong. A warm trickle was moving down between my thighs and I felt my belly knotting up again in the need to push on something.

"No!" I couldn't help the anguish in my voice and Earl came immediately. "No, this can't be happening! I can't be losing this baby!"

Earl caught me and lowered me to the bathroom floor. "Hang on, darlin'. The ambulance is on the way. Hold on."

But the trickle turned to a brook and I could feel my body pushing, pushing at something that could not come out. I would not allow it.

"She's coming, she's coming, she's coming!" I shrieked now, grasping at the towels Earl brought, twisting toward him, hoping to stop it all.

"Hold on, hold on!" His voice was too quiet for what was happening.

I could barely hear him through the blood and the pain that should not be there. Earl's hands were slimy with red. My legs came up of their own accord and I grasped my knees, curling unwillingly into a ball that would not do my bidding.

"Not now, not now…" I heard my own voice trail off as the blood gushed and my body rejected the little mass that was our child.

I don't want to remember that now.

The ambulance came and I went to the hospital where they did whatever they did to clean me out.

By the time I came home some days later, Earl, or maybe Carrie, had cleaned up the bathroom. There were even new towels in a color I did not pick out. That didn't erase the memories, however, and it took me a long time before I could go into that bathroom and not cry.

It was easier miscarrying twice more than it was delivering that first sweet one, only to find him already gone. After the horrible, sudden miscarriage in our own bathroom, I was very careful, but I was determined to try again. Earl wanted more children. We talked about it, surely, but he was cautious, ever cautious, and when I did announce each pregnancy, there was always an electric shiver of fear, barely noticeable, and most certainly never mentioned. I took to bed, I followed directions, I ate right, I lifted nothing. I could not carry another child. Finally, the doctor told Earl there would be no more babies. None. We cried. I lost the war. Of five children, only one survived. One. Everything that could have given us babies was taken out of me and life went on.

Margaret, my old college roommate, came. She came with all of my—deliveries. The angels that flew away from us and the one that survived. Only one she could be a godmother to. My saving grace. My Regina Marie.

Chapter 12
Betty

1964

I woke up fifty this morning. I moved into a new decade. I wondered if this would be my last one? I couldn't bear to open my eyes just yet. The glorious moment when I was almost awake, but barely almost, felt so protected, so soft, I couldn't bear to spoil the delicious feeling. Reggie was away at college, so I knew there would be no little girl pulling my hand out from under the covers, crying, "Mommy! Mommy! Guess what, Mommy? It's your birthday!" Dragging me out to see the spring sunshine and the "breakfast" she made for me with her doll's dishes and pretend food. Well, she outgrew that birthday innocence long ago. I still treasured the memory of those few years, long gone. Now I would get a card, a phone call, a spray of flowers, but I missed her childhood exuberance.

I reached over to Earl's side of the bed, but it was no longer warm. Was he up this early? Even though my eyes still weren't open, I knew it was early. The light filtering through my eyelids was still slanted and dim, not yet sunny as predicted. He should have arrived home from a business trip late last night. He called and said to expect him very late, if he somehow—I heard him laugh—didn't miss his connection. I opened my eyes, and realized he must have done just that, missed his connection. The covers on his side of the bed were turned back slightly, folded just as I left them the night before, and the light was still on in the kitchen. I could see the glow even through the haze of dawn.

Wait. I smelled coffee. That meant he really did make it home. But not last night.

"Earl?"

"Hey, darlin'! I'm just putting on some coffee and breakfast! Happy birthday!" he called up the stairs. "I've got something here for you!"

"I'm on my way!" My feet were already over the side of the bed and I followed the fragrance of fresh coffee. "Mmmm! Pancakes too!" I called down the steps, "Hope you made plenty."

He looked so good, standing there at the bottom of the steps. Fresh and gilded, somehow. His hands were behind his back, hiding my gift, I was sure.

Suddenly, he swept me off the stairs and into his arms. No gift there but the welcome embrace. "Look what I have for you, darlin'." He led me to the table.

I opened a blue velvet box that waited by my plate and a strand of pearls appeared, glowing mutely. "They're beautiful!" I whispered. "Perfectly beautiful!"

"Kind of to replace your mom's. I know you were supposed to get them when she died." He leaned into my hair and kissed the top of my ear.

"Well, I wasn't about to fight with my brother over them," I said, lifting them from the box and laying them against my cheek.

"I'm sorry I didn't get home on time. I did end up missing my connection and was delayed half the night at the station," he said.

I stopped him with a kiss. "You're here now, aren't you? That's all that counts. You're home safe."

"Heart and soul," he said as he drew me up the stairs.

I wore those pearls almost everywhere for the next two years. They were a warm reminder of Earl, whether I was in a cocktail dress or a housedress. Sometimes I took them out of their velvet box just to look at them. I heard the more you handled pearls, the more lustrous they became, finally reflecting the glow from your own skin tones.

As I put them away this afternoon, the angle of the sun was getting lower and, although winter was still a ways off, the slant of light reminded me that summer was as good as gone. In spite of that, I couldn't help my excitement at this new opportunity, late in the season as it was. I was going with him. Earl traveled a lot over the years we were married and I never had the opportunity to go with him. This time, I was going. Reggie was still in college and she really didn't need me to be available anymore. She'd grown into independence by then. Besides, Margaret was available in Madison in case something happened at the house or with Reggie. Only an hour away. That would do. I guess I became quite independent too.

This trip was special. This trip was to Europe. Reggie said I would be a fool not to go and, for once, I agreed with her. There was no reason to stay home. Even though Earl would be busy with his conference, I was quite comfortable with the idea of traveling around those old cities alone. Finally, I could actually view some of the beloved art I saw only in books. Certainly, I visited some grand museums here in the States, but Michelangelo's art still resided in Italy and the Mona Lisa didn't leave her home in the Louvre. Unfortunately, we couldn't get to Miro's or Picasso's home grounds, but even a taste of the originals would soothe my palate.

Earl was at work, trusting me to get our traveling things organized while he finished up what needed to be done at the office. So, I poked my nose into the attic to drag out the largest suitcases. They were sure to need airing. Earl's biggest hadn't been on the road for a couple of years.

The day was gloriously hot for so late in the season and I carried the suitcases out to the patio, where the air and the sun could get to them. Mine opened in a snap and spread across two lawn chairs, open like some great hippo's mouth, waiting for those little birds to come and pick the parasites out of its teeth. Earl's clasps didn't give so easily, and at first, I thought they were locked. Suddenly, the first latch popped open, so I knew I just had to work at it a bit. I broke a nail trying to pry the second latch, but it came open eventually. I would have to remember to ask him the trick, because he certainly wouldn't have much patience for a suitcase so reluctant to give up its contents. With a small sigh, it folded back, opening to the sun and breezes. A piece of paper, a receipt by its looks, fluttered up a bit from the bottom of one of the pockets as I coaxed the suitcase to open wide. I managed to trap the paper before it escaped, and took a closer look. The receipt for the pearls he bought me two years ago. Didn't the man ever clean out his luggage? I was highly amused. How sweet, I thought, until I saw the amount.

I couldn't help a small gasp. That was far too expensive, even if it was a milestone birthday! The amount was staggering. I looked again, sure I imagined too many zeroes. I must have missed the decimal point somehow.

But no, it was right.

I looked too closely. Under the column for quantity, there was the numeral two. Two. This didn't make sense. I looked at everything. I recognized the name of a well-known jewelry chain. I recognized the date when he was on a business trip to San Francisco. I recognized the handwritten "Mikimota Cultured Pearls" and the price. The two was still there. So was the final amount paid.

Why two? He certainly did not bring Reggie a string of pearls. Anyway, he stopped bringing Reggie gifts from trips when she left for college. Well, maybe he did bring a second strand back, and stashed it somewhere for a special occasion, her college graduation, maybe. But no. I was the one who puts his laundry away. I was the one who checked his pockets before his clothes went to the cleaners. I rummaged in every drawer, every pocket, for lots of reasons. He didn't store anything.

So why the second strand? No other woman would merit such a generous gift. No other woman.

Other woman?

Come on, Betty, isn't the answer obvious? My stupid brain still asked, "Why two?"

My heart knew why two. Two strands. Two women. The anger rising in me blindsided me. How could he? What did I ever do to him? I felt the heat build up inside and my mind went wild. My usual control disappeared, even as I struggled to maintain it. No good. Even if I wanted to be rational, I couldn't. My heart and head were in communion. Both recognized the audacity of this and sprang to my defense with well-intentioned anger. No, madness. If a neighbor called to me now, I would respond with words so vile, I would never be able to tell where they came from. I wanted to pull my hair and scream. I couldn't stand to be outside for one second more, the neighbors might see me. I would never be able to explain this uncharacteristic feeling of impending explosion. I left the suitcases and forced myself to walk into the house.

Once in, I raced up the stairs to our bedroom. It seemed the most logical place to slip into insanity. The closest thing at hand was my hairbrush. I lifted it to hurl it across the room. Suddenly, I saw nothing but blurs through my tears. I heard the little voice of my upbringing, saying, "Well-brought up girls don't throw things." I thrust the hairbrush to the floor and turned to my childhood solution.

I snatched a pillow off the bed and before my brain could connect with my hands, I pummeled the bed, swinging the pillow up over my head and bringing it down in hard even strokes. It was Earl's pillow and I wanted to kill it.

His side of the bed did nothing to soften my fury and I lunged for the brass footboard. The cotton corners of the pillowcase and the shell beneath gave way, and it suddenly snowed goosedown. The feathers floated up in the summer sun, settling in slow motion on my hands, my shoulders, my hair.

That slowed me somehow. Slowed me just enough to send me gulping and gasping into a torrent of crying. I could hardly get my breath. The pillowcase dropped to the floor and I dropped with it. With my arms wrapped around the brass bed, I tried to cry without noise, still worrying under it all that the neighbors would hear. What did I care if anybody heard? I was cracked and draining, but I couldn't bear to think of anyone else knowing.

While my breath settled into ragged hiccups, I let loose of the bed and turned to find that receipt. There it was, right there under my nose. Look at that. Two identical strands of pearls. He couldn't even come up with something unique for my fiftieth birthday. He gave us both the same thing. Was I no more than a— I couldn't even say the word—a woman to be paid off?

I stuffed the receipt in my apron pocket. I pulled my hand out, as if burned, even as I raced back down the stairs. Once outside, the suitcase lay gaping in front of me, inviting me with a leer that promised more secrets.

Both of my hands moved of their own accord toward the suitcase, though I was mentally screaming at them to stop. They frantically went through every pocket, every corner, every hidden fold. Nothing. I knew there must be more. Finally, I regained control, and I forced my hands to stop their erratic movement. I stopped searching. With cold duty, I began to methodically clean and wipe, trying not to think. My finger caught on a loose edge of fabric as a piece of the lining pulled away from the suitcase. Another corner of white, not moving in any breeze, was caught under the damaged lining, trapped there unwittingly, I was sure.

"My dearest Earl," I unfolded and read from a stranger's hand. Suddenly, I found myself sitting on the concrete next to the picnic table. I didn't know how I got down there, but the suitcase loomed large above me, and I felt like I was about to be swallowed whole. Still, I couldn't move. Couldn't cry out. Could barely think, though my mind was racing.

I forced myself under control. My body was cold and frozen in place, and my mind joined it. At least for then. Until I could see everything. What was going on? And for how long? I had to read the rest of the note while I was still frozen. Before I could think too much, I had to assimilate it all. All at once.

"My dearest Earl, my dearest, sweetest Earl," she wrote. I already knew it was a she, the handwriting was far too feminine for otherwise. And the pearls, of course. It had to be the same woman. "How can I let you go? After your gift—and Mikimotas yet!—"

There it was. The pearls. Two strands.

"I just don't understand it. We've been so good for each other, Earl, my darling Earl. I've never felt so safe as when we're together. I knew you were married before you told me. That telltale band of pale skin on the hand I've kissed so many times..."

I didn't think I could read more. My hands started to tremble.

"...I'll take you as you are, my dearest. I know we can't be together very often, but the past four years..."

Four years! That was impossible! No, not impossible! He went twice a year to San Francisco on business.

Stop. I couldn't listen to myself. I had to read.

"...have been the most glorious in my life. You rescued me when I had no one, nothing. I cannot give you up. The way you touch me, kiss me..."

My sight was failing. I was going blind.

"...lifts me so high that I cry out. You know I do."

I cried out too. But not from touch.

"Please, don't leave me. Last night, you said it was the last time. I can't believe you! Last night was ecstasy! Today, you won't answer my calls. I went up to your room, but you won't answer.

I'm writing this note in a last desperate effort to hold you. I want so much to hold you! People are looking at me, sitting here in the lobby, crying my eyes out writing this, but I don't care! The bellboy is coming with your luggage. I know it's not locked—God knows, I've unpacked it often enough!"

Her hands on his clothes. Her hands on *him*.

"I've said enough. I love you, Earl. I will always love you! Remember my touch, my lips, my cries. I hope they echo forever. With all my heart and soul, R."

She must have slipped it into a barely open suitcase, not knowing—or remembering, I thought bitterly—about the torn lining, sliding it inadvertently between lining and case, where it would not be found by—by him. But instead, inadvertently, unwisely, by me.

And then what? Time for me to run away?

My cold, rational self took over. Think, woman, think. He didn't return to that city since your fiftieth birthday, did he? No. No business trips, no pleasure trips. She did write that *he* was calling it off, didn't she? Yes, he called it off. She said so herself. The note was a desperate attempt to stop him and it failed. He came home. He came home to me.

He never read the note. He never read it. That much got through to me immediately. It was creased in only the places she creased it to have it fit in some obscure spot in a suitcase she didn't want to fully open. No other creases or evidence of refoldings were there. Earl would never have left it in his suitcase. I could picture him reading it, getting more agitated—angry, I amended—then crumpling it up and throwing it—no, dashing it into the nearest wastebasket. It was clear from her words, he was calling the whole thing off, he was walking away. The pearl necklace was meant as a farewell gift for services rendered. Services rendered. Obviously, she had savored the feel of his hands, his lips—

What drove him to her? Her vulnerability perhaps. His own needs perhaps. Four years he went to her. Plus, it's been two years since my fiftieth birthday, when he brought the pearls home. That meant it began six years ago. I was forty-six then, years after being told there would be no more children. Far too long in between for him to be thinking about the children I couldn't give him. It wasn't about children then. Didn't I satisfy him? No, that wasn't it either. I too cried out in the night from his touch and he from mine. We still satisfied one another. No, not that either. Maybe the same thing that drove me to rise to John those many years ago at the lake. There was a need then somehow too. But I recognized it. Earl didn't. I could understand. Maybe I could even forgive. I didn't know if I could ever forget.

All I knew was I couldn't ever think of it again. Earl walked away from her. Walked toward me. Back to me. I would not allow her to destroy that image of him coming toward me. I placed her behind him, where I couldn't see her for his bulk coming closer and closer toward me. Towards *me*.

That was the only thing I had to remember. Which way he was walking.

I stood up, shaky, and went into the kitchen, note still unfolded in my hand. The kitchen matches were over the stove. One should do it, but I plucked out two. Two. One for me, one for her. I forced myself to stop thinking.

Outside again, I moved as if underwater to the fire scar. It was the middle of the afternoon and the hedge screened me, but this time, I didn't care if the neighbors saw me. One match was enough, but I lit the second one anyway and watched the note blaze up in a brief fury, then crumble away to black scraps. Even while they were still hot, I grasped the flakes and rubbed them into nothingness. I scrubbed my hands together until there was nothing but ash. When I opened my fingers, it all blew away. I rubbed them clean on the grass and headed back into the house. I knew where the pearls were and I took the box, went into the guest bedroom and put them in the top dresser drawer. I never even opened the box. I couldn't look at them. I don't know if she threw her strand into San Francisco Bay, but as for mine, they were no longer really mine. They became, in that instant, hers, and I would never wear them again.

When I laid the receipt on Earl's dresser, I felt like an invader in my own home, but I did it anyway. His cufflinks anchored one corner of it to the dresser, but they didn't cover the numeral two.

We traveled to Europe and never spoke of the receipt under the cufflinks. I forced everything to the back of my mind, reminding myself that he was with me in the here and now, not with her. I faced outward and distracted myself with museums, galleries, palaces, all the wonders the Old World had to offer. It would have to do.

Chapter 13
Betty

1966

Reggie made it home safely from Europe, though when she came over to see us, she rattled around the house, as if looking for something she lost. I wanted to ask, but I knew she'd close up. She told me about all the wonderful things she saw and the hospitable people she met, but she confided few of the details I felt behind her stories.

I was in our pantry, with the door half shut, when Reggie and Sam came into the kitchen. I heard plates clinking and silverware scraping as they cleaned up and began to fill the dishwasher. They were laughing, as they always did when I saw them together.

"Were you surprised?" Reggie asked.

"Was I ever!" Sam said. "When did you plan this shower? You were gone all summer."

"Actually, most of it was done before I left. It was Mother's idea to have it at her house, so you wouldn't suspect."

"So, you and your mom are getting along, finally?" Sam asked, but she kept right on, as if it were only a rhetorical question. "When I got pregnant, my mom finally decided she better get her act together or she might not see her grandchild. I'd never keep her away from our baby, but she was being particularly stubborn. Eventually, she came around."

Out of sight, I waited for Reggie to respond, but nothing came through but the sounds of silverware dropping into the dishwasher rack.

"Anyway," Sam said, "the party was wonderful. I don't think I'll have to buy a thing. The stroller you got us is so cool. We love to walk, so it's going to get lots of use."

"I'm glad you like it," Reggie said. Her voice sounded relieved. I heard plates being stacked in the dishwasher.

"Are you kidding? I love it," Sam said.

The dish sounds disappeared and I pictured them hugging, and smiled when it was confirmed.

"Whoa! Big belly in the way!" Reggie said, "I suppose you won't be driving much anymore, with the baby coming in a few weeks."

"*I* don't have a problem driving, but Jim wants me to stick closer to home, just in case," Sam said. "But you're welcome to come to Madison anytime."

"I know, I know," Reg said, "but I've got so much to catch up on."

"That's what happens when you disappear for so long," Sam said. "Speaking of..."

There was a long pause. I imagined Sam sending Reggie a significant girlfriend look. The door to the pantry was half shut and I could see, by rocking back and forth a bit, a little of each girl. I watched a sparkle develop in Reggie's eye as she gave Sam a happy grin.

"So, what do you want to know?" Reg asked, then added, "Where's my mother?"

I deflated. Apparently, she didn't want me to hear.

"Where's your mother? What's that got to do with it? She's out on the patio, I think, cleaning up the wrapping paper and stuff," Sam said. "Now, come on. Out with it. Who was this Spanish dreamboat?"

That would be Carlos. He appeared in a couple of the photos from her trip and I got curious. But I refrained from probing. Earl, being the kind of father he was, didn't hold back on the questions. She told us how she met Carlos in Spain and that they shared a lot of interests. Though she didn't say so, I'm sure she fell for him, a handsome foreigner, to judge by the photos. All along, I had a feeling she gave us only an overview, not the details, on that part of the trip. Now might be the chance to find out the rest. I flushed, realizing I was trespassing into my daughter's private life. I was not just keeping my own counsel, remaining silent here. I should make some noise to forewarn them, then step out into the kitchen and leave them to their privacy. But I didn't do it.

"The Spanish dreamboat? Man, that's putting it mildly," Reggie said.

Well, it was too late now. I was stuck for the duration. Or, at least, that's what I told myself to quiet my conscience.

"I know the basics," Sam said, "but I want the gory details. Didn't you say he wanted you to stay in Spain?"

I stopped breathing, afraid to let out the gasp that threatened.

"Yes, he wanted me to stay," Reggie said. "I almost *did* stay. More than once, I wondered if I should."

I leaned slightly, in order to see Reggie's face more clearly, but she'd moved to lean against the sink and all I could see was the tilt of one shoulder.

"What would your folks say?" Sam asked.

I was wondering the same thing myself.

"I didn't think about that at the time. I told Carlos I had obligations at school and couldn't leave everybody hanging," Reggie said. "But, oh man, could he kiss!"

I pursed my own lips and clasped my hands in front of them to hold myself in.

"Kisses do not a lifetime make," Sam said.

My thoughts exactly.

"I know that," Reggie said, "but I wasn't exactly working with the whole deck of cards at that point. I just wanted him so bad. He was perfect. He was hardworking, considerate—"

"Handsome," Sam broke in.

Don't fall for looks alone, Reggie. I know you want more for yourself. I wanted badly to join the conversation.

"Oh, yes. That too," Reggie said. She turned enough so I could see her smile. Then she picked up a bowl and bent to the dishwasher and I lost the view again.

"So, what about now? Are you planning on going back?"

I felt my shoulders tighten.

"You know, I spent most of the flight home trying to figure out what was going on," Reggie said. "When I left Spain, I was certain if it was meant to be, it'd all work out."

More clanking of dishes and water running. Shut it off, I wanted to say. I can't hear. As if on cue, the faucet shut off.

"But the farther away I got," Reggie continued, "the more I wondered. Would it work out? Or better question, *could* it work out?"

Sam moved into my field of vision and I watched her nod.

"I thought of you and Jim," Reggie said, "how you guys had so much to deal with. I figured, if you could do it, I could too."

I squeezed my eyes shut. My hands hurt. They were clenched into fists. *Please, God,* I thought, then hoped I didn't whisper it aloud.

"So, are you going back?" Sam asked.

"When I got to London, I had plenty of time to look into costs and schedules."

Oh, Reggie! How could you help but fall in love in a setting like that? But take time to think! It was just a summer fling! I knew how close a girl could come to falling over the edge.

"So?" Sam's voice rose.

She seemed to demand an answer. I wanted one too. What *did* Reggie decide? Was she going back?

"So," Reggie said, "I almost put a ticket for Christmas on my credit card. In fact, all I had to do was sign the slip."

Her voice stopped, replaced almost immediately by a cry from Sam.

"Ach! Stop fooling around! Are you going back or not?" Sam's voice got louder.

I held my breath. *Come, Reggie, you're smarter than that. Don't you see what a mistake it could be? At the very least, get him to come over here first. If that doesn't seal it—* Reggie's voice broke into my anguish.

"No," she said. "I'm not. From a distance, it felt too much like a plotline for a novel, you know the kind. I figured I needed time to get some perspective. Yes, Carlos was wonderful, but would it last?"

I let my breath out so quickly, I was afraid it whistled. But they didn't flinch. *Good girl, Reggie. I knew you had a good head on your shoulders.*

"You'll never know, I guess," Sam said, "unless you change your mind."

Reggie's answer was swift. "Nope," she said. "I really spent a lot of time analyzing the whole thing—"

"*That's* a first!" Sam laughed. "Since when did you analyze before you made a decision? Anyway, I'm glad you're staying here. I'd miss you terribly. Your parents would too."

"My parents?" Reggie said. "My dad would be devastated, but Old St—"

Sam stepped on her words with, "Your mother would be broken-hearted if you moved to Europe, and you know it."

I wondered what name Reggie had been about to bestow on me. Old Stuffy? Much as I hated to admit it, from her perspective of twenty-four, I probably did look like an old fuddy-duddy.

There was a long moment of silence.

Sam's voice came again. "Where is she, anyway? I want to thank her for a great party."

I didn't hear Reggie's answer because of water running again. The dishwasher door closed, then the patio door slid open. Their voices, shifted to talking of baby clothes and paint colors, receded out to the lawn.

I sneaked a peek into the kitchen before I made a beeline for the stairs. All clear.

Sam called my name from the front yard as I closed the bathroom door behind me. Covering any questions that might arise about where I'd been, I flushed the toilet, washed my hands, and headed back downstairs.

They were just coming in the front door as I reached the turn in the staircase.

"There she is!" Sam said, delight in her voice and face.

I registered her happiness and heard her multiple thank yous. I know I squeezed her arm and patted her cheek. But my mind was fixated on my Regina Marie.

I opened my arms and, before she could react or protest, gathered Reggie to me. "I'm so proud of you, dear," I said, then stepped away so she didn't have the chance to refuse my gesture. I didn't want to embarrass both of us in front of her best friend.

As I stepped down the hall toward the kitchen, I could feel a laugh bubbling up inside. She made the right decisions without a bit of help. Good for her!

I heard Reggie say, "What was *that* all about?" followed by the beginnings of that old adage from Sam, "Don't look a gift horse..."

Chapter 14
Reggie

1967

"Yes, Mother, I got the package," I answered into the phone. "I just received it today. In fact, I'm opening it now." What on earth could she have sent me? It was June. Christmas was far away and my birthday was long gone. The card actually came on time this year. She remembered my birthday most of the time, but barely, it seemed. Sometimes, I'd get a card quite late. Talk about scatterbrained. I went back to wondering, *"Why now?"*

"Wonderful," I heard her voice as I tuned back in. "I had it insured, of course, but I wanted to make sure it arrived safely."

"Oh my!" I exclaimed as I pulled away the packaging and lifted the cover of the box inside. I immediately recognized the pearl necklace. "Your pearls!" Her pearls? Why would she send me her pearls? First of all, she wore them all the time. Come to think of it, though, I hadn't seen them for a while.

"You deserve them, Reggie. You worked hard for your Master's degree and I know how you love the necklace. It's time you have something special. I had all the enjoyment I can get out of those pearls. Now it's time for you to have fun with them."

"Mother, these are the pearls Dad gave you on your fiftieth birthday. You only had them a few years. They were your special present. I can't accept these." I couldn't help stammering, she caught me so off guard. Of all the things she could pick, this necklace would be my first choice. Don't tell me she finally got it right? She's giving me something I really *liked*? Something I *wanted*?

"My fiftieth, a special birthday, yes," she said. There was a small heartbeat of silence. "But I really want you to have them. It's far more fun to watch you smile now, than to have you inherit the pearls after I'm gone. Why should you wait until I'm dead to have them? Why should *I* wait until I'm dead? There's no pleasure in that. Take them now. That will give me the greatest pleasure."

A gift like that from her? And those pearls! I adored them. They were one of the few things that made me think maybe she did have a heart, if Dad loved her enough to spend that kind of dough.

"I—I do love them," I said.

She laughed at my admission. "I know. It just didn't seem quite right to give them to you until now."

My old discomfort with her resurfaced, even if she did gush over my Master's degree. I shook it off. She had to love me. I was her daughter, after all. But then again, we always kept distance between us. Was that normal for every mother and daughter?

Mother went on, "Right now seems a wonderful time. Getting your degree is a real accomplishment. These pearls are just a—well, a gift from heart to heart. The best for the best."

I wondered if that's what Dad told her when he fastened them around her neck, "Only the best for the best." Now she seemed to be talking more to herself than to me, but it broke through my defenses. In spite of myself, tears sprang up

I knew the pearls were not just for the Master's degree. Somehow, Mother must also see the pearls as a kind of consolation prize. Consolation because of Carlos who sent me a lovely little garnet ring for Christmas, then married someone else last month, married some European someone else. So much for love at a distance. When I told Dad and Mother about Carlos's Spanish bride, I saw her look at me with that unfathomable face. What was she thinking? She was not telling and I wasn't about to pry. But now, I thought she was trying in her own way to offer something other than just the pearls. It was tough in some ways, letting Carlos go. But like it or not, life would move on, with or without Carlos. Water under the bridge.

Holding the phone to my ear with my shoulder, I lifted the long strand of pearls from their box and draped them across my neck. They seemed still warm from the touch of her hands. Sudden warmth flooded me too. "Thanks, Mother," I said. "I love them. I—I love you."

"I love you too, Reg." Said without a moment of hesitation.

But I could almost feel the surprise. I couldn't remember the last time I told her I loved her. If it surprised her that I loved her, it sometimes surprised me too. But then, just as quickly as I said it, I mentally drew back, a bit embarrassed, to tell the truth. I fingered the beads.

"The pearls belong to you now," she said. Her tone changed. "Listen, I'd better let you go. You have lots of things to do and I don't want to hold you up. Enjoy the pearls."

"You can count on it."

"Okay, dear. Bye-bye."

I hung up and went to the mirror to admire the necklace. I loved that long strand of warm spheres. They had a mysterious life of their own, like unspoken lines in some black and white movie. *Casablanca* perhaps. I imagined the hands they moved through, hands which lifted them carefully out of oysters, hands which polished them with a soft pink cloth, pale pink, barely pink. Hands which raised them out of their satin lined velvet box, draping them, the pearls like nudes posing for a French Romantic painter, nudes with arms flung overhead, voluptuous breasts uncovered, eyes inviting, yet demure, somehow. I shook the romantic vision out of my head. I admitted it, I was smitten from the first. I dreamed of borrowing them for my wedding day, whenever that would occur, always adding the cautionary, "If ever." Still, I never imagined myself asking for them, even to borrow. True, when I was home, I would sneak in now and again to pull them out and hold them against my skin or even try them on, but never with her there. I didn't want to give her the satisfaction of seeing that I salivated over something of hers. When did she see I coveted them?

Now they were mine. A consolation prize, yes, of sorts. Consolation for her and for me, perhaps. As for the Spanish fling, in some inner reception room in my mind, I always knew I wouldn't be going back to Carlos. How hard to think those phrases, to admit them consciously. Suddenly, it all became brittle and real again. But the pearls were warm on my neck, a clear reminder that today was today, and what I had yesterday, though now beyond hope, was never beyond reach. I could always pull out that jewelbox of a summer and savor. Like the Hope Diamond, it was part of my own little personal stash, to be visited on hot summer afternoons when the sun was simply unbearable and the humidity too much to take. The pearls, on the other hand, would remind me of the hope of what was to come. Everything to its own time, and now, it was time to close the door and move on.

Chapter 15
Betty

1967

"Fifty-five, Betty, you're going to be fifty-five when you get that teaching license," Earl's voice was cautionary. "How long do you plan on using that thing? Is it really worth it." That last more a statement than a question.

"I'm going to be fifty-five anyway, license or no license. Do you really think I'm too old?"

"Not at all, not at all." That was not backpedaling. Just straightforward response.

"I think she's too old," Reggie put in, ignoring me and turning to her father.

I opened my mouth to reprove her, but Earl beat me to the punch, leaving me with an ugly frown on my face.

"Don't sass your mother! You know better than that." His face lost some of its thunder. "It's not the age," he said to her. "Do you think your mother really wants to spend those years driving back and forth, studying until all hours of the night? We're not twenty-five anymore, you know."

"Earl," I broke in. This was really my affair and they shouldn't have been haggling over it, or over me. "This is something I've wanted to do for a long time. This is something I am going to do. If it's too much, I'll know. Education is never wasted." A phrase I heard him use over and over.

"You're right, darlin'." A smile washed over his face. He knew I was right. "Of course, you've got every right to try it on for fit. More power to you."

He did love me, and gave me plenty of leeway in what I wanted to do.

I decided I needed to get my mind sparking again. Anything to concentrate on other things. I could have gone back sooner, I suppose, but I felt disconnected somehow. I needed to immerse myself in my art again, needed to get some pats on the back from people in the field, people I respected. That meant taking a class here and there just to get my feet wet, and then exploring some new media, pottery, for one, as well as complying with state regulations for teacher certification.

It took me three years, but I did it. I went back to college and got certified so I could teach art again. I didn't regret a moment of it. I stepped back into an art studio as a teacher for the first time in years. It felt so good. So natural. Earl, in spite of some early skepticism, never opposed me. I'm not sure what I would have done if he had.

After—well. After the pearls. He could not believe—I know he couldn't—that I didn't walk out on him. Oh yes, he found the receipt for the two strands of pearls. I know he did, because it disappeared from his dresser. He knew I found it. He knew I knew. For weeks after that trip to Europe, he sat at the table for meals or in his chair with the paper and watched me carefully, steadily. He never said a word, but that in itself said more than I could have wished for.

When I gave Reggie the pearls, there was an almost audible sigh, as if he had been holding his breath. After I found the receipt, I never wore the pearls again, never even took them out of the velvet box. For two years, I wore them happily and often. Then, never. Reggie used to take them out when she thought I wasn't watching and hold them to her neck, but I would never let her borrow them. She knew how I once loved them, and I was careful to give the impression that I didn't want to lose them or have the thread break. She thought I was protecting a precious treasure. She was wrong. Yes, Reggie always wanted them—but I did not. In fact, I couldn't even touch them. I put them, intact in their velvet box, into the guest bedroom's dresser drawer. When Reggie received her Master's degree, the summer after her European trip, I sent them to her. They were consolation for the pain she'd endured over Carlos, but far more than that, they were a mute congratulations. I was so proud of her.

Earl noticed it all, of course. Noticed that they disappeared from use and noticed when I packaged them up to send to Reggie.

In giving her the pearls, I was really the one given a gift. A small opening, a small chance. Neither Earl nor I broached the subject of the necklace since it disappeared into the dresser drawer. I knew he was full of guilt and, yes, sorrow. He should have been. I didn't mind that at all. The guilt was an angel with a flaming sword, standing at the gate to our garden. I remained in the garden, sitting under a great spreading tree, but there was that angel. The way in was no longer clear.

I was afraid. I think he was too. That much lay palpable between us, even without words to define and refine what we were both feeling. What led him away must have something to do with both of us. "It takes two to tango," my mother used to say. Maybe it went back to that first baby, to my inability, or maybe it was unwillingness, to share that kind of pain with anyone. I doubted I would ever know for sure. But I would not take all the blame upon myself. It was, in the end, his decision. His decisions, really. Both of them, both the going out and the coming back.

I called Reggie a few days after I mailed out the pearls, just to make sure she received them and to try and tell her how proud we were of her. As I spoke on the phone, Earl waited with his paper lowered just enough to see safely, like a knight at an arrow slit. "I want you to have them, Regina," I said. "You deserve them. And your father has given me plenty of beautiful things to wear. The pearls are yours now." I ended our conversation and said goodbye.

Reggie knew, of course, the necklace came back with Earl from one of his business trips. Came back for my fiftieth birthday. I knew the truth lay closer to the fact that *he* came back with *them*, rather than the other way around.

I couldn't bear to bring it up with him. Not then, not now. I didn't want any details, sordid or not. I didn't want excuses or reasons. I thought I came to terms with all of that. I just needed— something. Some sign from beyond the gate. I knew he waited for me, the woman in the garden, to signal somehow. He figured he'd know the sign when he saw it. I knew how he worked. He'd recognize the sign, he said with his eyes. He was sending his own signs, but I was unwilling to allow them past the angel at the gate. Until now.

I was careful not to look at him, but I saw out of the corner of my eye the newspaper went to half-staff, and his defenses stood down a bit more. An innocent enough movement. But I knew.

"They'll look grand on Reggie," he offered, then gave me a quick glance, a pure and raw question.

"Yes," I agreed, "they will."

The flames died out and the path lay open at last. The angel was still at the gate, but safe passage was guaranteed. We couldn't ask for more at the moment.

Chapter 16
Reggie

1968

When I got to the art gallery for the show, the rooms were already full. A few of my mother's pottery pieces were displayed on various size pedestals close to the door and I caught glimpses of more of them farther back as people ebbed and flowed through the rooms. Photos and paintings filled the walls, and artists were busy pointing out details or simply looking smug. It was an honor to be invited to show here. As I moved in, I heard snatches of conversation and listened for my mother's own quiet voice among the hubbub. Amid the political comments, the appreciation of the local wine being served, and the esoteric verbal reviews of the works and their artists, I heard, practically in my ear, "So, what do you think of this piece?"

Tony! I would recognize the particularly rich tenor anywhere. "I think it's a piece of crap," I said, without turning around.

"What?" the voice behind me rose in what sounded like surprise.

I glanced over my shoulder to throw Tony another barb and stopped cold. It wasn't Tony. It was two men, both strangers, clearly talking to each other, not me. One of them smiled at me as if I were a misplaced child and, with a little wave of his hand, walked away. "I...I...I...." I sounded like an idiot. I felt my face run the entire spectrum of reds, right on out into infrared and back to ultraviolet.

"You don't like it," the second man said, no question this time. "Don't worry. It's not mine. And, personally, I don't like it either." He smiled. And what a smile! Everything came to a complete halt.

"I'm so sorry!" I finally sputtered. "I thought you were someone else!"

"I hope not the artist," he said.

"Good Lord, no! I hope no one else heard me." This man must surely be convinced I had too much wine.

"I doubt it. It'd be pretty funny if they had. Honesty in an art gallery. How refreshing." The stranger's whole face brightened, like summer lemonade, when he laughed.

His laugh was infectious and it was pretty obvious he was not laughing at me. His hand was already out. "I'm Tom Mackensie."

Direct eye contact. Nice. I added out loud, "I'm Reggie, Social Blunderer."

Tom had wonderful eyes. The rest of him wasn't bad either.

I tried not to stare, but he was the best-looking male in the room. Bright blue eyes below sandy hair. Tan with a light glitter of freckles across his nose. He was tall, taller than I, but not towering, and he wore his body like a comfortable and well-designed sweater. I thought he might be the best-looking male I ever saw anywhere, anytime.

"Listen," he began.

I couldn't help but try to guess which classic pickup line he was going to use. After Carlos's goodbye of two years ago, I went into a bit of a spiral, though it was hard to admit it at the time. Carlos sort of hit me between the eyes, both coming and going. After a few letters and that lovely garnet ring for Christmas, I thought maybe he was interested enough to pursue—well, I was wrong, considering he got married the following spring. What bothered me was he didn't even have the nerve to write himself. His aunt added it to one of her letters, and that hurt. However, I didn't become a nun. I dated, but nothing until now struck me with the sudden shiver of Tom Mackensie's eyes.

Tom's voice came through the cloud of my thoughts. "Listen, I know you probably know all the best pickup lines, but at the moment, I can't think of one. So how about a straightforward introduction from someone we both know? This is an invitation-only art showing, so who do you know? We ought to be able to find someone in common to vouch for both of us." He looked around. "How about that lady over there?" he added. "Do you know her?"

What he doesn't know won't hurt him, I thought, as I recognized my mother standing in front of one particularly oddly balanced piece of pottery.

Tom craned his neck and went on. "That's one of the artists, but I don't know her. I only know her work. She has pottery and, well, let's just put it this way, most of it is nothing I'd spend my hard-earned money on."

I laughed, to myself and out loud. Well, let's just see where this goes from here. I don't think I want to reveal that particular little secret yet. Let's see if he can stick his other foot in his mouth. "So how did you get here? If you don't know that artist, or the others, then how did you get in?"

He glanced down, bringing himself back to me. "I don't know *that* artist, but I do know *this* one." He reached out and corralled an older man with thick dark hair tastefully speckled with silver. "This artist has those weird wall plaque thingies."

The older man turned at the sound of Tom's voice and smiled. I went from confused to aware. They had the same strong chin and the warmth between them was obvious.

"Reggie, this is my father, Sam Mackensie. He'll vouch for me."

"Oh, you think so, do you?" Then, to me, Tom's father added, "He holds himself in high regard, but he's really a nice guy. Luckily, he mostly takes after his mother, so anytime I want to, I can say I don't know him."

They sparked off each other, clearly enjoying the banter. I liked them. Just like that, I decided I liked them both.

Sam offered his hand. "You're Betty's daughter, aren't you? I admire her pottery so much. I'm so glad she was able to exhibit with us. She sold two of her pieces this afternoon." He tipped his head in the direction of the potter that was my mother.

"Your mother? She's your *mother*? Oh-h-h…" Tom's realization of his blunder washed slowly from neck to forehead.

"Aha!" I couldn't help but pounce. "The shoe's on the other foot now, isn't it? Listen, personal taste is personal taste. To be honest, there are some of her pieces I don't care for either. But I do like most of your father's work."

"Ah, don't try to butter me up now," Sam said, then turned away in response to a hand on his elbow. He threw over his shoulder, "Be nice to each other. You both come from talented people who happen to be wonderful too. Go have fun."

"*I* don't even like some of his stuff. You don't have to play nice just to make me feel better." Tom waited until his father was out of earshot. "But thanks for the thought."

"Sympathy is never a bad thing," I said. "Shall we take a look at some of the other exhibitors' works? I know we're on safe ground there. We can say whatever we want to about a non-relative."

His smile charmed me again. "Truce. Let me, madame, extend my arm to you and let's wander through the galleries here and see what trash we can uncover."

I tucked my hand into the crook of his elbow and we set off on what was sure to be an adventure. As we wandered, he reached out to kiss the cheeks of several women artists he said he admired and shake hands with a few men. I rode along on his popularity, enjoying every moment. My inner voice kicked in with, "This one is not going to get away." That thought emerged unbidden, like the first spring robin. It caught me by surprise. I didn't even have him. How could I possibly lose him? I didn't even have him yet.

Chapter 17
Reggie

1969

Two months. Was it really that long? We'd been dating two months? Tonight was the real test. He was taking me to the opera. The opera! Can you imagine, me at the opera? Yes, we met at an art gallery, but opera was in a league of its own, kind of like the mountaintop for hoity-toity music lovers. I hoped I'd be hoity-toity enough for him, although I knew he wasn't that way at all. He just loved the music, that's all.

The doorbell rang and I rushed to answer it. It had to be Tom. He called from work and told me he'd pick me up at six o'clock. I rarely ran late, but he wanted to make sure I'd be ready.

I wasn't ready.

When he stepped in, I had a shoe in one hand, a mascara wand in the other, and my toothbrush clenched in my teeth. "Mmff," I said, indicating he should make himself at home in the living room while I finished.

"Sorry," he said. "I know I'm a little early."

I glanced at the clock in the hall as I headed back for the bathroom. It was 5:40. When I finally got the toothbrush out of my mouth, I called out, "A little early?! Twenty minutes is enough for a full shower and no makeup. Or full makeup and no shower."

"Don't talk with your mouth full of toothpaste," he hollered. "Just hurry up. We've got a hot date tonight."

"Did you remember that we need to swing by my parents' place first? Did you find that glaze Mother asked you about?" By that time, I had my shoe on and my mouth rinsed.

"Of course," he answered. "I can find anything. Are you about ready?"

"Almost," I called, adding in a mutter, "almost stabbed myself in the eye, that is." I finished up the final touches and walked out to meet Tom.

He sat on the arm of the big chair by the front door, right where the light cascaded across his shoulders, looking out the front window at my little birdfeeder. When he heard me coming, I saw his head swivel in the late sunshine. Pinpricks of light scattered as he moved to meet me.

"Mmmm. You smell good," he said as he buried his nose in my hair and kissed the top of my head.

"Chanel's best, just for you."

"I like it."

"Well? Didn't you say you were in a hurry?" I giggled. How silly to giggle, but I couldn't help feeling lighthearted around him.

"We do have a deadline," he said. "I suppose we'd better get going. You look great, by the way."

"Not so bad yourself."

"Come on. Let's get the glaze to your mother and then we're outta here."

"That was incredible." I couldn't believe I actually enjoyed opera, but it swept me off my feet.

He opened the car door for me. "*The Magic Flute* is usually a good one to start with. It's got great music, great costumes and, in this production, a chance for a stage designer to go nuts. Did you see that set? It was unbelievable."

I actually went to an opera. The Hiking Queen of the Heartland went to an opera. Will wonders never cease? "I never thought you'd get me into a production like that—" I avoided the word opera— "but, you know, I really like it. Well, I liked *this* one. I can't say the same for others."

"Not a problem. You can love rock and roll and still hate Elvis. You pick and choose, just like everything else. Take what you like and leave the rest."

I knew what I liked, and I wasn't about to leave him behind. But I didn't want to go totally bubbly and sappy on him just yet. It wouldn't do to scare the poor guy off now, would it?

"What say we go get a beer? Enough of this highbrow stuff for one night. Mozart's made me thirsty. I think he'd appreciate that, don't you?" he asked.

"In this get-up? You want me to go into a bar dressed like this?" I laughed. In truth, I was willing to go anywhere with him. Would we look out of place? Who cares!

"Sure," he said. "My mom used to tell my sister, 'A little black dress can go anywhere.' I heard it so often I almost went out and bought a little black dress for myself."

His teeth were perfect. What a thing to notice—his teeth were perfect! But I was noticing everything about him. I liked everything too. "That's okay," I said. "You've got yourself a little black dress. I'm in it."

"What luck," he said. "I didn't even have to go shopping." He brought my hand to his lips and kissed the tip of my index finger. "Let's stop at that pub out in the boonies. What's it called? Draco's Dragaway? It's just a hole-in-the-wall, but they've got some great imported beers. I know they serve food too. And there's a pool table."

"A pool table! Actually, I love to play pool. I wonder if I can work a cue in this dress."

"You can work anything in that dress," he said. "But yeah, you can play pool like that. You'll get a few looks, but that's okay. So will I."

"Yeah, but you can leave your jacket and tie in the car. There isn't much I can take off." I stopped. "I didn't mean—"

He smiled broadly. I could see his teeth, even in the dark. "Take off what you can, then. Or what you want."

This was going in an interesting direction. "Let me leave these in the car then," I said, taking off my pearl necklace and dropping it into my evening bag. It slithered to the bottom and nestled between my handkerchief and a tube of lipstick. "I don't want to look too overdressed and I don't want to lose my pearls. Can I leave my purse in your glove compartment?"

"Sure," he said. "But I don't think there's too much you can do to look casual. You're bound to attract attention. You're a bombshell in that dress."

"Good thing I'm with the bombardier then," I shot back, pleased with his compliment.

• • • •

Twenty minutes later we parked in the tiny lot next to the bar, taking the last spot way back in the corner. Tom turned off the car, leaned over and ran his hands up the back of my neck and into my hair. "Come here, you," he said, his voice husky.

I couldn't see his face, but I could hear his voice pitched in a tone that said, "Don't ask me to say this in daylight." Then he did say it.

"Reg, I'm falling for you."

"Oh, really? Is that why you were flirting with every good-looking woman in the theater? We could hardly get out of the lobby!" I joked to hide the rising flutter in my stomach.

He chuckled. "I can't help it if a lot of women know me." He kissed my ear.

"Like Casanova," I said. "A lot of women knew him too." The jitters in my stomach were expanding.

"Now, let me talk, before I lose my nerve," he said. "Since I met you at the art gallery, you're in my head all the time. I plan what I want to do on the weekend and it always includes you. When something good happens, I want to call you. When something bad happens, well, I want to call you then too." Silence. A full silence, though, not one of those awkward, awful silences. Then he leaned over even more and pulled me to him. I hoped he felt how easily I leaned into him, because I wasn't able to say a word, my throat was so full. He touched his nose to mine. "What do you say, kid?"

"I knew when I met you that you were special," I managed to get out. Then my voice cleared. "I don't know where this is going and I don't want to guess right now, or have you guess either. I just know when I'm with you, I'm—happy. No, better than that. Satisfied. Satisfied and warm."

"I like that. That's good." He tilted his head and kissed me. "I love you, Reg." He said it so quietly I wasn't sure I heard right. I hoped I did. But before I had a chance to even react, he said, "Let's go play some pool and destroy the moment."

I loved him for that.

Chapter 18
Reggie

1969

"Dad?" Where was he? "Dad!" I checked the kitchen. Not there. "Where *are* you?" Standing in the middle of the living room, I sounded like the school's tornado siren.

"What's wrong, Reg? Are you okay?" Dad came clattering down the stairs. "What's going on?"

He came loping across the living room and stopped within breathing distance of me. His eyes stared at me, and he reached for my hands. It suddenly dawned on me, I was scaring him.

"Look!" I said quickly. I brought my left hand up between our noses. The diamond sparkled just like all the romance stories promised it would.

"Ah!" he said. "Where'd you get that? The dime store?" A chuckle.

My dad the wit.

He folded me in his arms. "Really, honey, it's beautiful."

I started to giggle and could barely stop myself. "I am *so* happy! We figured next summer. Is that good for you guys? I've struck gold. I feel like I've moved right on up to the angelic choir. No longer human. I love this man!" Finally, I got control of myself and stopped jabbering.

"Does your mother know?" He held me at arm's length.

I shook my head. "I think she's outside."

"Well, c'mon. Let's go tell her." Dad slid open the patio door and waved me out. "Betty, get on over here! We've got some good news!'

Mother swept off her garden hat, pulled off her gloves and came toward us.

I held out my hand, without saying a word.

She grasped my hand in both of hers. "It's beautiful!" Mother said. She startled me when she opened her arms and folded me in to her. "Oh, my darling, congratulations! So, where is your wonderful man? I need to congratulate him on his exquisite taste."

I almost missed the compliment, I was so distracted with thinking about Tom and our engagement.

Mother liked Tom from the beginning. When the chance offered itself, they sat over coffee and talked. Not that I minded her taking a liking to Tom. Almost everyone did. But I never knew my mother to talk so much to anyone. They seemed to talk about everything, from silly to sublime. I felt a little bit jealous, of course. Well, perhaps more than a little bit. Mother never talked to *me* that much. Didn't serve up coffee and advice. Eventually, I retreated to a "fashionable distance," as she would call it, close enough to be congenial and even affectionate at times, but not so close as to be mistaken for full-out dependence. Actually, when I thought about *their* conversations, it was mostly Tom talking and Mother listening, laughing and commenting appropriately. I accepted this arrangement, sometimes even disappearing whenever Tom pulled up a chair to join her in the kitchen. I didn't want to listen to Mother's "Uh-huhs" and "How nices" and "What did you do thens." I was just glad there was no tension between them, that she liked him. It made everything easier.

"Where's Tom?" Mother asked again.

"He'll be here in a minute. He said he'd leave the women to themselves until the shock wears off." From the driveway, I heard a car door slam. "Here he comes now." I turned to the door, hardly able to contain my happiness. "I feel like I'm flying!"

I saw Mother smile. She said, "Hang on, you don't have your pilot's license yet."

Her eyes glinted with humor, but the softness of her lips and the tilt of her head said there was more under the surface there. I almost missed it all as I performed a deep curtsey toward her, but I did glance up in time to catch—what was it?—something.

"Well—" I began, but I heard Tom come through the door, and everything flew out of my head but my darling man. I turned to go in the kitchen. "Nobody's perfect," I called back to her, heading for Tom to bring him out to the backyard. "Maybe someday I can fly. But for now, come on, bring out the orange juice! And the vodka! Let's have a toast in the backyard." I heard my voice trailing off behind me like stardust.

Chapter 19
Betty

1970

Reggie wore my dress. It was just a simple little dress. Brocade with long fitted sleeves and points that extended down the backs of my hands, like those medieval gowns, and a very long train that fanned out full behind me. The only lace I wanted were insets in the bodice and a band around the veil. I carried a pearl rosary and a single white orchid, which became my going-away corsage. I felt like a queen with that elegant dress. My mother had it sewn for me and I loved it. I still love it now. I was delighted Reggie asked to try it on. I couldn't begin to tell her how much it meant.

•　　•　　•　　•　　•

"Mom," Reggie came bursting in the door, "you kept your wedding dress, didn't you? I mean, you didn't just stuff it away somewhere where it's collecting mold, like in the basement, did you?"

"Yes, of course, I kept it." I held my breath. "One does not just pack that kind of thing away and then forget about it. I know right where it is. It's in the back of the closet in the spare bedroom, wrapped in black tissue paper. My mother had it cleaned while your father and I were still on our honeymoon."

"That's the last time you saw it, when you took it off for your honeymoon?"

"No, my dear. I took it out every year on our anniversary to see if it still fit."

"And?"

"And," I said, "it still did. At least, for quite a few years it did. Once we started—once we had you, it didn't fit anymore. That's when I packed it away for safekeeping. Do you want to go and get it out? You'll see the box on the top shelf, way in the back."

"I'll be right back." I heard the tail end of Reggie's voice as she headed off to get the dress.

I hoped she wanted it to wear for her own wedding, although I wasn't sure. Sometimes Reggie was so hard to read. I remember when I got married, I wanted to wear my mother's wedding dress, but it turned out to be a gray watered silk suit, with lace cascading over the bodice and along the cuffs of the blouse, more for traveling to the Twin Cities, as they did for their honeymoon, than for a formal wedding. "Remember," my mother told me, "ladies in those days couldn't always afford a dress to wear just once. This was a dress I wore on my honeymoon, and even once or twice that first year, before I decided I needed to retire it." She couldn't bear to get rid of it, though, and neither could I. I still had it stored in another box, wrapped in black tissue.

Reggie came out, dropped her jeans right there in the middle of the living room, and stripped off her shirt. Two minutes later, she stood backed up to me, waiting for help with those thirty-two little satin covered buttons. In a flash, I remembered exactly how many buttons followed each other like lemmings up the back of the dress. It fit her perfectly, just perfectly.

"You know," I said as I buttoned, "my mother and I laughed ourselves almost to wetting our pants over these buttons." Unconsciously, I counted as I fingered each loop. Sure enough, thirty-two.

"What on earth about? They don't seem very funny to me."

"If you peeled your finger instead of a potato, the idea of trying to finagle all of these little things into these teeny loops without bleeding all over— Well, I guess you had to be there." I chuckled. I didn't have a bandage on my index finger, and I wasn't struggling with the buttons. What strange memories came up out of nowhere! Suddenly I was my mother and Reggie was me. I was back, far back, in my mother's parlor, vestiges of which were in the furniture right here in my own living room. It pulled me up short, that sense of continuing life, unseen futures, mortality. I remembered all of the years with Earl, all those stories stretching out behind us, many of which were too insignificant and mundane to share with anyone. Many more were forgotten. How sad it was we didn't always perceive the everyday, the simple, as the fragments that build up into the vessels of our lives.

But then Reggie wiggled and I was back in real time. Maybe we were immortal in a way. Reggie, even though she always held herself at a small distance, was so dear to me. I impulsively wrapped my arms around her waist and rested my cheek on her back. "You are a dear, you know," was all I could manage before my voice lost its power. "I love you."

I felt her back straighten, perhaps in surprise, and she patted my hands at her waist.

"I love you too, Mother," she whispered and neither one of us moved for a long moment.

● ● ●

"There you go," Tom said as he placed the last pin to attach my corsage. He insisted on coming to the back of the church himself and pinning on his mother's and my corsages. He leaned over and planted a kiss on my cheek. "I'd give you guys a big hug, but Reggie would kill me if I squashed everything before we even get into church." He spotted the groomsmen waving from the front of the church. "Gotta run. Love you both." He was off. I went toward the bride's room to see if anyone needed help. Earl's tie— Reggie insisted on him being there in the bride's room with her—

needed straightening, but that was all. We were all set to walk her down the aisle together. Her request, to my surprise and delight. I turned to my daughter. She was radiant.

Reggie reached out and touched my corsage as I neared her. "The flowers are gorgeous. And look at our dress! We didn't even have to alter it. How perfect is that? I think it's a good omen."

I smiled at her.

"You and Daddy have such a great marriage. Everything you've dreamed of, I'll bet, and more. You guys have always been so happy."

She talked to me more today, more than usual. Love loosened her tongue, I think. She fingered the pearl necklace she chose to wear. My mother's pearls now belonged to my brother's wife. These were the other pearls. Without warning, tears lined my eyelashes, and it was too late to turn away.

"Oh, Mom! I didn't mean to make you cry!" She seemed truly concerned.

"You know how I always cry at weddings. I'm just so happy for you, Regina," I covered. The thought surfaced from where I interred it with flowers, candles and prayers for the dead. *My dearest, dearest Earl...I tremble at your touch....*

Nothing was quite as perfect as it looked. But Reggie heard what I wanted—no, needed her to hear. What she needed to hear were not the inevitable sorrows. Not mine, certainly. We all had enough troubles of our own. She didn't need to take on the burdens of others.

I was suddenly sure I didn't give her nearly enough to survive, much less thrive. Why didn't I tell her to watch, to wait, maybe even to talk more? Was that even the answer, to tell her more? Maybe it was better to go in somewhat blinded by the force of early love. Love, if it was true, would grow over the long run, not flare early, like fireworks, and then fall into the lake, fizzling as it fell. My own love for Earl had its ups and downs, and there certainly were times I wondered if I made a mistake marrying at all. I was, after all, the lonely only, destined to remain a spinster. In that earlier day and age, it was anathema to stay single. Now? Maybe not so bad.

But that would mean missing all the mornings waking up with my legs tangled up with Earl's, feeling the heat creeping like early morning fog over to my side of the bed. It would have meant missing my darling Regina Marie, pink and slippery, but freshly mine, freshly born, the one who survived. I would have missed Earl's insistence at making breakfast on Sunday mornings while I read the paper. "Nope, darlin'," he'd gently push me back onto the couch, "my turn in the kitchen. Today is the Lord's day of rest, and you rest too. Besides," there was always an endearing twinkle in his eyes, "I love to cook breakfast. It's the only meal I can't ruin." True enough.

I would miss the pain too. The gardening, painting, and staining blisters. The sore muscles, the rain on newly cleaned windows, the wrenched back from lifting a stone too big to be lifted. The physical pain was really the easiest. The other pain was a lot harder. I wouldn't mind missing that. All the differences, big and small, that must be dealt with. The pearls. The poor dead babies. Still, I couldn't choose which of those to excise, which to bypass. As searing as some were, I was who I was because of all of it. Every bit of it.

Maybe the old saw was true. Steel tested in fire and all. I could only hope the me of today was stronger than the me without all of the struggles. We never would know, would we—what we might've been? What if, what if? Futile, certainly. I was alive and kicking, having moments and days and years of happiness, contentment, satisfaction, call it what you will. Sometimes I even reached ecstasy, when I knew without a doubt this was indeed the right road to be on. Not too many of those, but they were there, like trillium, appearing one year in the woods and not there at all the next. It was enough to keep me looking.

"What are you smiling so secretively about?" Reggie's voice entered the edge of my mind.

Now was the time. Give her all the strength I gained over the years. Pour it out. Excite her. Love her openly and freely. Speak all of the hidden words.

"I'm just thinking about your dad," I said. Damn! The unbidden, unspoken oath surprised me.

The moment was gone.

"Help me fasten this veil a little tighter, would you?" She fiddled with her hair, tangling the edge of her headpiece in a hairpin. "What are you thinking about him?"

She bent her head to me and I began to maneuver the hairpin out of her headpiece and into place. Damn, damn, damn. This time, a deliberate thought. But I couldn't go on, the flow was wrong. "Well, how I grew into knowing the whole man. No one knows everything about their spouse, I think. But stick around long enough to find out who it is you really married. Sometimes the results can surprise you."

"Mmmm."

She stood very still and I realized this might be my only chance to say anything of value. My hands slowed.

"So, what are your words of wisdom for me on this day of days?" she said.

Was she reading my mind? "Darling Regina. Listen to your heart." It slipped out of its own will. What else could I tell her on this day of days?

"That's it? That's all?" She giggled deep. "No 'watch out for loose women hanging around your husband'? No 'never say no'? There must be more to making a successful marriage." She was suddenly serious.

"Just listen to your heart, darling. Don't rush. Listen." I smiled. Of course, there was so much more, but I couldn't tell her any more. She would come to know, she really would. We all did, eventually. I couldn't see the road ahead of her. She would have to deal with her own potholes and repavings when the time came. She didn't want to hear about roads wearing thin and I wasn't about to spoil her day. "Just listen to your heart," I repeated. "It'll tell you what to do."

She removed her attention from me and focused it on the few wisps of hair not yet perfect. She frowned a bit into the mirror, then turned, perhaps projecting her thoughts into the church and the day ahead of her. Suddenly, she gave me a hug full of baby warmth remembered, and of depth so profound, she was gone before it reached the bedrock in me.

"Your heart will help you," I said again, as much for my benefit as hers.

Chapter 20
Reggie

1970

I was nervous.

Believe it or not, I wanted my mother. If she said as little as nothing, somehow I knew it would calm me down. I turned around and there she was, straightening Dad's tie. They looked good together. I watched her smile up at him and, in the look he gave her, it was clear he adored her.

"Mother!" I called to her across the bride's room. "The flowers are gorgeous. And look at the dress! It fits perfectly! I think it's a good omen." My hands moved up to align the pearl necklace, the one she gave me, the one Dad gave her for her fiftieth birthday. My favorite necklace. "You and Daddy have such a great marriage. Everything you dreamed of, I'll bet. You guys are so happy." I thought I saw tears flash into her eyes.

"Oh, Mom! I didn't mean to make you cry!" I said.

"You know how I always cry at weddings. I'm just so happy for you, Regina." She looked me up and down.

I was sure she remembered her own day in this very same dress. I knew it would delight her I wanted to wear her dress. I tried it on more for shock value than really wanting to wear it for my own wedding, but once I got it on, I was entranced. It fit like a glove and made me look taller and slender. For both of us, it was surely both a surprise and a triumph.

For me, right now was one of those rare threshold moments, a sense of standing on one side of an open doorway. Not quite ready to step through, I stood gathering my nerve, like a jet engine building up enough power for takeoff. I wanted to step through with a sense of determination and clear choice. It would come down to a pure and simple personal choice. This would be the only chance to ask questions on this side of the threshold.

Mother smiled. A little, almost secret smile. She was far away from here, someplace pleasant, I bet.

I deliberately looked deeply at those around me, especially her. I wanted to remember the pattern of the lace on Mother's shoulder, little whorls of paisley, tiny pearl drops, thick curves. Her flowers, roses blending from mauve to cream, each petal extending from the tightly packed base, bending like a Swan Lake ballerina. Her lipstick, outlined carefully so it wouldn't bleed out beyond the self-defined boundaries, bowing up as she smiled, oblivious to my gaze. I was determined to burn every little detail of this day into my memory so I could pull it out, and smile, as Mother was undoubtedly smiling over her own special days.

"What are you smiling so secretively about?" I broke into Mother's personal reverie. "Tell me."

She only whispered, "I'm just thinking about your dad."

Of course she was. How sweet! "Help me with this veil, would you, please? What are you thinking about him?"

She gave me some platitudes about sticking to your man and all. "Mmmm," I said, waiting for more. I tried to stand very still as she worked on my veil. "So, what *are* your words of wisdom for me on this day of days?" It sounded so flippant, but this time, for once, I was honestly serious about wanting my mother's opinion.

"Darling Regina. Listen to your heart." She looked me straight in the eye and didn't even hesitate.

Did she mull over what to say to me for a long time? I wasn't sure. "That's it? That's all?" I tried to show her I was serious about this.

"Just listen to your heart, darling. Don't rush. Listen." Mother smiled and touched my cheek, adding, "Just listen to your heart. It'll tell you what to do."

That last seemed to be spoken more to herself than to me, though she never broke eye contact as she anchored my veil and stroked my hair gently. But Tom was waiting and he tugged at the edge of my mind like nothing else. I checked myself in the mirror one last time. As Mother dropped her hands from my hair, I started for the door. At the last minute, I caught sight of her face, remembered how she hugged me and told me she loved me when I tried on her wedding dress, and a sudden rush of pure love lifted me. I went back and hugged her like I hugged her when I was a kid, tight, without guile or inhibition. I broke away quickly. I couldn't do more, I was so overflowing. Dad stood in the doorway at the far side of the room and I floated away to him. Clear love for both of them welled up unbidden. I could hear the florist behind me, instructing my mother about my bouquet.

The moment I reached my father, right on cue, the church bells started to chime and we both laughed spontaneously.

"Well, well. Listen to that, will you?" Dad had the warmest chuckle of any man I knew, even Tom. "Wasn't there a song in an old musical about hearing bells when you fall in love?"

"Oh, Daddy!" I laughed with him. "I love you so much. Tom is going to have quite a struggle to get up to your level."

"Tom will do just fine," he said. "Just don't expect the poor guy to be perfect. Nobody's perfect."

"Is that your advice for me today? Don't expect perfection? But look at you. Mother got such a deal when she captured you."

His eyes seemed to darken just a bit. I knew the look. He was about to say something profound, and I had better catch it the first time around because he would only say it once and then probably deny ever having said it in the first place. He was such a softie underneath all of that man-of-the-house exterior. He took my chin in his hand.

"Regina." Now I knew he really was serious. He knew he had my attention. "Remember, we're all only human, trying our best to get through this life. What we do, we sometimes don't see..." He stopped. "Well, sometimes we don't always think. That's why we marry people who can help us think. If you're lucky, you've got a man who will help you think when you're sure you can't anymore."

I waited. This was more than he had strung together in a long time.

"If he can unkink your mind, then cherish him. Those kinds of partners are few and far between."

There was the pearl.

Tom—I saw him through the half-open door to the sacristy at the front of the church—did "unkink" my mind. Plenty of times, he helped me step outside of my skin and take stock, helped me see the decisions I needed to make.

"Yes, Dad," I whispered as I kissed his cheek. "He's a good man. I'll remember."

Rich notes of Bach swelled into the church and it was time to take my place at the end of the procession. Mother came over and handed me my flowers. Calla lilies flowed down the front of my gown, studded with pearl clusters where the stamens had been, all of it clouded with baby's breath. Dad offered me his arm and Mother lightly slipped her gloved hand into the crook of my elbow. I wanted both of them to give me away. Tom moved out to the front of the church and stood, hands folded, slightly shaking, I thought, though I couldn't really see at this distance. But I could see his smile and the set of his shoulders. What a comfort he was, strong and gentle, able to enfold me and yet not suffocate. I was so lucky.

I leaned and kissed each of my parents, burning the feel of their cheeks into my memory, willing myself to hear every note of the lovely organ processional and feel every step down the aisle. I wanted this pink and cream marble path etched into my mind so I could tread it anytime I wanted. Every anniversary, every moment of lovemaking, every experience we would share, I wanted to remember it all. I wanted to be able to see this aisle as the beginning of a long and fulfilling partnership, together heart and soul.

"Time now, Reggie," I heard my father whisper and I took the first step.

Chapter 21
Betty

1972

"Well." It was a long, satisfied sound from Earl, matching the apple cider's steam that languidly curled and twisted above our cups. Earl sank down in the chair nearest the fireplace and reached a free hand over to grasp mine.

"Yes, well," I echoed. "What a lovely afternoon for just relaxing."

"I didn't think I'd ever get that snow off the walk, the stuff was so darn heavy." He balanced the cup on the wide arm of the chair and leaned back, letting his eyelids droop.

"You know, you're not as young as you used to be—"

"Sixty, darlin', I'm only sixty. Still a lot of spunk left here."

"I know, I know. I'm sixty too, remember. Still and all, we're going to start slowing down one of these days. They say sixty is a kind of benchmark. That you start—well, not being able to do the things you could before. It's a borderline, I guess."

I didn't sound too sure of myself. I honestly didn't see myself slowing down. I could still dig up the garden in good time, although it took me a bit more sweat these past couple of years. I could run the snowblower as well as Earl could, and sometimes did, but he loved to get outdoors, even in the coldest weather.

But I could see the years took a toll on him. More than on me. The traveling for work diminished, but the headaches and pressures only increased. When he was on the road, the job had its own kind of defining rhythm, the kind of rhythm that apparently wasn't the same as in the smaller orbit of an office building. The company was large and his place was not at the top, but in the middle somewhere and off the road. Both of those conditions took a lot out of him. Or put more onto him. I knew he felt the weight. Maybe he could tote it more lightly when he had the freedom to set his own schedule for traveling, but now that option, that independence, wasn't there. It was not that he was terribly unhappy or he hated his job; it was just, he set his sights on retiring in a couple of years and that was driving him. Like a horse headed for the stable. A horse pulling an awfully heavy load, and unable to jettison anything yet.

He sat slouched in the chair as I rocked my head to see him better. Yes, there was a lot more gray hair, where there was hair left. He could be a full-fledged abbot, the tonsure descended so far from the crown of his head. If I didn't bow to his demands and do some appropriate trimming, he'd be sprouting wiry stray hairs from ears and nose, but he was fastidious about making sure those were destroyed in short order. I couldn't help but smile.

He opened his eyes and turned to me, returning my smile. "Still can't keep your eyes off the ol' man, eh, darlin'?"

"You always were the best-looking man I knew." I matched his tone.

"Still am." He smiled again, but somehow, it looked more like a brief painful twinge. "Better looking than Tom."

He was baiting me. We both agreed when Reg married Tom two years before, that Tom was probably one of the best-looking men either one of us had encountered.

I laughed outright. "Better looking than Tom for certain. He doesn't have your stylish hair or your boyish charm."

"My stylish hair, eh? At least he's got hair."

"I like yours better," I said.

"Want to see my chest hair?" he teased. "I think I have four or five left."

"Oh, my! Are your parents home? We wouldn't want them catching us, now would we?"

He stood up and swept me into a bear hug. "I don't care if they catch us. Let's go to bed."

I started to say, "I'll rinse out the mugs," but he backed me toward the stairs. The mugs would wait until tomorrow.

• • • • •

"Betty?"

"What time is it?" I came awake slowly.

"Two-thirty."

"Are you okay?" I was fully awake now. Earl never stirred once he was asleep. Something was wrong.

"Just a cramp or heartburn or something, I think."

I turned on the bedside lamp and saw his face, drawn and worried. "Do you have pain in your chest? In your arms?"

"Maybe heartburn," he said, but the small creases and crevices around his mouth deepened as he clamped his mouth tighter.

"When did this start?" My voice turned urgent. "Did you have pain when you were snowblowing?"

His shook his head once and I could see that he was unable to answer more than that. He clenched his teeth tighter.

"Hold on," I commanded as I dropped my feet to the floor. "Hold on!" I called back over my shoulder, on a dead run for the kitchen.

Why couldn't I remember what to say, who to call? My fingers went numb as I picked up the receiver and tried to get the short sequence of numbers right. I couldn't seem to do it and, in desperation, punched 0, over and over. Finally, a voice asked, "May I help you?" and I spilled out what I hoped was a coherent sentence or two.

My mind deserted my body and seemed to be standing over there near the mixer somewhere, observing. "Get over here!" I wanted to holler frantically, but nothing came out and I remained disembodied, floating.

When a low "Ah!" reached me from the stairwell, my mind finally leaped back into my body and took over. I didn't want to move, but I could and I did. I gave all the information they needed, then left the receiver dangling as I sprinted toward the stairs.

Earl made it to the living room and lay slumped back in the overstuffed reading chair, both hands on his chest, like an Aztec priest ready to plunge his hand in and sacrifice his own heart. His eyes were open and his mouth was no longer clenched, but pleading, silently pleading for help.

"They're coming, hang on, they're coming, hang on, hang on," I babbled, even as I heard the wail of a siren moving closer. I got the message correct. At least I did something right.

I was going to lose him, I just knew it, but in this strange situation, as he looked up at me, alternately squeezing his eyes shut and grasping for my hand, I dared not let him know this. Even though I couldn't smile, I locked eyes with him, chanting my mantra, "Hang on, they're coming, they're coming."

Suddenly, they arrived.

I was gently moved aside. I stood where he could see me as they carefully moved him to the stretcher, all the while talking and taking information. I lost track of what they were doing, realizing at the same time that it really didn't matter. They were in charge now, and I could let go of that part of it, at least. But I couldn't bear to and my mantra changed to a constant question, "Is he going to be all right? Is he going to be all right?" What a stupid question to be asking right in front of him, part of my mind demanded. What if they say no? Then what were you going to do? But I couldn't seem to stop my mouth from forming the words. I felt one of them hand me my shoes and help me into my coat.

As they moved Earl out the door, a young lady stepped up and forced eye contact. "Come on, you can ride in the front. It'll be better for the ambulance attendants to have a little more elbow room in the back. Do you have your house keys?" She asked as she led me out the front door, ready to pull it shut behind us.

There was a heaviness in my pocket and I realized that my keys were with me already. How they got there, I had no idea. That mind standing by the mixer must have grabbed them off the counter when I wasn't paying attention. "Um," I stumbled, "right here." We moved quickly off the stoop and I felt like I was being swept into hell with only this tiny girl to guide me.

I was helpless. How terrible that feels.

*   *   *

Hours later, Reg, Tom and I hunkered down in what should have been a very pleasant waiting room. There were flowers and subdued lighting, magazines and a telephone. Utilitarian tables settled on one end, and two couches and three floral chairs huddled on the other. We were within reach of one another on the comfortable end of the room, but I was not comfortable. None of us were.

We should have been. The doctor came out and told us that Earl had suffered a heart attack, but that he was stable and should recover. Protection in that "should." I would rather have it "would," but the doctor was being cautious.

We had no time to breathe smoothly yet. We did know everything looked good, but we were still chewing on that. When they let us in to see him, all too brief a meeting, Earl smiled wanly at me and squeezed my hand quickly.

"We don't want him to tire," the nurse took my elbow, "but you can come back in anytime you wish. You just need to be quiet and let him rest as much as possible. He's sedated right now, and probably won't remember much. Take some time, now that you've seen he's going to be all right, and get yourself a cup of coffee. Walk a bit. But you can come back in anytime."

Back in the waiting room, Reggie looked tentatively at Tom, then blurted, "Daddy works far too hard. Maybe he shouldn't wait two years to retire." Her voice trailed off.

"Yes, he does work too hard," I said. But then I thought to myself, I don't know how ready he is to stop working. I honestly don't think he's shifting into the retirement mode just yet.

"Maybe it's time for him to hang it up." Reg's voice interrupted my thoughts.

"I'll go get us something to drink." Tom stood abruptly. He could sense a family crossroads here. I knew he was astute enough to keep his opinion to himself until he was consulted.

"Reg," I said, "your father is still capable of making his own decisions. I'm not going to force anything on him. I certainly don't want him thinking he can't take care of himself, that he's suddenly become the dependent one, the child that needs to be parented." I nearly bit my tongue at that. I didn't want to offend Reggie. She was only trying to help. I hope she didn't think—

"Mother," she broke in, "I'm not trying to tell you guys what to do. Only, I don't want him to—to overwork himself."

I felt she was about to say "to kill himself," but caught herself.

"Reggie, believe me, at the first indication from your dad, I am going to leap right in there and talk about it. I don't want the job to take him away from me." Whether he was ready for retirement or not, I was not quite ready to think of life without him. "Or anything else, either, if I can help it," I added as an afterthought.

• • •

We moved smoothly into recovery and rehabilitation, with trips to therapy and a change in diet and exercise. I used my sick days and took time off to take care of Earl until he felt comfortable alone again. Each day, we stepped into our little routine. Earl poured out the cereal and I brought out milk and fruit. We both switched from regular to decaffeinated coffee and stopped eating sweet rolls and bacon. Then we'd go for a walk, greeting all the early morning dogs along the way. Earl always wanted to stop and pet each one. We finally took to carrying those little doggie treats in our jacket pockets. We'd ask for permission from the owners first, of course, but we made a lot of four-legged friends on those ramblings. The doctor assured us, as long as the temperature was reasonable and the roads not icy, we were perfectly safe walking outdoors. When we couldn't do that, we took turns using the treadmill we bought and set up in our bedroom. Earl even bought a little television so he wouldn't get bored. Sometimes in the evening I'd read out loud to him, if I found a newspaper or magazine article which sounded interesting.

On the last Saturday morning before I went back to work, Earl took my hand as we walked and said, "Darlin', what do you think of ol' Earl here calling it quits? Retiring, I mean." He sneaked a peek at me.

Reggie's concern, which had always matched mine, in spite of how I placated her at the hospital, flooded over me. With hardly a break in stride, I said, "If you feel you are ready, then I am all for it." We flashed each other very bright smiles. So, this would be it then. I didn't even have to work at convincing him.

He had me type up a letter of intent to retire and that was that. He retired. Of course, it wasn't quite so smooth, but after a couple of months, he plotted out the paths of the men he was training and he was off. In June, he cleaned out his desk and walked away. With school out for the summer, we both felt this was the best timing. We could spend the entire summer together.

In all the time we had left, he said he never once regretted that move. He said he knew he was heading for retirement anyway and this heart attack was a blessing in disguise. He said he'd learn to cook, he always wanted to and, if I wanted, I could keep working. Well, I did want to. I had only been teaching for a few years and loved it. So, we negotiated and I kept teaching while he took care of the house. It was good for both of us. I came home to hot meals and he got to nap in the middle of the day. We both knew it was a win-win situation.

Chapter 22
Reggie

1972

"All right, all right, all right! Let's get these groups wrapped up here!" I bellowed across the room. "Come on back, gang, before the bell rings! I've got a couple more things to clue you into before your presentations tomorrow."

Papers shuffled, backpacks thumped onto the tables, and the chaos of the end of a normal high school English class began. I stood in the middle of this mess, timing to see how long it would take them to get everything back. I put my fingers in my teeth and blew one of those earsplitting whistles. Everyone froze in place and the noise level dropped to nothing. It always amazed me, I actually trained them well enough at the beginning of the year, so now I could get their attention quickly.

"Okay, gang," I said, "the list of who presents when is posted over here on the wall. Just remember that ar-ti-cu-la-tion counts. Costumes and props too."

"Can't we use scripts?" a voice whined from the back of the group.

"Nope. Them's the rules, folks. No scripts, no notecards. Either improvise or memorize. Your choice."

There was a general groan, but they knew the parameters already, so it was more a knee-jerk reaction than anything else. The bell rang and the clatter began again as they made their way out with various Goodbyes and See yas. Just as it quieted, the speaker on the wall crackled and the administrative assistant's voice came on. "Mrs. Mackenzie? Would you come down to the office, please?"

"Be right there," I answered, but before I even made it around the corner, Mrs. Ketka, the principal, rushed up, waving a letter.

"The summer workshop for teachers? You've been accepted!" she announced grandly. "It looks like my recommendation worked. They accepted your application to co-teach. I'm *so* excited for you. Congratulations!"

I had put the application into the back of my mind, hoping beyond hope to participate as an instructor, but knowing it was a long shot. What did I have to offer? Apparently, enough. This would be a real feather in my professional cap. Best of all, I'd have a chance to connect with peers just as interested in teaching writing as I was, and excited about sharing what worked and what didn't. I couldn't wait for summer.

* * * * *

"Whaddja tell 'em?" Tom's question was pretty casual when I got home and told him, but I knew he was deeply interested.

"I told them yes, of course." We agreed that, if the invitation came to teach at the summer conference, then I should go, even if it meant I would be away for two weeks. What I didn't tell him was I had a fleeting moment of doubt before I accepted the position. Dad's heart attack of a few months before was still near the top of my thoughts and I hated to leave him behind. I knew Tom would just say, "What're you worried about? Your mom treats him like a king. Go. Enjoy yourself. If you're that concerned, I'll stop over there every day." We wouldn't exactly argue, but he seemed to see Mother as an angel of mercy, while I pictured her as someone who waited in the shadows, which gave me an unexpected chill. I shook off the thoughts. "I called right away and said I'd love to co-teach," I said.

"Excellent," was his immediate response. "You deserve to get away and show off your professional stuff. I get to do that often enough. You should too."

"Well," I couldn't keep the smile off my face, "our department has worked pretty hard on developing this team approach. It's about time we shared the joy."

Tom pulled me into his lap and nuzzled. "I'm so proud of you. Nobody works as hard as you do. Go off and enjoy yourself."

I toyed with the idea of asking him to come with me. In fact, I had my mouth open to do just that when he said, "You might want me to come along, but I'm going to hang around here. I can catch up with some work without your goddess-body to distract me."

"Are you sure?" I asked. "I'd love to have you come." I meant it too.

"Naw. I really do need to get stuff done here and I can't take it along. Don't worry about me."

It didn't take much persuasion. I was going, one way or another. Too bad Tom couldn't come, but I knew he could use the time without interruptions. It would give us a better summer once I got back. More time for each other, more time to goof off once in a while. This way both of us won. That made it even better.

Twelve days down, two to go in our summer conference. Final projects and outlines were in. The gorgeous college campus, the consistently warm weather, someone else to cook meals—it was all coming to a close. But no time for thinking about that. Right now, the four of us teaching the workshop sat surrounded by papers in my room.

"How come we always meet in here?" I whined about the invasion, as usual.

"You are the only single in a double room, you jerk."

I was well aware that Jane, at first exasperated that I was the one lucky enough to snag the largest room, was by this time only teasing.

Michael added, "That couch came in handy."

"Only for stacking tons of papers and projects," I said. I hadn't sat on the couch since the first day, almost two weeks ago. It was always full of one thing or another. This time, the four of us were inundated with finished projects.

"We have got to get this stuff organized." This came from Miriam.

Michael made sympathetic noises.

"Wait." Jane sounded like she hit gold. "Let's just divvy these up."

"Yeah," Michael leaned her way. "Why don't we—"

"Right!" Miriam jumped in. "Jane, you and I can take half, and Michael and Reg can take the other half."

"Sounds great," Jane agreed.

We shifted the chaos into two piles.

"Honestly," I stood like Lady Justice with her scales, papers in each hand, "sometimes I think teachers are worse than students. We just don't follow directions very well. I'll bet some of these people chased balls into the street when they were kids."

Miriam laughed. "Maybe that explains some of the eccentric behavior around here."

"Come on," Michael said. "Some of us were ordered into the street. 'Why doncha go play in the street, kid?' Good ol' Mr. Schmiedl. Always loved the neighbor kids."

"Okay, I think that's it," Jane announced. "All divvied up. Want to get started on it right away?" This was directed at Miriam.

"Why not? We have time. Nothing going on until dinner tonight."

"Don't we have conferences?" I wondered about those who needed to bounce ideas off one of us before getting up to do a presentation in front of the whole group.

"Nah," Jane replied, "we have all afternoon off. Besides, they know where to find us, if they need us."

"Makes sense." I sat down with a stack of projects in my lap. I glanced at Michael and raised my eyebrows, a good signal developed between us over the past week or so.

"Yup," came an immediate answer to my unanswered question, "we might as well get going. We ought to be finished before dinner."

The four of us clicked from the first day. The two weeks were almost over now, but I felt like I knew these people forever. "You guys are the best," I blurted. "I wish we had more time together." Although the others seemed to be sublimely unconscious, I was quite aware, soon we'd be back to the normal rat race.

Turned out they weren't unconscious at all. Just quiet, up until then. We all began talking at once, all but Michael. Michael sat looking down at his hands, playing with his watch, his one annoying habit. "This," loud and imperious from him as he looked up, "is why God invented telephones, guys."

In a half-rest in this waltz, time suspended and we measured each other. One lovely brief moment when our little corner of humanity came together. Unexpectedly, Hemingway's *The Moveable Feast* emerged from my mental mists. The expatriates partying in Paris and sharing that special bond of travelers coming together in a foreign land. But that ended badly, didn't it? Drunken brawls, insanity, and one form or another of suicide? Well, that was *not* us!

"Come on, you guys. Yeah, yeah, yeah, I'll miss you too, but let's get rolling." Michael could break the mood. Always the kidder. He turned away pretty quickly though, and underneath it all, I caught out of the corner of my eye the emotion behind the joking.

Jane and Miriam packed up and headed out the door. Jane threw back over her shoulder, "We'll see you guys at dinner."

I had just enough time to get out, "Great," before the door swung shut again and they were gone.

"Okay." Michael rubbed his hands together. "What's first?"

"You really are going to miss the Wicked Witches, aren't you?" I teased.

"Yeah, you in particular, oh Great Witch of the West. You have been my particular thorn this week."

"Come on. What will you do without your three buddies? I don't want to lose touch. I don't think we've drained our brains enough yet, do you?"

He was still smiling, but the teasing look was gone and he said, "We are a great team, aren't we? Yeah, I wish you guys could go home with me. The house is pretty empty since the ex left." He glanced over, the twinkle back. "I could use a new Witch to order me around."

"Man, I can see why she's gone! Did she take the gingerbread door with her when she left?" I had no idea why Michael's wife left him—he only shared that she left him, not the other way around—but I couldn't understand why he didn't find another "Witch." He was one of the most interesting, tolerant men I ever met. With a sudden shimmer, I realized he reminded me a bit of Carlos. The same good looks, the same intelligent eyes. Lord, doesn't that go back a few years!

I picked up the nearest project and raised my eyebrows.

"Three hours. That has got to be a record." The couch, previously stacked with projects, was empty. It was quite a challenge to get them critiqued before dinner, but finally, we closed up the last ones.

"Quite a collection, eh?" Michael stood with hands on his hips and admired the pile we created on my bed. "I'm going to stuff these into a box before the whole thing topples and we have to start over." He picked up a nearby box and carefully began stacking the projects inside.

"I am *not* starting over." I rubbed my eyes. "We made a list of the ones we got, remember?"

Finished, Michael plopped down on the couch. "Man, my eyes are ready to fall out."

"Mine too," I said. My words were almost unrecognizable as I oozed back into the corner of the couch, pushing my arms up over my head and squeezing my eyes shut. "I am stiff as a brick." I stretched my arms up as far as I could, forcing tight muscles to uncrimp.

"Love to help." Michael's voice was too close. He reached over me, stretching for a paper on my desk. At least, that's what I thought. His breath was on my face as he moved over me. His hand covered both of my hands stretched up over my head, imprisoning them in a warm, soft grasp. I kept my eyes shut tight, unwilling to either look or move. I felt the soft hairs on his arm graze my forearm. He hovered, poised on hands and knees, mere slivers of daylight between us, waiting for a sign.

From outside somewhere, I felt my body go calm. "Why are you relaxing?" my mind shouted. "Shut up," my other half retorted.

I felt him over me, and opened my eyes directly into his. Like a bird coming to the nest, he settled gently onto me, full length, closing the daylight between us, keeping his eyes on mine. To my own amazement, I remained still. Not limp, just quietly attentive. My mind stirred somewhere across the room, observing, not complaining, not warning. Just silently chewing its fingernails.

I shut it out.

Michael reached down, kissed my ear and whispered, "This is what I thought about all week," then kissed my neck.

I couldn't believe I was watching all this. Watching from across the room and not responding or rebelling. It was exhilarating in a strange way.

"You're smiling," he added. "That's a very good sign." He balanced, bent down and kissed the edge of my ear again, lingering.

I shivered and he slid to kiss my neck. Only lower this time.

He looked up, gave me a pixie smile, and kissed me, a slow full kiss.

Suddenly, my body stood at attention. Everything was poised and ready and I sank deeper into the couch, borne by the weight of him, the heady, warm feel of him. Michael kissed me again, then shifted his weight ever so slightly and slid his hand behind my back, pulling me to him.

I was still at attention. "I—" That was as much as I could get out. I wondered if I even wanted to get more out.

"Am I hurting you?" he whispered. "I'm not exactly a lightweight."

"No." It was the only conceivable answer for the moment.

"You're still smiling." He smiled back into my eyes and moved his hand down between us, tugging at the elastic of my shorts.

I could not believe I was still so calm. How could I be? I was a married woman and I was enjoying this. I should leap up and throw him off. I should never—

In reality, I was churning inside. In spite of my life with Tom, I found this fascinating. Michael stirred me. A lot more than I cared to admit, that was for sure.

He kissed the corner of my mouth softly. He touched me in all the right places. I felt myself turning to him. Very little remained between us as he pressed us together again.

"I—Wait." That was my voice. Was that my voice? I heard myself say out loud, "I—Wait," while my mind was telling me, "Why 'Wait'? Why not 'This is wonderful'?" Because it was.

At my words, he rose slightly and the sliver of air between us reappeared. "Lord, don't stop me now," he implored in a whisper and leaned in.

I squeezed my eyes closed again.

"Don't. Michael. Please." Like notes forced out of a tired horn, breathy, but on key.

He withdrew to one knee and elbow. When I opened my eyes, his leg was still draped across me as he looked at me carefully.

With real effort, I forced myself back. "Okay. I'm sorry. No, I'm not. I don't know what's going on." My mind ran over from the other side of the room and clambered back into my body. All of the words came rolling out at once. All of the words my mind would say, had it been home the last few moments.

"Michael, I'm really sorry— " I could go no farther.

"It's—I—uh—I misread the signs, I guess."

Signs? What signs? Before I had a chance to follow that thought, he pulled back from me completely and stood up.

This happened much too fast. I managed to bring my arms down to a more natural position, but nothing else seemed to be functioning.

"Come on," he said. "I didn't mean to scare you, and I am certainly not the kind of guy to, you know, take advantage if you don't want this." He offered his hand to help me up. I looked directly into his eyes, but I couldn't stretch out to take his hand.

"Don't worry." He lifted an eyebrow. "I'm not going to pull you into my arms and try and force you or anything. I'm not that kind of guy," he repeated.

I felt he was telling the truth, like a little boy caught standing in the kitchen with a garter snake in his hand: "Yeah, I brought it in the house, but I'll take it outside now." The look was disarming and I finally reached for his hand.

"Better rearrange your clothes," he said as he pulled me to my feet. "People will wonder." The smile, though a bit sad, was genuine and I began to breathe again.

"Look—" I said.

"No, don't try to explain or anything. What happened, happened. For me," his eyes softened nicely, "it'll be a great memory to fall back on in hard times. Someone found me pretty attractive. It'll be better than caffeine."

I couldn't help but laugh outright at that. Though I couldn't very well tell him—or wouldn't—I felt the same way. Someone else found me attractive. Someone else wanted to flirt. Someone else wanted to be with me. Someone else wanted to make love to me. What a high. Better than caffeine.

"I need a little time to myself right now," I said. That was obvious for both of us.

"Thought so. Me too." He tilted his head, raised his eyebrows and added as he grabbed his things and headed for the door, "I'm gonna go sulk awhile." Then that brilliant smile and he was gone before I had a chance for another word. It seemed clear in those last looks that this would stay between us.

What did I do—almost do? Did I really lead him on? Well...yes, I guess. From his point of view, maybe I did. We understood each other so well. We built up such a friendship— Friendship? Where I saw friendship, he saw invitation. Duh, Reggie! Smiles, linked arms, arm punches, laughs, little signs. He misread them all. All it took to bring it out was one tight t-shirt and a stretch on a couch!

Still...I couldn't help but smile. That was a little too close. But what a high. Better than caffeine indeed.

•　　　•　　　•　　　•　　　•

"I'm home!" I hollered as I dropped my bags in the front hall. "Tom? Where are you?"

"Back here! I'm in the kitchen."

I heard a chair scrape back from the table and Tom's voice increase in volume as he came closer.

"Hey! Am I glad to see you!" He said as he came padding down the hallway in his familiar old sweat socks. "I thought you were driving home later this afternoon?"

"Yeah, well, I decided to head out a little early. Did you miss me?" I was laughing by that time. He wrapped his arms around me in a bear hug and lifted me off the floor.

"Miss you? Good Lord, woman! No one was here to listen to me complain. No one laughed at my stupid jokes. Yeah, I missed you. The house is complete again." He planted a kiss in my hair and set me down. "Did *you* miss *me?*"

"Darling," I said, "you are the cream in my coffee. How about that?"

"Boy, are we getting sentimental," he said. "Come on. Come with me to the kasbah. Speaking of coffee, there's a fresh pot all ready."

He leaned down and gave me a deep welcome home kiss, warm like chocolate. I wrapped my arms around his waist and squeezed hard.

"Whoof!" he huffed. "What a hug! You really missed your old man, huh?"

"You'll never know how much," I said. "Other coffeehouses are fun, but homemade coffee is the best. Come on, let's get that cuppa."

Chapter 23
Betty

1973

I couldn't believe it when Reggie told me she was pregnant. She was in her early 30s, which was late for a first baby, but she always took care of herself. She was healthy and certainly ready for a baby. The pregnancy gave her no problem, not even morning sickness. Of course, I was delighted, but there was also that nagging voice in the back of my head which always seemed to appear when I really didn't want to hear it. "What do you think? Is it hereditary?" the voice questioned. My other half flinched. I knew exactly what that voice meant. Losing babies. Dead babies.

Why couldn't I just relax and enjoy Reggie's time in the sun? She was so carefree and happy. I'm sure she didn't think losing a baby would happen to her. In fact, I didn't know if she even gave any thought to it. Certainly, we never talked about it.

Being pregnant, the last thing she needed to hear was my story—stories—of heartache. She did know of miscarriage in my life—but not how many there were. I didn't want her to worry about the possibility of having the same problems I had. I could do all the worrying for her about that. She could concentrate on enjoying the novelty of having a baby growing within her. I, in my usual way, kept my own counsel and was able to make her see only my happy face. I banished the ugly little voice to a mental back closet. She never knew the odds were against me, and might, just might, be against her too. Sometimes ignorance really is bliss.

"Betty?" Earl's voice called from the patio. "Betty? Betty! Phone!" The volume went up as I heard the screen slide open and the automatic stamp of his feet on the little braided rug.

"I'm in here!" I called, though he could probably see my feet propped up on the footstool in the living room. "Who is it?"

By this time, he was standing next to me, offering the phone. Even before I slid forward in the chair, he was on his knees next to me, his hand over the phone.

"It's Reg. She's in labor. She sounds really excited."

There was a small heartbeat as we exchanged glances. We knew what this phone call meant. We knew what was supposed to happen next. Supposed to happen. Could I keep my fears out of my voice? Over the years, I had plenty of practice of doing just that, but this was one time I didn't want anything to go wrong. That would be something I could never fix, never take back.

I took the phone.

"Yes, dear?" It really was more of a statement than a question, but the rising inflection helped me keep myself under control. According to Earl's look, Reggie didn't tell him much.

*   *   *   *

Over the past months, I watched her blossom, really blossom, almost right before my eyes. With every new visit, I charted the growing globe of her abdomen like early sailors must have watched the far horizon as they emerged pristine through the Straits of Gibraltar into the uncharted Atlantic Ocean. Astonishment that the far horizon curved, actually curved, like water droplets on a table. The promise of more to come, far more than could ever be imagined.

That was what it was like for my pregnancies too. Astonishment at watching my own curve move from a gentle, rolling hill to a steep parabola. Reggie seemed to feel the same, seeing her belly expand beyond what must be humanly possible.

She had friends with children, but until now, I didn't think she realized what she would become. The power she wielded. The Venus of Willendorf. That early artifact with heavy pendulous breasts and protruding, fecund belly. The vision of that woman, the fertile, filled woman, was far more erotic than any other nude I ever saw.

"Mom?"

I came back to the moment. "I'm right here," I said. All she really needed to know was that I was indeed right there.

"I wouldn't have called you, it's really too early, but Tom insisted."

Was she too old? Maybe not. It was her first baby. Wasn't thirty-one too old though? Too much could go wrong. I couldn't let any of that come out through my voice.

"Mm-hmm. How do you feel?"

Earl shook his head and smiled. He was still crouched next to me and I gave the top of his head a little tap. What a silly thing to ask, I was sure he was thinking, but I was only trying to slow things a little.

"Actually, I feel great. My stomach is so tight, if I bounced a quarter on it, it'd probably launch into outer space."

We both laughed. Earl hoisted himself up from his haunches and headed for the other phone.

"Dad is going to pick up the other phone. Have you timed your contractions? I hope they're not hitting you too hard." I heard a soft click on the phone.

"Hi, Daddy."

"Hi, little girl. How are you doing over there? You want us to come over?"

Earl's voice betrayed every thought. We wanted to be there. We wanted to hold her hand. We wanted to make sure this one, this first one, any of them, weren't lost. We knew, of course, it didn't matter what we did.

"Oh, Daddy, no! Tom and I want to do this by ourselves." She was excited, ebullient. I was holding my breath and she didn't hear the undertones in Earl's voice.

"So, tell me," I stepped in on top of her last words, "how are those contractions coming?"

"Only every twenty-five minutes or so. Sometimes closer, but not too regular yet. But regular enough to know this is probably it." She sounded remarkably calm.

I remembered my babies and not knowing exactly what to expect, especially with the first one.

"I just wanted to let you know I'm in labor, and we'll keep you updated," she said.

"Listen," Earl's voice was velvety calm, under control, "anything you need, you just holler. It's probably better if we just kind of stay out of things for the time being. But we can be there in an hour if you need us."

Poor Earl. He must have felt more helpless than I did. At least I knew what Reggie was going through. Tom would be able to help her. They wouldn't let Earl anywhere near me once I got into the hospital. Tom would coach Reggie through. They filled us in on all the latest breathing techniques, and all the little tricks for getting as comfortable as possible. "Are you calling from the hospital?" I wanted to know.

"Oh no. Heavens, no. It's far too early. They told me when to come in, and I'm not going in one minute before I have to. I'd rather be able to walk around here in between contractions. My back bothers me if I lie down. I figure gravity ought to do its part." That last with a little chuckle.

"Okay, sweetheart. Listen, keep us up to date, but we'll get off the phone right now so you can—well, so you will be able to concentrate." I didn't know how else to put it. I knew she had a lot of work ahead of her, and she didn't need us breathing down her neck. Or Tom's either.

"Thanks," said between clenched teeth, I thought, and I rushed to say goodbye. She was clearly having to deal with the beginning of another contraction.

"Bye, sweetheart." Earl recognized the signs too. "We're pulling for you."

There was a moment more, then Earl hung up the phone. At the click of the disconnect, I suddenly felt my own belly tightening. I knew it was my imagination—call it sympathy pains—but I was right back, thirty-three years back, into that young body, tightly pregnant with the boy. I even remembered how sexy I felt. Like a flood coming down a dry wash after a heavy rain, the pain of all of it rushed toward me and it took all of my will to turn it aside into the flat, parched land that blossomed into the baby who became Reggie. One gone with the flood, one here to stay.

Oh, how I missed that boy!

"Hey, darlin', you okay?" Earl was back on his haunches next to my chair. He reached out and touched my hands, my hands spread spider-like over the small globe of my belly, cradling emptiness.

No, not total emptiness. I was fecund once. Once I was the Venus of Willendorf too.

"Oh, Earl—" It was all I managed before my voice broke and I reached for him with my eyes. The rest of me seemed to be frozen in the past.

He lifted my hands and kissed my fingers.

"I know, darlin'." Even he couldn't say it would be all right. "Don't worry. She didn't hear it."

I knew exactly what she didn't hear and I was glad he recognized it.

We sat silently hand in hand. I was still scared.

Chapter 24
Reggie

1973

After the first couple of hours, I knew I was in labor, but I wasn't getting contractions on a regular basis. In spite of that, I just knew this was the real thing.

"Go ahead, call her. Call your mother, Reg. She'll want to know." Tom clipped his words, a sure indication he was verging on impatience.

"Do you really think that's a good idea? We're going to get them all worried. They'll be up all night when they really shouldn't be, or need to be. What can they do, after all?"

Tom sighed. "Give them some time to figure out—"

"Who's going to come and stay with us, and for how long. Personally—" I began, then stopped abruptly. A definite gathering of belly muscles. A wave that flowed down my abdomen. My fingers splayed out across my belly, as if I could feel the contraction rippling within.

"What is it? Another one? Are you okay?" Tom's voice was solicitous. "Maybe we better just head to the hospital right now."

"No, no; it's fine," I answered. "The doctor told me not to come until they're firm and regular, neither of which is going on right now. So far, they seem to be about twenty-five minutes apart—"

"That's regular, if you ask me," he interrupted.

"Yeah, but he said five minutes apart, and we're not that close yet." I spoke as if he too was feeling the hardness of my skin, the heaviness that wanted to descend and push. I cradled my big belly, one hand caressing the top and one pressing up on the bottom. I could no longer feel where foot or elbow or head was situated.

Earlier in my pregnancy, although not that much earlier, I realized with a small shock, I was able to discern the round buttocks, the sharp little heels pushing out my rib cage. Tom scoffed. I took his hand and guided it around the map of my abdomen. When the baby kicked, he didn't draw his hand away, as I expected, but instead knelt down on the floor and put his cheek to my belly, saying something about miracles.

Tom shifted his hand to the small of my back. "How's your back doing?" It was sore for the past couple of weeks from the drag of gravity on my off-balance body.

"Push," I begged and he kneaded pressure into me. "That feels so good."

Tom kissed me on the back of my neck and even then, in the midst of paying attention to my body's response to the baby, I could still respond to him.

"Too bad I'm a bit preoccupied right now," I turned to say in his ear. I felt his lips smile against my hair.

I wondered as I quickened under his touch, *How can I feel two things at once, pain and desire?* The contradiction pleased me.

"You are so beautiful." His voice was soft and honest.

I felt beautiful. He was always able to do that for me.

"Call your mother," Tom whispered in my ear.

I laughed, unexpected even to me.

Tom sat back, giving me elbow room.

"All right, all right," I said. I knew I was beaten. "Just for you, my dearest, just for you, I will call my parents. Then we can worry about getting this twenty-pound baby out and not concern ourselves about relatives."

When he handed me the phone, I couldn't remember the number. I felt the beginnings of another contraction.

"It's two—" Tom began, but I cut him off almost immediately.

"All you had to do was start me. I've got it now." The ache unexpectedly subsided. I punched in the numbers and listened for the ring. It was still early and they wouldn't know who it was. It could be anyone, a friend asking about tomorrow's meeting, a colleague with a piece of news—

"Mother?" But no, it was Dad. After a quick "Just a sec. I'll hand off to her," she was on the line. She asked me if anything was wrong. "No, everything is fine. Tom and I just wanted you to know, I've gone into labor. Not to worry, because my contractions are only twenty-five minutes apart, and it's too early to go in yet."

Tom began to massage my back, working on the lower curves where the pressure from the inside was starting to hurt.

I heard a click and the volume coming from the other end dropped a bit. "Hi, Daddy." He still called me his little girl and, though I always frowned wickedly at him, we both knew I loved it.

"Hi, little girl," he said, right on cue. "How're you doing?"

I could hear the worry in his voice. What was he so worried about? People had been birthing babies forever. This was just one more. I was only concerned the pain would overwhelm me somehow. But then, women gave birth between beet rows on hot afternoons and got up to finish picking the row before heading home from the fields.

"Listen," I said out loud to him, "we just wanted to call and let you know what's going on. We'll keep you posted."

Both sets of our parents were, of course, ready to drop everything and come over to help in any way they could, but I wanted this beginning to be with Tom alone. As with every other family, the grandparents would be around plenty before long, and I needed some time with the three of us alone. I wanted time to recover and then to savor the sweet bundle all crunched up inside of me.

My skin was stretched taut. Another wave was building on one shore and moving out across the expanse. This time, the contraction drew in tighter, pulling me forward. Because of that belly, I couldn't bend far, but I suddenly wanted to bend over and push down hard with my hands. Tom increased the pressure on my back as I gritted my teeth.

On the phone, I was sure they could hear the change in my voice. Dad said a rather abrupt goodbye, apparently uncomfortable in the ignorance he felt toward women about to deliver. In his day, men were banished to a waiting room, never to see the miracle. I was surprised to find out most *women* were never really around for the birth either. Their bodies were working away, but they were spared the pain of those final contractions when the doctor administered gas and took over the hard work.

Mother never talked with me about her pregnancies. Dad did mention that there would have been other babies, but for miscarriage. Maybe she thought I'd be scared off by the primitive birth techniques of her day to talk about any of that. As for right now, I was only concerned about being able to handle my own pain and delivery.

"We'll call you with more news later." Tom took the phone. Still pressing on my lower back, he said to my mother, "Don't worry. She's a trooper; she's doing fine. Not to cut you off, but—" Apparently, Mother said goodbye then, because he dropped the phone onto its cradle without removing his other hand from my back. "Well, that takes care of that." He turned his full attention back to me. "Now it's just you and me, girl. How are you doing? That one seemed stronger."

"I think we better go pretty soon." I couldn't help speaking cautiously. That last contraction took me by surprise. It was strong and very definitely different from the others. I could feel that the baby slipped lower and I was busy trying to tune in to what my body expected of me. I desperately wanted a shower.

•   •   •   •   •   •

It was a foolish idea to shower first. I was almost three hours into what the nurses called hard labor and I was sweating like a long-distance runner miles out from the starter's gun and not knowing exactly how far down the road the finish line was.

"No," Tom said, "she doesn't need anything. She's doing fine."

I didn't even hear the nurse come in. In the middle of a contraction, I didn't have the strength to change my focus to protest his decision on my behalf to forego painkillers.

"She's doing great," a nearby voice repeated. "She should deliver within an hour, based on what we're seeing here."

An hour! Maybe I can do that. I think. Not really much choice now, is there? I couldn't hold onto Tom's hand anymore. I was afraid I would break the bones in his fingers. Switching my grip to the headboard, I squeezed as hard as I could. Though I folded myself together as much as possible, the nurse pulled my feet out and into the stirrups at the base of the table. I lost leverage just at the moment I needed it the most.

"Come on, sweetie," the nurse encouraged, "push down on these. Scootch down here a little farther."

She picked the absolute worst time. I was in the middle of a really hard contraction. The only order that was coming from my body was *Push!*

As if she heard my thoughts, the nurse warned, "Don't push yet, dear. The doctor will be back in just a moment."

I spat back mentally. *Like hell! Since when were doctors out in the fields with mothers delivering? Were those women supposed to wait too?*

But the doctor did appear and instructions came fast and hard.

"All right," he commanded, "I want you to rest in between, even if just for a moment. This is hard work and we want you to save every bit of strength you can for the final push. You're doing great."

His voice was far too calm for me. Because he never gave birth, but only watched, I felt my confidence ebbing. But he snapped me back to attention with "Now, push! Push hard!" His voice had gone into General of the Army mode and I eagerly responded. Tom helped lift my shoulders and I began to work. I felt the rhythm. I was stretched to the limits of my capacity.

"Once more, Reggie. Once more will do it."

The nurse emerged from behind Tom's head, gently moving him aside as she took over his position. "Hurry up!" she urged. "Go watch your baby being born!" She lifted my chin towards the base of the table.

I saw Tom peering over the doctor's shoulder. The nurse and I worked in tandem, she encouraging and lifting, me straining. Not a moment later, I felt the baby's head slide clear of me, then the shoulders, and suddenly, a shout.

"It's a girl!" both Tom and the doctor cried together.

I started to cry. Tom's glittering eyes met mine and he came up and gave me a gentle kiss.

"Well done, Mama. We got ourselves a little girl," he managed to get out and cradled my sweaty head in the crook of his arm. "A baby girl!"

"Baby Emily," I whispered.

"Baby Emily." The wonder of the miracle was still in his eyes. "And she's perfect, just perfect."

I was exhausted, but I didn't care. It was all worth it.

Dad and Mother came to see Emily in the hospital, but the three of us came home alone. We said we wanted a few days to ourselves and both sets of parents honored that. But it wasn't long before Dad asked if they could come over and help us out and, incidentally, he added with a little chuckle, see their granddaughter. When they walked in, Dad came right over to me, took my head in his hands and gave me a big kiss on the top of my head. He said, "Congratulations! You did a grand job on that baby girl. Now, let's see her," and proceeded to sweep Emily out of my arms like a pro. Mother hung back, as usual. It seemed as if she didn't want to get in anybody's way, but I wanted her to gush and coo, like a grandmother should.

"Come on, Tom," I said, as I pulled him toward the kitchen. "Help me get some coffee together."

When we were alone, I hissed, "What is wrong with that woman? This is her first grandchild! Why is she acting so stand-offish?"

"Give her a break, Reg," Tom said. "Maybe she just wants to give your dad first shot."

"I don't get it. She's acting like she doesn't even care," I said.

"Don't kid yourself. She cares," Tom said.

"How do you know?" I said.

He shook his head. "Did you see her eyes? Anyway, maybe she needs a little time getting used to being a grandmother. She's a loving person. She loves Em. She just doesn't show it much yet. Wait and see."

He turned on the coffee grinder and drowned out any potential response.

When we walked back into the living room with Tom bearing the tray of coffee and cookies, there was Mother, settled into the big rocker, her face only millimeters from Emily's, her lips whispering something I couldn't hear. Tom and I both stopped spontaneously, caught in the moment. Dad saw us and gave a secret little smile. I couldn't believe what I saw—Mother cuddling and cooing. My tears came unbidden and caught me by surprise. Mother looked up just then and our eyes locked. I saw tears on her cheeks too.

"I'm so proud of you," she said, almost too quietly for me to hear. "She's beautiful."

"Mom." I couldn't say a single word more. I walked over, knelt on the floor in front of the rocker and kissed my daughter. I felt my mother's breath on my hair.

When my happiness bubbled over into laughter, she joined me. We huddled together, three generations of girls. I felt as light as a dream.

Chapter 25
Betty

1975

I didn't want to interfere with Reggie and Tom, so when Em was born, I reminded myself to hold back just a little, get the lay of the land first. But it took all of my control, when they took her home from the hospital, not to call and offer to do anything and everything for them. I knew how it could be with a new baby. Of course, I didn't really know in the same way Reggie knew. When Earl and I went home that first time, it was horrible, not wonderful.

Earl got impatient and, after a couple of days, called and offered our help. I could hear the forced lightness in his tone and hoped Reggie, his little girl, wouldn't ask us to wait any longer. When Earl turned and gave me a thumb's-up before hanging up, I practically flew into the car.

Earl climbed into the driver's seat. "Look at you," he said, pointing at my feet. He started to laugh.

I was carrying my shoes, because I didn't even change out of my bedroom slippers. So much for maintaining calm. On the ride over, I composed myself and was under control by the time we arrived at Tom's and Reggie's. Earl just plowed right in and took Em right out of Reggie's arms, saying, "C'mere, little one." Then to Reggie, "You gave me another sweet girl to love." When Reggie and Tom went into the kitchen to make coffee, Earl came over to the rocking chair where I was sitting and handed Em down to me.

"Oh my!" I whispered as I drew her in to me. My every pregnancy spun through me, unreeling like a high-speed highlights film, until it stopped at the small bundle that was Reggie. And now, here was her child. I folded back Em's blanket and caressed her tiny toes, then bundled her close again. I ran my finger along her hairline, fine peach fuzz, then around her ear. I touched the palm of one little hand and Em grasped my finger. She looked up at me, slightly cross-eyed the way some newborns are, and, I swear, I fell into her just like that. Cradling her, I lifted her close to my face and said, "Welcome to the world, little one. You are a lucky baby, you know. You have the best parents in the world. And your grandpa and I love you from the bottom of our hearts." My heart was full with more, but I wasn't sure how to put it into words. I nuzzled baby Emily's nose, unbidden tears filling my eyes. "You and I are going to be special." *Now where did that come from?* I knew even then it was true.

Across the lovely baby months, I attended Em whenever I could, although I stepped back for Reggie and Tom, of course, but also for Earl. He loved children and I couldn't be selfish about our first grandchild. When we knew the three of them were coming to visit, we'd rummage through the old toys, pulling out stacking blocks and rings and things, hoping we were remembering what would fit with Em's age. But she wasn't particular. Like her mother, Em was equally entranced with blocks and trucks, miniature kitchens and windup cars, even when she could barely sit up alone, much less do anything more than stuff things in her mouth. Eventually, almost all the toys came out. Earl would sit on the floor with her, but Em preferred me, reaching out chubby arms for me to pick her up. I tried not to be too possessive, but Em wouldn't have it. If I tried to hand her off to Earl, or even Reggie some days, she squealed until I took her back. Maybe she felt my heart beat and discerned a kindred spirit. I was secretly elated.

As a toddler, when she didn't see us for a week or so, she pestered Reggie and Tom until they brought her over. One day, she came running in while I was busy in the kitchen. She wasted no time pushing a chair over to the counter so she could help. We got out measuring cups and spoons, so she could dip out sugar for the cookies. She dumped more on the counter than in the bowl, but it didn't matter.

"What dat?" she asked and pointed at my apron.

"That's an apron. Would you like one too?"

"Uh-huh!" She bobbed her head.

I pulled out the shortest one I owned and wrapped it around her twice, tucking it in so it wouldn't trip her up. She rushed off to show Earl, but was back in a moment.

Earl came with her. "How about a bath?" he said to Em. "Gramma can finish the cookies and we'll be back before they're out of the oven. Maybe you can even have one before you go to bed."

Em clapped her hands and tried to untangle herself from the apron, but her fingers were too little. Earl and I both started to laugh, but at the look on her face, we stifled it. We let her struggle a little, but I couldn't watch her frustration very long. Once she was out of her clothes—all of them—Earl chased her to the bathroom and I finished the cookies.

I could hear them in the bathroom, Em calling for me once in a while, then shrieking as Earl squirted her with a watergun. The cookies finished, I curled up in the big chair in the living room, and let my mind replace Em's chatter with Reggie's.

They sounded so much alike. When Reggie was little like that, she used to love it when Earl would help her take a bath. At first, he was cautious, but he soon found out bathing a toddler could be fun, if he didn't mind all the water on the floor. He bought a squirt gun, then another when Reggie got to be three, so they could have water fights in the bathroom. I just looked the other way. They had just as much fun sopping it all up with the bath towels. Now, he was having the same fun with Em.

However, when Reggie was young, all too soon she didn't want either one of us helping her in the bath anymore. I still retained rights to a final check, until she was ten. When she turned ten, she put her foot down. "Mother!" she said when I asked to come into the bathroom. "I can do it myself!" And that was the end of that.

I imagined the washcloth, steaming with warmth, draped over her face. I set my forehead against the doorframe and willed my mind to calm. "If you're sure…"

"I'm fine!" she said.

Earl came toward me down the hall on his way to our bedroom. He stopped and put his arms around my waist. "Hey!" he called to Reggie. "Are you done? 'Cause your dad needs to get in there soon. This house only has one bathroom, you know." He kissed the top of my head, then said to me, "I'm getting my pajamas on. Hope she's out of there before I get back." He wiggled his eyebrows.

I heard the gurgle of the water as Reggie pulled the plug. "I'm out, Daddy," she called. "I'm drying off. You can come in in a minute."

I headed back downstairs before she came out. I'd have to trust she did, in fact, wash everywhere. She always accommodated Earl, even when she was a toddler. Daddy's little girl, I guess. I was delighted she went to him so often. She wasn't intimidated by him, like some children were by their fathers. I wanted that for her, a closeness with her father. I didn't mind she ended up going to him first. I was just glad we had her at all.

Before I knew it, Emily was three years old, going on thirty-three. I went from Gumma to Gramma. She wanted to call and talk on the phone. Though Reggie started the conversations, Em ended up talking longer than Reggie. Well, I stood back and let Earl have his moments in the sun with Reggie, his daughter. But I won't let that happen with Em. Earl had Reggie; I had Em. Isn't it silly? I found it easier to talk to a toddler than to my own daughter.

Reggie put the glitter on a lovely Christmas with the announcement she was pregnant again. A new Mackensie baby. Am I worried again? Of course. But I'm bound and determined not to let her see it. I doubt I can keep my fears from Earl, though. We've been through too much together to hide anything very long.

Chapter 26
Reggie

1976

It's the country's Bicentennial and here I am, stuck in a hospital maternity room again, not even able to see the fireworks. So okay, I just gave birth to the most beautiful baby boy the country has ever seen. But it would sure be fun to show him the fireworks.

"Can't we go up to the garden terrace and watch them there?" I asked Tom. I inserted a little whine for good measure.

"Lady, you just had a baby two hours ago. Isn't it enough Tim was born on the Fourth of July?" he said. "He's gonna play that for all its worth, you know."

I laughed and pulled my knees up to my chest, hugging them to me. "Timothy Earl. My dad's going to be so happy."

"Speaking of your dad, here he comes," Tom said, as my dad ushered Mother into the room ahead of him.

"So, where's the little guy?" Dad's booming voice reached me before he did. When he got to me, he shuffled me into a great big hug. Mother actually rubbed my arm gently, before grasping my hand and rewarding me with a smile.

"Come on," Tom said, pulling the wheelchair over to the side of the bed. "We'll show you. Visiting hours are still on for the nursery."

Tom helped me off the bed and into the wheelchair and expertly steered me out into the hall.

"We're so glad you called, dear," Mother said. "I was just biting my nails, hoping you'd have an easy delivery."

"Easy as pie," Tom said.

I tut-tutted. "Easy for you to say, big guy." But it was an easy delivery. When I wasn't hungry for the picnic lunch at noon, I knew something was happening. We left for the hospital shortly after and made it before my water broke.

Tom swung me around in front of the nursery windows, where the nurse moved to pick up Timmy. He was one of the few babies born on the Fourth and his plastic bassinet had a tiny flag drawn on his nametag.

"Isn't he gorgeous!" Mother said. "Your little Yankee Doodle Baby!" She had her arms linked in the crook of Dad's elbow and I watched her lean into him.

"This was a quick delivery," I said. "The doctor said if we're going to have more, I better camp out at the admitting desk next time. I'm a real baby factory."

I watched my mother's face crumple just a little and she looked up at Dad, then at me.

"I'll be right back," she said, slurring her words together in haste. "Where are the restrooms?"

Tom pointed back down the hall, then waggled his finger to the left, and she set off, giving what looked to me like a mangled smile.

"She okay?" I asked automatically.

My dad cleared his throat and shoved his hands in his pockets. He and Tom exchanged glances.

"*Is* she all right?" Tom asked.

I felt concern rising in my throat.

"Yes, yes, everything's fine. This just brings back some pretty hard memories," Dad said.

I'm sure the blank look on my face, coupled with my palms up gesture, prompted him to go on.

He cleared his throat again and looked down the hall, as if to see if anyone, Mother in particular, was in range of hearing. "Well, your mother had—well, she had lots of problems with having babies. She had miscarriages and lost—" His voice caught and ripped, like an old coat torn from a rusty hook. "She lost our first baby when he was born."

"I knew she had a miscarriage, but I never knew she lost the first baby!" I said. I wanted to save him the pain of going on. "I mean, I knew I was the only one, but—"

He stopped me with a gesture. "She didn't want you to know, didn't want you to worry about having babies yourself. So, we figured it was better not to tell you. Maybe that was a mistake, but I don't think so."

"I'm so sorry, Daddy. I didn't know. I didn't know I had a— a—brother or sister?"

"This is incredibly bad timing, Reg, but yes, you had a brother. He died at birth. The umbilical cord was wrapped around his neck. The others, well, the others we just didn't know. But they were all hard on your mom." He pulled a hand out of his pocket and ran it across the top of my head, ending with a pat on my shoulder. "They were hard on me too."

"Oh, Daddy! I'm so sorry," I said. I wanted to say more, but my throat closed up. What else could I say, anyway? There was no way to take away pain like that. I couldn't imagine losing either one of our sweet children.

"Here comes your mother," Tom said, his voice barely audible.

I missed an entire chapter in my mother's life. How could I miss that? Yes, I knew of one miscarriage, but Daddy said "others," plural. I never knew. And why was there never a hint, not one, about a lost child? I had a brother. Had. Where was he now? I was sure there was no headstone in the cemetery. Why, why why didn't she tell me? As she got closer, I realized now wasn't the time to bring anything up anything like that. She wanted my pregnancies to go smoothly—God, how she must've worried!—and now, I wanted all of us to enjoy the new baby, not mourn those lost. I could give her that small gift. I arranged my face to a more appropriate smile.

When she reached us, I couldn't look her in the face, but I reached out a hand to her, and another to Daddy. "We named him Timothy Earl," I said and watched a wave of happiness wash over my father's face. I looked back to the nursery, and saw the reflection of my mother's face in the window, next to the nurse, who now bent to return Tim to his bassinet. On my mother's face was the most peaceful look I ever saw her wear. There was an inner glow of sorts, and I was reminded of the angelic look on her face when I caught her first holding Em. Her face was quiet and it looked like she came to terms with all of the babies in her life, not just mine.

Chapter 27
Betty

1976

Mexico. I've always wanted to go to Mexico.

Earl persuaded me, even though it would be late summer and hot, we should take another big trip and Mexico would be a good place to visit. It's been eleven years, no, twelve years since that trip to Europe, and it was about time to take another one. The tour sounded like it was covering all the places we would want to see—Mexico City, ruins, beaches, charming towns. Sure, we'd be traveling like Americans, air-conditioned bus and all, but Margaret and Bill said they'd go if we'd go, and that sealed the deal for me.

•   •   •

"So, darlin'," Earl said, ignoring the unending jungle passing by our over-sized window, "isn't this great? Wandering around with our own guide and our friends. No responsibility. No bosses to answer to."

I knew where this was heading. He was retired for three years now, ever since that first heart attack after the snowstorm. I was sixty-three, just like he was, and he kept trying to set me up for retirement too. I think he was lonely at home, all by himself. No one to share coffee or conversation during the day. He puttered around, but I think he missed me. I knew I was sixty-three, my hair was white, gravity continued to do its work on my body, and I was into sensible shoes, but, my dear, I was not quite ready to hang it all up. September would begin my eighth year of teaching, and I thought I was finally getting the hang of it. I was still having too much fun. Don't get me wrong, it was a lot of work, but I didn't keel over of exhaustion, or let lumps of clay splatter all over because I couldn't handle the potter's wheel anymore. A smile escaped the corners of my mouth as I pictured my pristine art room with blobs of clay shooting everywhere, a Dr. Seuss and the Cat in the Hat kind of picture. Of course, Earl heard none of this, considering I often talked only within the confines of my own skull, and there wasn't too much company in there to listen, at least not yet, thank goodness.

"Aw, look at that, she's smiling. Must be thinking of how wonderful it would be to go out to New England in the fall when the leaves are turning. When you don't punch a clock anymore, you can get up and go whenever you want."

I rolled my head lazily and connected with his eyes. We played this game for quite a while now and I was getting pretty good at it. "Send me a postcard, will you? I should be somewhere in the middle of a ceramics unit about then." I kissed my finger and drew it down his nose.

"Can't talk you into it, eh?" He sighed and leaned over to kiss my hair.

I turned to check out the window. The green wall still slid by, smooth and just beyond the edge of understanding. The solid bottle-green turned mottled, then resolved itself into individual trees loaded and overloaded with varied shapes and colors, all greens and browns of one hue or another. The bus was slowing. We turned into a parking lot that was hiding within all of this jungle.

"Well, folks," a disembodied voice came thickly out of the speakers above us, "we have arrived at the world-famous Mayan ruins of Chichen Itza. We have a full morning to explore these glorious ruins, and then we'll provide you with a lovely lunch spread and allow a little time for relaxing before we head back. We'll be able to avoid the hottest part of the day this way and you can catch a siesta in our air-conditioned bus on the way back."

The voice of our very capable tour director droned on about a guided tour and I tuned out, knowing Earl would remember all the details. I floated off to be with Reggie for a moment, she and Tom and a five-month old baby brother for Em. Our sweet Emily! And now a boy. It was a flawless pregnancy for Reg. She hummed about, busy as could be. Never a moment of sickness or discomfort. That second delivery went so quickly, she barely had time to call a neighbor to take Em before they were off to the hospital. It wasn't an hour later the baby was born. How quickly things went for her! And how different for me. How easy for her. How difficult for me. Every time, how difficult.

We drove over to see our new grandson, of course, and I thought about our own car ride before our little Teddy fought to be born. I wouldn't let Earl see my chin quiver and my eyes fill. I watched the fields and the woods stream by, craning my neck as if looking at distant birds when the memories got too close. Well, it was a second chance, perhaps. Our own boy reborn whole, I couldn't help thinking. They named him Timothy Earl, and Grampa was proud as could be.

"...step when exiting the bus." I was sucked back as Earl shifted to stand.

"Okay." I moved over to his seat and grabbed my hat. "Let's explore."

The tour guide's khaki back swung ahead of us as we came back down the path from the sacred well and headed for the main pyramid.

"Anyone who wants to climb the pyramid should probably do it now, before it gets too hot," she warned over her shoulder.

"You want to do this?" I asked Earl.

"It's not that steep." He threw me a sideways glance and took my hand. "C'mon, let's go."

He read my unspoken question perfectly. The stones of the pyramid's steps frowned and dared us. Stacked tight, they provided little encouragement. My foot fit, but barely, on the rough tread, and I had to step as high as a drum majorette to reach the next one. It was a formidable, precise pile of rock. Earl sidestepped up, balancing carefully, hand wrapped around the almost-vertical chain provided for guidance. Not many others joined us.

When would I be back here? I always asked myself the same question when faced with something I ordinarily wouldn't do. This time, it was the height. That and the narrow steps, inviting, even challenging, a misstep that would claim just one more sacrifice in order to keep the life-giving sun turning another day through the sky. I might never get back here. When that was the answer, I shoved misgivings aside.

I concentrated on each tall gray step, lifting myself up. I remembered how hard it was sometimes, just like this, to go up the basement steps, hoisting a full basket of wet laundry. Halfway up the pyramid, I stopped for a breather, just as much for me as for Earl, who stopped once already. I knew if I turned around, I'd lose my nerve to get to the top, so I rested standing up, facing the rock, examining the green and gray plants crawling across and around the fine cracks.

When I reached the top, I intended to holler some triumphant epithet over to Earl, but all that came out was a wheeze. Where was Earl? He should be right behind me, but, as I turned, the spectacular view was lost to me in my concern. Ah! There he was. "Hey! You down there! Hey, handsome!"

He stopped a few steps below and managed to raise his hand in a brief wave. I couldn't see his face for the brim of his hat, and I didn't hear any response either. Just that wave.

He rose off the step and finished the climb.

"You okay?" I asked. I squeezed my eyebrows together the better to focus in the intense light.

"Yup." He draped his arm across my shoulder and pecked me on the cheek. "That is one long climb."

Even though I was terrified of looking down, I did it anyway. The steepness of the pyramid made me sway. "No wonder people let themselves be killed once they climbed up here! They were either so tired, they didn't care anymore, or they died of a heart attack. This is stunning!" The jungle marched out before me like miniature broccoli heads packed tight. The canopy of the tree tops frothed like tiny bubbles, packed tight and nubbly. The emerald green was so bright, my eyes hurt. Texture and color mixed, reminding me of Magritte paintings, so real and yet so impossible. "Just stunning," I repeated.

"Unbelievable," Earl echoed. "How could they possibly build something like this? How did they find their way around from one town to another?" His arms inscribed a great arc over all of that green.

"Indeed. One of the great mysteries of life."

We circumnavigated the small temple built on the top, identifying all of the other buildings we could see, some rising strangely and suddenly out of the jade and lime green mat spread before us.

"Ready to go back down?" Earl said.

I pivoted to him, but he was stepping down gingerly onto the first step. He turned and sat on the top level of the pyramid, patting the stone next to him. Bill and Margaret came around the corner of the temple and eased down on the top platform next to us.

"I never would believe it if I hadn't seen it with my own eyes." Margaret shook her head.

"Okay, let's go." Earl stood, shifted sideways and started down.

"Hey! What's your hurry?" Margaret called down after him, then sent a dismissive hand wave too.

"See you at the bottom." I skootched over the edge and carefully planted my feet. I could go down facing out, but I opted to turn a little sideways. Cheap insurance, I thought to myself. Why take a risk? This pyramid saw enough dead people already.

Earl moved methodically below me and I watched the top of his hat swaying in his own personal rhythm. He reached the bottom three steps ahead of me and plopped onto the last stone. From the back, I saw the sweat trickling over the creases on his sunburned neck. Just as I got to him, he dragged the hat off his head and it flopped to the ground, carried by its own weight and not by his direction.

"Earl?"

Margaret heard my call for help even as Earl made a small move to turn toward me and slumped sideways instead.

"Earl!" It wasn't a question anymore. Earl's face was flushed scarlet and his breath rasped in his throat. "Help! Margaret, help! Anyone!"

"Hang on! We're coming! We're almost down!" I heard the anxiety in her disembodied voice even as Earl's cheek bumped onto my shoulder. I felt Earl's exhalation like an angel's breath on my cheek.

"Darlin'."

I went numb.

* * *

Looking back, I honestly didn't know how I made it. If Margaret and Bill weren't there, I would've died myself.

Margaret took care of me while Bill took care of—I couldn't say "the body." I just couldn't think of Earl that way. Bill took care of Earl.

It was difficult, I was told, to get, well, to... How could I say this? When someone died in a foreign land, there were so many hurdles to jump, so much paperwork. It was hard on Bill, and Margaret too, to try and get everything taken care of.

I don't remember much of it.

Our minds shut out what we cannot handle. I heard that so often, but now, I knew it was true. I remembered blips, but only that. Nothing to create a whole fabric from. Just moments.

Holding Earl's head, me sitting awkwardly, twisted on the step. Signing for an ambulance to take him to the airport. Something happening in the middle of the night so we could get Earl back to the States as soon as possible. Was it true that if we kept him there longer than twenty-four hours, he had to be embalmed in Mexico?

I didn't remember getting from one place to another, but I did remember the feel of afternoon heat and middle of the night cold as we worked to get back home. Or rather as Margaret and Bill maneuvered to get us all home.

I stayed numb through the entire funeral, clear through the service, the interment and the luncheon that followed. I remembered it all, but I didn't remember what I felt. Maybe I felt nothing.

Reggie and Tom were with me every moment, one or the other. Em, my precious three-year old, helped. She took my hand and sat on my lap, playing with my jewelry. Reggie hung on Tom more than she did on me. I never saw her so distraught. She burst into tears at the slightest provocation. As we stood in the receiving line at the wake, friends would come through and say things like, "He hardly got to know your little Tim," or "I'm sure you are going to miss him terribly. You two were so close." These sent her into recurrent sniffles or outright sobs.

I, on the other hand, couldn't seem to cry. Even when they played "How Great Thou Art" as the funeral recessional, I didn't cry. Ever since that moment at the foot of the pyramid, I was turned in on myself. At that time, as I reached Earl and he slumped against me, he breathed "Darlin'." No one could ever understand the depth of meaning in that one cherished word and I held onto it as tightly as I could.

• • • • •

Two weeks after Earl's funeral, Margaret drove over to spend the day. The last thing she said to me after she closed the car door, ready to go home, and slid down the window was, "It's a good thing you're still working. That'll save your sanity." She squeezed my hand, then kissed my fingers.

For whatever reason, her words and actions released the tightness in me. Maybe she brought me back into the living world, a place I wasn't sure existed for me anymore. I spent the rest of the afternoon crying into Earl's pillow. But as the sun started to respond to the horizon's pull, I moved out to the back porch, picking up Earl's old floppy hat at I went, the hat he wore in Mexico. I put it on and wore it all evening. When I went to bed, I put it on his pillow. For months afterward, I wore it while I was cleaning or cooking. Sometimes I just set it at his place at the table and left it there all day. Sometimes I took it to bed with me. A couple of times, Reggie stopped by unexpectedly and caught me with it on. "What are you wearing that old thing for?" she asked and I never could articulate how it was gradually warming me up. I knew how she loved him, but my love ran in a different direction. I don't think she really understood, and it was beyond me to try and explain.

Finally, the same year I retired, I retired the hat. Well, not totally retired. When I bought my new car, I put it in the back window. Margaret advised me, "No one will know you are traveling alone that way. They'll all think you have a man with you. You'll be safer." But the real reason I put it back there was so I could see it when I checked my rearview mirror or looked over my shoulder as I backed out of the garage.

But that first night of release, I sat on the back porch, Earl's hat pulled down low, and told myself over and over, "I will survive. I will survive."

Chapter 28
Reggie

1977

"Tom, I don't get it." I was curled up on the couch, nursing a Bloody Mary. "It's been six months and I can't figure her out."

"Figure what?" Tom was involved in his newspaper and his eyes surfaced over the top edge, but it didn't sound like he was with me yet.

"My mother. She didn't even cry at Dad's funeral. In fact, I haven't seen her cry at all," I said.

"Yeah?" Tom lowered his paper. "Some people are like that." He didn't sound very concerned.

"This is my father! How can she not care?" I didn't want to sound obnoxious, but this was bothering me. I was frustrated.

"You don't think she cares?" Tom held the newspaper aside. "Of course she cares. Earl was her husband for—how many years? She must miss him a lot."

"I don't see anything there," I said. "She just closed herself off."

"See?" Tom said. "Doesn't that prove it? She can't talk about Earl's death. That doesn't mean she doesn't care."

"But she doesn't show a thing! I still break into tears at the most inappropriate times. I hear some father at the playground calling out, 'Where's my little girl?' and I cry. Sometimes, when we're out for dinner, I spot one of his favorite dishes on the menu and I can hardly restrain myself." My voice got louder and I tried to keep it from cracking. "I catch a whiff of Dad's aftershave and look around, expecting to see him. How come I'm the only one who's suffering?" My breath caught and I couldn't go on.

Tom set his paper on the floor and moved to the couch, next to me. He took my Bloody Mary and set it on the coffee table. "Look, you're not the only one." He stroked my hair.

"I'm sorry. I didn't mean...I know you loved Dad too," I said. My heart hurt. I didn't mean to leave Tom out. I leaned back into him and closed my eyes. I felt his arms go around me. "Why can't Mother feel like this?"

"She probably does. We just don't see it," Tom said.

I tightened in his arms. "Now, there's nobody left," I said. "Dad's gone." My stomach twisted. "Everybody's gone. My brother and...and babies I didn't even know about." My brothers and sisters. I didn't even know which. A shiver rippled across my shoulders, in spite of Tom's body heat behind me. "How did she handle those other deaths? The miscarriages? And my brother? How did she feel when she lost my brother?" I looked up at Tom, then tucked myself back into his embrace. "I can't imagine losing a child. Why didn't she ever tell me?"

"I don't know," Tom said. "Maybe she didn't want to scare you. Maybe she and Earl just worked it out themselves. It happened a long time ago, you know. Maybe she just didn't want everyone fawning all over her. I don't know what she was thinking."

"Yeah, but don't you want to share some of that with your family? With your friends? I couldn't go through stuff like that without support from someone."

"She's got support from someone," Tom said. "She's got us."

"Right." I couldn't help feeling a bit confused. Mother never shared many of her feelings with anyone, as far as I could tell.

"She'll come around when she's ready," Tom said. "Stop being so hard on her."

"But I am suffering here! She won't talk to me about it either. All she does it set her lips in this thin little line and walk away. How do I know she's grieving, if she won't show me? We can't give her support, because she won't take it." My voice sounded petulant, even to me. I backed off a bit. "If she's feeling so bad, why can't she share that with us? She sure doesn't act like she feels terrible."

"Reggie," Tom said. His voice no longer had such a soft edge. "I'm sure she does. Probably worse than you do. Just because she won't tell us doesn't mean she isn't feeling it."

"How do you know?" I felt myself getting defensive. "Oh, that's right. You and Mother are pretty close." I stopped myself before I said something I'd regret, and sat up, causing Tom to withdraw his arms.

"What are you saying?" Tom asked. "You think she'd tell me something she wouldn't tell you? Come on, Reg." He humphed and shook his head.

"I know, Tom. I'm sorry." I turned around and touched his cheek. "But I still don't get it. I sometimes wonder if she truly loved him." I tried to settle back against him, but he shifted slightly and I ended up with a sharp shoulder in my back. I recognized his annoyance. "All right, all right. I admit, she loved him. And I know he adored her." I tried to settle back again and this time, Tom didn't rebuff me. I relaxed, feeling his heart beat on my back.

"He sure did," Tom said.

"I still don't get it. She is so matter-of-fact about Dad's death. She—she's so *cold*."

"No, she's not," Tom said. "Look how she hung on you at Earl's funeral. You don't do that if you don't love someone."

"She probably doesn't even remember doing it, she was in such a fog. She probably thought it was you, not me, she was using for support." I felt Tom stiffen behind me. I shifted the subject. "Dad always did such wonderful things when I was little. He was the one who gave me a bath, at least until I got old enough to do it myself and threw him out. Mother didn't do that."

"Maybe you just naturally went to him for everything. You know how Em and I are."

I could tell by his tone Tom was trying to be conciliatory. I turned around and sat on my knees in front of him. "But you weren't there. You didn't see how Mother held back. She always let Dad do the dirty work."

"Dirty work? Well, yeah, I guess bathing a tomboy would be dirty work." He laughed, but I could see it was meant to lighten my mood.

"No, I mean he was my rock. When we went someplace, Mother never took my hand; he did. He's the one who taught me to ride a bike," I said. "She's always been distant and now she's downright cold. No feelings, no heart." I felt anger swelling in me. "She just doesn't care. Never has."

Tom sat back, pulling away from me. "How can you say that? This is the woman who cherishes our children, who lost, I don't know how many kids herself. Don't you think she's entitled to a few scars? What's the matter with you?" He frowned and I saw the color creep up his neck, like a sunburn rising from under his shirt.

"There's nothing the matter with me!" I was feeling defensive and anger seeped out in my voice. "I can't stand being around her like this! She's freezing me out!"

"I was the one standing on the other side of her at the funeral, if you remember. Didn't you feel how she was trembling?" His voice rose to match mine.

"I don't remember," I spat out, even though I did. I wondered at the time if she was going to faint or stumble, but she did neither.

Tom stood up. "You're being selfish, Reg. For Pete's sake, look at it from her side of the fence. If you say your mother is unfeeling," Tom said, "then you are being just like her. You could care less how she feels inside. She's lost her husband. Can't you let her grieve in her own way? I bet Earl would understand her need for privacy. *She's* cold? You got the market on that today." He went for the door. "I'm going for a cup of coffee. It'll give you some time to come to your senses." He grabbed his jacket and was gone.

I sat frozen on the couch. Cold and unfeeling? How could he say that about me when I fought that in my own mother for years? Rage rose up in my chest and I couldn't sit still. I stood up, grabbed my Bloody Mary and downed it all in one gulp. I wanted to throw the glass against the wall. My hand shook as I set it down on the coffee table, before I turned and ran into the bedroom. I slammed the door behind me a hard as I could and collapsed on the bed. In my fury, I started to cry. Pulling the pillow to me, I let everything flow out in those tears. I missed my father more than words could say. I hated my mother for her hard demeanor. I even hated Tom, at the moment. I hated him for calling me cruel and heartless, like my mother. I hated him for insisting on seeing feelings in her, when I couldn't. All the times we were together— Dad, Mother, me—spiraled through my head, always with my mother in the background, standing aloof from it all. Tom didn't know her then, didn't see how important my dad was to me, partly because my mother set herself aside, just like she was doing now.

I felt helpless. I was so tired of it all. Exhausted, really. My tears slowed a bit and I heard my heart beating out, "Perhaps. Perhaps." I turned over on my back so I didn't feel it anymore, but as I drifted off to sleep, a sleep to escape the world, I thought I heard, "Perhaps Tom's right."

Chapter 29
Betty

1977

I heard the door from the garage open and turned to see Reggie step into the kitchen. I waited for the kids or Tom to come bubbling in after her, but no one followed.

"Hi...Mom." Reggie tossed her purse onto the counter and held up a finger. "I'll be right back," she said, and headed out the door, leaving it open behind her.

My hands were slippery from cracking eggs over the mixing bowl and I moved to rinse them off before investigating what she was doing. I was still drying my hands when she reappeared, carrying a rather large box.

"Can you get the door, please?" she asked. With a thud, she set the box on the table. "Thanks."

I shoved the door shut with my hip. "What's all this?" I flicked the towel at the box, then hung it on the oven door handle. "Where are my grandbabies?"

"Um, don't let me stop you. Are you baking cookies? Mmm! Sure smells good in here."

That was a bit strange, as I didn't finish mixing the dough yet, but I let it go. What on earth was she running on about? She acted as if she didn't even hear my question about Em and Tim. They must be home with Tom. On top of that, she sounded as nervous as a child waiting to go on stage. *Okay,* I thought, *I'll just pretend everything's normal.* I turned back to add the last egg to the bowl.

"So, what brings you out today? Did the family catch the fragrance of bakery, clear over at your house? Did they send you over to reconnoiter?" I threw a smile back over my shoulder. Which she didn't see, because she was digging in the box on the table. Picking up my spatula, I turned on the mixer.

"I—I just thought you might want some company," she said, raising her voice to be heard over the noise. "Tom's busy today at home, and he said he'd take care of the kids. So, I decided...I, well, I brought lunch."

The eggs weren't really folded in thoroughly, but I turned off the mixer and craned my neck so I could see her. Her back was to me. She moved the box to the floor and began unpacking. I was afraid to let go of the counter, for fear I'd fall, so sure I was of being asleep and dreaming, or perhaps cautious of what she'd say next. I couldn't bear to break the spell. Reggie, bringing me lunch of her own accord? I saw her lift out her favorite lace tablecloth. I turned around so she wouldn't see the tears in my eyes.

"Sorry for the noise," I said, "but I'll get this finished before we sit down." I cranked up the speed and the eggs and sugar flew into a creamy blend. I hoped she didn't hear me catch my breath. My heart raced with the mixer. I slowed the speed to add the dry ingredients and willed my heartbeat back to normal. By the time I had the cookie dough completed, I was under control. I turned off the mixer and lifted out the beaters. I held one out to her and smiled. When she was little and I was baking, it was the one time she'd hover around the kitchen, waiting for the leftovers. Frosting was always the best.

"Wow! Did I time that right," she said, taking the beater from me and pirouetting to lean against the counter. "Mmm. Chocolate chip. Mmm." She stuck her tongue out to catch an escaping chip. "Remember how you saved the edges from the pie crust?" She inspected her beater carefully.

"Yes," I said. "I used to roll it out and sprinkle it with sugar and cinnamon and bake it for you."

"That was the best," she said. "My own little piecrust. Whoops!" The beater touched her nose, leaving a dollop of dough behind.

"Here, let me get that," I said, reaching for the dishrag.

"Oh, no you don't!" She backed off. "Nobody's getting any of *my* cookie dough!" Her tongue snaked out, but couldn't quite reach, so she took a swipe with her finger, curling the dough over into her mouth. "Dad used to try the same trick," she said, then froze in place.

She was staring at me and I found I was unable to take my eyes off her. The look seemed to last forever. I saw fear, at first. I think she was afraid of saying "Dad" in front of me, afraid of what I might do or say, or even, maybe, of what I wouldn't. Fear was rapidly replaced with guarded caution, then simple anguish, if anguish can be called simple.

"I'm—I'm—" she began, but I interrupted her.

I stuck the end of my beater in my mouth and waved my hand at her, more to keep myself from saying the wrong thing. I popped the beater out and said, "The only way I kept him from stealing your cookie dough was to give him the other beater." I smiled at her, took a last lick of my beater and set it in the sink. As I moved away, I saw her visibly let out her breath. I stood with my back to the counter. "So, what's next?"

"You just keep on doing your cookie thing," she said, "and I'll set the table and get lunch out."

"You know where the dishes are," I said, but she already had a cupboard open and was pulling out plates.

She shook her head. "Don't worry about a thing. It's all under control."

I couldn't see her face, but she sounded delighted. A timer dinged, announcing the oven temperature was at the proper setting. I set to dropping cookies onto cookie sheets and shoving them into the oven. I filled the last sheets, listening to Reggie bustling about behind me. I heard the snap of a tablecloth being spread out. Then, dishes clinked and silverware tinged. I amused myself with imagining what was going on behind me. When I closed my eyes, I smelled dill and mayonnaise, then fresh bread or rolls. I heard a loud pop and spun around. Reg was brandishing an open bottle of wine. She stepped aside and, with a flourish of the corkscrew in her other hand, revealed the table.

My plain kitchen table was resplendent with lace tablecloth, linen napkins, plates of chicken salad, fragrant bread and crystal wine glasses. A small nosegay of fresh flowers graced the center. I couldn't suppress a small gasp and my hands flew to my cheeks. I walked all around the table. "Look what you did!" I hoped she didn't think I was reprimanding her. I added, "Look at this lovely luncheon! You outdid yourself, my dear!" Her smile spread, looking honest and delighted. Then, without warning, her face lengthened and her eyes opened wide. My heart fell.

"Cookies! Your cookies!" she said.

"Oh my!" I wheeled, grabbing oven mitt and turner. I whisked the top sheet out and slid the cookies off onto the cooling rack. They were a lovely golden brown, not burned at all. I whistled a breath through pursed lips. "Just in time."

"They're perfect. Do you need a taste tester?" she asked, taking a few steps my direction.

"Not yet. You'd burn your tongue, for sure," I said, brandishing the turner, threatening to slap her fingers if she went for one. She knew I was teasing. I could see it in her eyes.

We stood there for a moment, then I turned back to the oven to shift sheets and put another in. What did I see behind her eyes? I couldn't read her and was afraid I'd mistake her motives if I asked. Why *was* she here? If it were bad news, she would burst out with it as she came through the door. If it were good news...well, what could it be? She probably would blurt out any good news too. So, why? "I'll be done here in a little bit," I said. "Is it all right if we wait to eat until these are finished?" I pulled another cookie sheet out of the oven. I didn't want to turn around just yet.

"By all means, finish. Then we'll have some cooled and ready for dessert," she said. I could hear her footsteps retreat toward the table as I slipped the last of the cookies into the oven. She said, "I'll pour us each a glass of wine."

She delivered my glass, but I waved her off with my potholder. "Set it on the table, will you, please? I don't want to knock it over."

Reggie sipped and wandered around the kitchen while I finished up the cookies. I wanted to watch her, but that would be far too strange. So, I busied myself with jobs to keep my hands and mind occupied. Reggie seemed a little nervous, but, finally, I let it go. Maybe she needed some time away from all the little things calling her at home. Dusting, cleaning the bathroom, cooking, all those things that have to be done over and over. With Tom taking care of the kids, this would give her a small reprieve. That must be it. She needed to get out a bit. I was the lucky recipient and I shouldn't be looking for ulterior motives. Just enjoy.

"Okay," I said as I turned off the oven and slid the oven mitt back into its drawer. "All done. I'll let the cookie sheets cool and wash them later. Let's eat."

With a flourish, Reggie pulled out my chair and guided me in. She took her own seat and raised her wine glass. "To...to us," she said and reached over to tap her glass against mine.

I took a matching drink to hers and smiled into her eyes. My heart was so full I couldn't respond with anything more. "Yes, to us," I said, finally, while she took a sip of her wine.

We ate and tried to carry on a conversation. Reggie never seemed comfortable making small talk with me, and today was not really much different. I helped her where I could, but we were tiptoeing around each other. Finally, I said, "This food is so good, you're going to have to forgive me if I can't carry on a coherent conversation. Let me savor and we can always talk when we finish eating." After that, she seemed to relax without the pressure of having to hold up her end of a dialogue.

I popped the last morsel of bread in my mouth and washed it down with a sip of wine. "You know, your father used to tell the most wonderful jokes." I figured this would be a subject we could negotiate without too much discomfort. If she thought I wasn't able to handle talking about Earl, this would show her I could. "I wish I could tell jokes like he did. One that was really cute was about a doctor." I chuckled a bit and picked up my wine glass again.

"So, tell me, already," Reggie said, finishing the last of her chicken salad.

"Well, I'll try. I'm not sure I can remember it all. Let's see. A doctor calls his patient and says, 'I have some good news and some bad news.' The patient says, 'Okay, give me the good news.' The doctor says, 'You have twenty-four hours to live.' 'If that's the good news,' the patient says, 'what's the bad news?' 'Well,' the doctor says, 'I forgot to call and tell you.'" Somehow, that didn't sound right. I pursed my lips and glanced at Reggie. "That's not it, is it?" I said.

"Well, not exactly," she said. She looked a little embarrassed, but I thought that might be because she thought *I* was embarrassed.

"Do you remember what it's supposed to be?" I asked. With that look on her face, I was sure she did.

She cleared her throat. "That was Dad's favorite joke," she said, looking at me sideways. "He used to tell me that one all the time. It gave him such a kick, even when I rolled my eyes. Maybe because I rolled my eyes." The skin around her own eyes crinkled with the memory.

I waited. I didn't want to rob her of a sweet memory.

Finally, she said, "The punch line is 'I forgot to call you yesterday.' See? The guy doesn't even have twenty-four hours anymore. Sick, isn't it?"

Then, we both laughed at the pun. "Sick, yes," I said. "I'm sorry I couldn't remember it right." I shook my head at my poor performance.

"Don't worry about it." She shoved her chair. "I'm going after some cookies."

I was glad I didn't have to recover verbally. I poured a cup of coffee for each of us.

Two cups and a few cookies later, Reggie exclaimed, "I am stuffed! I'll help you clean up."

"Well," I said, "let's just clear the table."

We stacked the dishes in the sink. She tossed her napkins into the box, on top of the empty chicken salad container. While Reggie folded the tablecloth, crumbs and all, into a neat package, I picked up the empty wine bottle and dropped it in the garbage bin under the sink. A whole bottle of wine! In the middle of the day yet! A giggle worked its way up my throat and bubbled out. I hiccupped and put my fingers to my lips.

Leaning over, Reggie slid the box toward to the back door, but she stopped and looked at me a bit askance, as if she wasn't sure what she heard. Then she shook her head and gave the box one last shove. "A little tipsy, are we? It's a good thing we had a couple cups of coffee or I'd have to go home and take a nap."

Little did she know that's exactly what I planned for this afternoon. I wasn't exactly tipsy, but I was nice and warm in my tummy. A stretch in the recliner would be quite welcome.

"Come on," Reg said. "I'll help you with the dishes."

But I shook my head. "No, no. There aren't that many. I'll just leave them in the sink and do everything together after supper. You need to get back to your lovelies. Poor Tom must be overwhelmed by now."

"Not at all—I hope," she said. "He's one of the modern ones. Even changes diapers. I love it."

Earl didn't do any of that until Reggie was a little older. He always said he was afraid he'd drop her, so he waited until she was beginning to walk. When she headed right for him, he melted, and it was all over but the shouting. He helped her do anything she asked him to, even "go tinkle," as she put it. I pulled myself back to the present. "You are one lucky girl, Reggie," I said.

"Don't I know it. This gives me a breather and gets me out of the house." She ducked her head as if embarrassed. "I had a good time today." In one fluid motion, she slid her purse off the counter and into the box.

"So did I." I hoped I didn't sound too weepy. "Let me hold the door for you."

Reggie bent and picked up the box, less of a burden now that we consumed most of what she brought. "Be right back." She squeezed out the door and headed through the garage to her car.

I waited at the door, craning to see if she got everything into the trunk. She strode back to my side, edging past me into the kitchen.

"I need a drink of water before I take off," she said, going to the sink and filling a glass. "Wine always makes me thirsty."

"Are there rest stops along the way? We consumed a lot of liquid, in one form or another," I said. A little joke, I hoped.

She took it as such. "I have bladder strong like bull!" She displayed her biceps, almost spilling the water in her glass, and laughed deeply, putting on a Santa Claus tone. Setting her glass down in the sink, she said, "Okay, time to run."

I barely had time to say, "Thanks so much for the lovely lunch," before she was at the back door once more.

She pushed open the screen door, then let it swing to again, without going out. Before I knew it, she had me in a bear hug, the kind of hug she didn't give me since the day she got married. Then, it was the exuberant, spontaneous overflow of emotion from a young woman going out to meet her great love. Now, the hug held the hidden fragrance of exuberance, but it felt more deliberate, more thoughtful. The depth astounded me, took me by surprise, pleased me beyond measure. She stepped away before I could do more than begin an embrace.

Reggie stopped at the back door, one hand on the handle, the other smoothing her hair. "I—I had fun." Then, a flash of a smile.

"We should do it again," I said, surprising myself at being so outspoken. "Come anytime. Next time, I'll treat you. But you come here, so you get some time for yourself." Now I appeared to be the one running off at the mouth. My mouth ran down and I found myself smoothing my hair in imitation of her. I shoved my hands in my pockets.

A brief moment, barely a breath of time, then she said, "Thanks, Mom." And she was out the door.

"I love you!" I called out to her, not expecting her to respond, or even hear me.

But she did.

"Back at ya!" came her voice, drifting to me just before she closed the car door.

I stood at the back door until she backed out the driveway, then I rushed down through the garage to watch her drive away. I stayed until I couldn't see even the imagined exhaust from her car. I hoped this would last.

Chapter 30
Betty

1980

The movers were putting the last piece of furniture in place in my new condo.

"No, put that over there. Yes, that's it. Right against the wall. Perfect."

Well, sort of in place. At least, everything was in the rooms I wanted it in. It was a start.

Everybody told me not to make any changes for the first year after Earl died and I didn't. I went back to teaching in the fall. I stayed in our house. I didn't even buy a new car as we planned to do the following spring. In many ways, all of that routine, normal as it could be after there was no more Earl to set my rhythm by, helped me find my way. Margaret and Bill drove over once a week, like clockwork, all summer, until I told them school was starting in a week and I needed to clean out the cobwebs and get ready to embark with another boatload of young minds and hands. They still called faithfully and we visited each other when we could. Even Reggie called once in a while, though she never talked long.

Over the years, I managed to find my own rhythm, set and somewhat slow. But steady and pulsating softly, not dying or diminishing as I thought it would be. The students looked to me for guidance and, though they didn't know it, gave me a tangible reason to go on. I signed the contract. I couldn't let them down, now could I? It didn't feel that easy in the beginning.

I went three years beyond normal retirement age for no other reason than retirement at sixty-five still scared me. What would I do with all that time on my hands and no Earl to share it with? At first, I didn't take into account the Betty of before, before my teaching certification, before working an eight-hour day, before all of that. That Betty managed just fine when Earl was traveling or working.

So, this year, I quit. Just walked into my principal's office in February, that most bleak of months, and told her I wasn't coming back She accused me of picking the darkest part of the winter to tell her. She kept hoping, as she said over and over throughout spring, I would change my mind and stay on.

But even in the depths of the indigo day, I knew the sun was right around the corner. I was ready.

In March, I bought a new car, retiring the old clunker. The new one smelled like floor polish and linseed oil, don't ask me why. Our old car, Earl's car, smelled like Earl. Old Spice aftershave, even though the kids tried to get him into something more contemporary. And leather, the old car smelled like leather from the seats, though the car was old. The fragrance remained, arising anew on damp days when jeans grated the aroma out of the seats.

The new car didn't have leather seats. I never did like them. They popped and burned and sometimes even squealed as I slid out on hot summer days. They cracked and creaked worse than an old man with ancient hips when I slid in during the cold winters. The new car had fabric seats. I'm sorry, Earl, but I love them.

The last month of school, I bought a condo. Thirty years ago, I didn't even know what the word meant, nor did I ever see one. I made the decision myself, but I must admit, I had a lot of advice. Since retirement, Reggie and Tom, dear as they were to me, behaved as though I were the child and they were the parents. Honestly, sometimes I had to bite my tongue—literally bite my tongue—when they started handing down their opinions. I listened, I always listened, but I kept my thoughts to myself and pretty much did what I wanted to anyway. Now, that didn't mean I ignored what they told me. That would really be acting the child. No, I listened, sifted, and passed judgment. Often, they had a lot to offer.

The moment I announced my retirement, they were on me to move.

"Mother," Reggie began, with an imperious tone hiding behind soft words, "don't you think it's time to get into a smaller place? A place where you don't have to do so much work?"

The idea was, of course, enticing, but I still loved to do a lot of work. Gardening, sweeping the walk, even washing the windows. I still cut my own lawn then, and enjoyed it too. The deciding factor had nothing to do with not being able to do the work. It had to do with Earl.

Of course, I missed Earl, and he was in every nook and cranny of the house, even though I managed to part with his clothes and his other belongings. But it wasn't that Earl haunted the house. It was Earl and the winter.

This past winter was a howler, a real howler. Snow up to my knees sometimes, and that meant digging the driveway out, brushing off the car, going out twice, or sometimes more, in an evening to shovel or snowblow so it wouldn't get too deep to handle.

The last big snowstorm of the winter, the second week in February, drove me to it. As I shoveled off the front stoop and did a general cleanup where the snowblower couldn't reach, suddenly Earl was beside me.

"Hey, darlin'." His whisper floated directly to the top of my brain.

I even stopped shoveling, it seemed so tangible. But when I listened, all I heard was the shimmer of the breeze through the pines and the small clicks of maple and elm branches snapping their fingers.

I knew what he was telling me.

"Remember my heart attack. Remember. Do what you have to do. Do it now."

The next week, I went in to hand in my resignation for the end of the year. Then I visited a realtor. The car was just a bonus.

Now, I was in a new condo. Although the furniture was there, boxes and bags were scattered everywhere. But that was fine with me. I felt like I came full circle. Back on my own, but with a lot more know-how. I allowed myself to settle into the overstuffed chair Earl and I bought with our wedding money, the overstuffed chair which was already reupholstered twice, and was due for a third. It still smelled a bit like Earl. I wouldn't get it redone. Not just yet. Maybe never. I'd see. I learned never to say never.

"Mother?" Reggie's head poked around the corner of the front door. I didn't even have time to close the screen when the movers left. The purple and pink, red and white impatiens planted by the management appeared to come out of her left ear and followed the curve of the walk behind her, making a small rainbow of color with Reggie the pot of gold at the end.

"You look tired," she said, stepping through the doorway.

"I should be! I just moved forty year's worth of valuables into this place. Now all I have to do is unpack it all—No, that's all right," I said as she reached to pull the tape off one of the boxes. "I'll get to it."

Her mouth closed abruptly, even as she withdrew her hand from the box.

It would do no good for her to argue and she knew it. As I unpacked, I wanted to finger every piece. Everything I owned came with attached memories, and I loved replaying them like old home movies, grainy, mostly black and white, but endearing in spite of it all.

"I brought over the last box of art supplies. Where do you want it?" She asked over her shoulder as she headed back out to the car.

"Put it in the spare bedroom. That's going to be my studio." I closed my eyes and our old house came up like a slide on a screen, frozen in time. The flowers bloomed—impatiens, too—and the big maples hovered protectively over the front porch. An intruder stepped into my line of sight, and the house was suddenly no longer mine. Small children took form on the porch and I heard baby laughter from inside. The mother, the intruder from my peripheral vision, scooped up her children, kissing each on the top of their heads. The house enfolded them now, not me. The vision faded, leaving me not with a feeling of emptiness or regret, but with a feeling of fulfillment. The other mother, the family that now claimed our house as theirs, would feel us within it, and it would protect them and give them strength somehow.

When Reggie called from the front door, under a cumbersome box, I was up and back where I belonged. I belonged here, now. It felt right. Once she was in, I turned to reset the opener on the screen door and let it close softly behind her.

"Just down there." I directed her with a little wave as she sidled past me and duck wobbled down the hallway under the weight of my colors and pads and brushes.

"What are you going to do about your pottery work?" Her disembodied voice was followed by a distinct grunt as she relieved her arms of the weight. "You can't have a wheel in here, can you?"

"No," I assured her, "there just isn't the room for it. I could go into the basement, but I don't like working without a lot of sunlight. But there's a studio not too far from here. Within walking distance, actually. I discovered it on one of my exploration walks. The owner was very nice. He said we ought to be able to work out something. That was after I took over a number of my pieces to his shop for consignment. But I'm thinking of going back to watercolor. I used to do a lot of that. I loved it. Your father always said my colors were so wonderful. Reminded him of the best of his dreams, he said."

I turned to Reggie and we shared a small smile. She no longer waited with her eyes looking sideways and her mouth moving as if it didn't know whether to settle on a smile or a tight little line. She didn't say anything—she never would, anyway—but I think she felt me harsh and cold for not sharing my feelings. Truth be told, for a long time, I couldn't even think Earl's name without crying. When others were around, I held back, but, nonetheless, I felt the droplets collecting heavily behind my lids, before settling back into the ocean inside.

Since February, I was able to shift gears a little more. Earl was always with me, of course, but his name no longer brought in the tide, and remembering little things about our lives together no longer felt like an iron-tipped whip on my heart. He became my household god, my hearthside protector. I still turned to show him something extraordinary, or to share some intimacy. But for a long time, he wasn't there, except in the worst sense. In the sense of emptiness, of lack.

Now, he was there. There was a fullness somehow, a depth to the water, a measure to the tide. When I needed, his voice was with me. I was most definitely not hearing voices, you understand. That would be crazy. I only knew all was right with my world now, and I would never be alone again.

"Okay." Reggie rubbed her hands down the thighs of her jeans. "I think we've got it all."

"Goodness, I hope so. I have no room for anything else. I don't even know where I'm going to go with all this stuff."

"Oh, you'll find a place for everything, I'm sure. Besides, there's always Goodwill."

We both laughed, not quite sharing, but together. I couldn't count the trips we made to Goodwill already.

"You need me for anything else? I'm willing," she offered. "If not, I'll go pick up the kids."

"Where are my lovelies, anyway?" Em, my special girl; Tim, with the typical energy of a boy, the spitting image of his father. "Someday, Timothy Earl," I would hug him and tell him, "you're going to be a real heartbreaker. You're the best-looking man I know." I didn't tell him Earl and I said the same thing about his father.

"They're with Tom's mom. Actually, Em is at the movies with a little friend. They wanted to see—oh, I don't remember what. Some Disney confection. Tim is 'helping' his grandma cook up some special sauce, some old family recipe. He's supposed to bring home supper for us. I hope he does. I could use a break." She dramatically swept her eyes toward the ceiling.

"Amen to that."

"So, anyway, do you?"

"Do I what?" My mind lost track of where we started.

"Do you need more help?" she repeated.

"Nope." I reached out and turned her for the door. "Go get your lovelies and my favorite grandbabies. I'm just going to grab some lunch and take stock here. I'll do a little at a time, I think."

"I never knew you to do something a little at a time. But," she raised her hands in a gesture of surrender as she headed toward the door, "who am I to get involved? Just let the old lady work, I say." She tossed off an informal wave. "Bye, Mom. I'll call you tomorrow and see how far you rearranged the piles by then." A small smile and she was gone.

I sighed and stretched gratefully. It was all here, ready and waiting. My next life.

When I turned to survey the boxes and piles, "Welcome home, darlin'," whispered at the back of my mind.

Chapter 31
Betty

1985

Good Lord, where did all the years go? Tom and Reggie were married fifteen years, now, and throwing a big party to celebrate. What was the fifteenth anniversary anyway? Paper? No, that was the first. Silver for twenty-five. Diamond for fifty? I couldn't remember. I headed for my studio and rummaged through the top desk drawer, that one drawer everyone has with all sorts of flotsam and jetsam no one wants to throw away. At least, not yet. Somewhere in there was a little book with all of those fun facts: conversion charts for the metric system, substitutions for certain foods or cleaning substances, what message certain flowers conveyed, what each anniversary year meant. Sure enough, there it was. The little blue book was tucked under a bank book and an envelope with the key to the safety deposit box. A few pages in, I spotted "Anniversary Symbols: Fifteenth Wedding Anniversary. Traditional flower: Rose. Traditional gift: Crystal. Contemporary gift: Watches. This anniversary does not have any gem associated with it."

The perfect gift for Tom and Reggie's fifteenth anniversary? According to the booklet, watches. Well, they did have crystals, didn't they? I chuckled, with no one to share the joke with at the moment. Sometimes that made jokes even funnier. No explanations or apologies necessary.

What would be perfect? I didn't want anything big or pretentious. It just wasn't Tom or Reggie. She loved things carrying memories of the past or of favorite places. Tom appreciated anything. No, that wasn't true either. Tom loved anything Reggie loved. That and simplicity. Unlike Reggie, however, Tom took his time deciding the kinds of things he would surround himself with. But once he decided, he remained satisfied. Like his recliner. When they were shopping for a new chair for Tom, Reggie fell in love immediately with an oversized rocking recliner and wanted to take it home right away. Tom insisted on waiting until the following weekend, when they could visit two other stores and see what else they could find. She pestered him about the perfect color, the comfort, the ease of operation, but though he took her persuasive attempts in good humor, he would not be dissuaded. After another round of shopping and running back and forth between stores in order to "test drive" each, as Tom put it, he finally settled on the first one they looked at. Reggie harrumphed over all the time wasted, in her viewpoint, but Tom pointed out he would never know, and would always question, if they didn't take the time to shop thoroughly. He still had the chair, in fact, and used it so much, it was nearing the point of needing reupholstering. Unless they wanted to start the shopping process all over again. I didn't think Reggie was ready for that.

I smiled. Reg and Tom: counterparts. For the most part, they bore each other's quirks with gentle humor, though sometimes Reggie lost her temper with his insistence at attention to details. "Whatever," she would comment, and then turn and walk away. He would stop in mid-explanation, shake his head and sigh, then move on to other things. Not much seemed to bother Tom. I really like him for that.

But their anniversary gift. What was I going to give them? I really wanted something meaningful. Perhaps Earl's watch. That would touch Reggie's heart, I was sure. She loved her dad and still missed him, I knew. When they came to dinner or she dropped off the kids for a day of fun, anytime she came in, she stopped at the framed photo of him I had on the little table by the door. It was taken just before we left for Mexico. His mouth was open in a deep-bellied laugh and his eyes looked directly into the camera. He was toasting me with a glass of apple juice. I took the picture at breakfast a few days before we left, in order to test a new camera we bought for the trip. I asked for a big smile and he came back with a little "tea party" smile, which looked more like a grimace. "Come on, Earl," I said, "give me your best."

"Do I get a reward for being good then?" he asked.

"Sure," I said. "I'll tell everyone I was naked."

He burst into laughter at that—which I had counted on—and I snapped the picture just as he raised his glass to toast me. Then, he did get a reward. That's the part I never told anyone.

When I finally had the roll of film developed, over a year after the trip, the first photo I saw was that one. I forgot about it, being so wrapped up in losing him. I wasn't going to have the film developed at all, but thought better of it just before I dropped it into the garbage. When they came back, I was so grateful for having that last lovely photo of him, far more meaningful than the pictures of Mexico, though he was in some of those, too. I cried, fit the picture into an antique frame and propped it on the table by the front door. He was the first one I greeted when I came in the door and the last one to admonish, "Watch the house, please," when I went out. Reggie always stopped and paid a little obeisance when she visited.

I knew what I would give them for their anniversary. The juice glass in the photo. It wasn't really crystal, but it was a very well-done cut glass piece. In fact, I had two of them. At one time I owned a set of eight, but over the years, the number declined, some cracked, some broken. Now there were only two, one for Reggie, one for Tom. She would recognize them, I knew. I would wrap them in some vintage, rose-printed paper that would top off the requirements for a fifteenth anniversary. Perfect.

• • • •

The party they planned to celebrate their anniversary was a backyard picnic, the best kind, in my opinion. As I got out of the car, I smelled hamburgers and brats on the grill and saw coolers full of beer and soda along the side of the house. Even though I heard party noises coming from the patio in back, I still went in through the front door, as I always did. I dropped off my gift in the living room and went into the kitchen. Tom and Reg told everybody just to bring themselves, nothing else needed. But they all insisted on bringing something anyway, so the serving table and counters were overflowing. Fruit salads and coleslaw, at least three kinds of chips, baked beans—two different kinds—watermelon slices, and too many other things to name. The riot of colors swept down the counter and right out the door as neighbors and friends carried bowls of food in and out. Tom was at the stove, concocting a homemade barbeque sauce.

"Hey!" he said as he spotted me. "How's my favorite mother-in-law?"

"I brought a variety of cookies. I couldn't decide which kind to make, so I just made some of each. Oatmeal—"

"You better hide those," he said, "or Reg will gobble them all down. I hope you made up a special package just for me or I won't get any at all."

"Well, you'll just have to move quickly. But I did make those double-duty brownies you love."

"Stop right there. Those definitely get hidden. Do me a favor and put one in my mouth right now, will you? I have to keep stirring this stuff for a couple of minutes or it'll burn."

I found room on the counter and opened the container.

"Look," he said. "Just take that little one out and shuffle the others over. No one will notice it's missing. Put 'er right in there." He opened his mouth in anticipation.

I obliged and watched as he tilted his head back and sighed in chocolate delight. "Tom, you are one of my most appreciative audiences. The kids just eat! You savor."

"I do have style when it comes to complimenting the ladies I love."

"You love me only for my baking. I know that old song-and-dance. Flattery will get you anywhere."

"Flattery will get me another brownie, I hope," he said.

I didn't even try to conceal the space left by the second brownie. "So, what are you giving Reggie for this anniversary? You're always pretty creative," I said.

"You know, this year I think I outdid myself. She's always complaining how she doesn't have enough time to get the flowers and all that stuff looking the way she wants. So, I hired a landscaping service. What do you think?" He stopped stirring momentarily, waiting for my reply.

"I think that's a wonderful idea," I said. "She loves flowers and, you're right, she really doesn't have the time to do it up the way she'd like. You always come up with the best ideas."

"Glad you like it," he said, turning back to his sauce. "It always seems to work out when you approve."

Reggie's voice appeared at the patio door behind us. "So, what are you two doing? Tom, isn't your sauce finished? I'm dying to try it. It's a new recipe."

"Just taking it off the heat," he said. "I was telling Betty how nice your flowers look this year."

"Are you kidding? I didn't get anything in this year. I just wish I had more time," Reggie said.

Tom and I shared a quick smile. Yes, it would be the perfect gift.

    •   •   •   •

Presents were supposed to be banned, but people brought things: a bottle of wine, a gift certificate to a favorite restaurant, homemade bread, that kind of thing. My little offering pushed to the back of the end table seemed so insignificant, and perhaps a bit too personal, that I never said a word when it was almost overlooked in the hubbub.

"Wait," Tom said and reached out to stop Reggie's hands from crumpling up the used wrapping paper. "There's one more over here." He walked over and picked up my gift, then handed it off to Reggie. "Who's this one from? Must be your mom."

Reggie looked over at me, her hands quiet for a moment.

"Roses for a fifteenth anniversary," I said. "That's why the roses on the paper."

She shifted her gaze to the package, then began to unwrap it, not tearing it off the way she had the others. Tom sat down next to her. She handed him the paper and set the box on her lap.

"You need some help with that?" he asked as he set the wrapping paper on the floor.

Reggie shook her head and pulled the top off the box.

I packed the glasses in lots of tissue, but folded it back a bit, so the glasses would be visible when they opened the box. Now, I was holding my breath. What did I expect? I guess I was afraid there'd be nothing to expect, no reaction. Tom peered over the edge of the box and tilted his head. I knew he was wondering why I gave them a pair of simple juice glasses.

At first, Reggie looked quizzical, her forehead crinkling up. Then her face burst into sunshine.

I let out my breath and sent out a silent prayer to Earl. *Thanks.*

Reggie plucked the glasses out of their protective bed and held them up for all to see. She was laughing when she turned to Tom. "This is Dad's juice glass! Remember the photo by the front door, where he's lifting this?" Tom nodded and took one of the glasses from her. "That is my absolute favorite picture of him. He's so happy. That's how I remember him. Thanks, Mother."

Tom glanced at me and smiled. I hoped he didn't see the hurt in my eyes. Yes, of course, I knew she'd react that way—Dad's glass—but perhaps I expected too much. I wanted her to see two glasses, one for each of us, Dad and Mother.

"We got one for each of us," Tom said, and leaned in to kiss her on the cheek.

I had no idea if he was aware of what he just said, but it salved my heart a bit. I saw a bit of Earl and me in the two of them. Two people who loved each other. Two old glasses. I felt myself blushing. It was such a small gift. I thought it to be momentous when I decided to give it, but now the gift seemed too petty and too personal, all at the same time. Those glasses held memories for me, but I knew they couldn't be transmitted just by filling them with orange juice and swallowing them down. Some memories would die with me, others might float off, meaningless after a number of years. I couldn't explain all of this to them. They would have to find their own use for the glasses, pour them full of their own orange juice, their own memories.

Tom stood up and came over, holding out his arms. I rose to meet his quick hug. After a moment, Reggie followed. When I embraced her, I said in her ear, "May you have many good memories of us when you use the glasses."

She pulled back and looked me in the eye. I thought I saw questions there, but she only said, "Thank you. We will."

Chapter 32
Reggie

I grabbed the bowls of leftovers on the picnic table. "Tom?" I called into the kitchen. "Where are you?" I spotted him, slightly out of focus through the screen. He was tying up a garbage bag full of paper plates. "Can you open the door for me, please? My hands are full."

"Be right there." He gave a last twist to secure the garbage, then stepped over and slid the door open.

"Thanks." I scooched through and set the bowls of leftover potato salad and fruit salad on the counter. I turned to him and blew the hair out of my eyes. "What a great party! Of course, as usual, all the ladies hung on your every word. How do you do that, anyway?" I smiled over at him. After fifteen years, he still made my heart skip.

"Natural talent, I guess," he said and put his arms around my waist. "Just remember, you're the one I go home with."

"You're already home, silly," I said, draping my arms around his neck.

He kissed the tip of my nose, then held me at arm's length. "So, do you like your gift?"

"I love it. I can't wait to see what they can do with the yard." I stepped back from him and clasped my hands together. "Can I tell them what I want planted? Colors and such?"

"You can do whatever you want to, babe," Tom said. "They were very accommodating when I set it up. All you have to do is call them and they'll come over and do as much as you want them to." We started to load the dishwasher.

"This is going to be great. Thank you *so* much." I stopped and cocked my hands on my hips. "What did you think of Mother's gift? I didn't know she still had those old glasses."

Tom said, "Pretty good. Just the right size too."

"That's it?" I said. "Just, 'They're the right size'? I think it's kind of strange—well, I mean, I know she figures it'll give me something of Dad's to remember him by—"

"Won't it?" Tom asked. "I thought it was kinda neat. Now you've got something of his. Fortunately, she thought of me too. I don't think it's that strange, do you?"

"Well, no," I said, "I guess when you put it that way." I remembered Dad sitting at the breakfast table with me, pontificating on any and all subjects, talking to me like an adult, slurping his orange juice in that very glass. "Yeah, lots of good memories." Tom was right. I could see Mother and Dad bustling around each other in the kitchen in the morning, concocting breakfast, Mother pouring juice and delivering it as if it were liquid gold.

"There you go," Tom said, hefting the garbage bag to take it outside.

"Wait!" I gave him what I hoped was a coy smile. "I have a gift for you."

He set down the garbage bag. "You gave me a gift," he said. "I love the new golf clubs. It'll force me to take some time out to relax. How come another gift?"

"This one is just for you," I answered. "Just between you and me. Hang on a second, I'll go get it."

Two weeks before, when the kids were home from school, I corralled them in the kitchen. "Before you get yourselves all grungy, I want you to do something for me." I picked up my camera and pointed out to the backyard. "C'mon, I want to get a nice photo of the two of you."

"What for?" Em asked. "We got school pictures."

"Yeah," Tim said. "I want to take my bike out. Do I hafta change clothes? Do I hafta wear a suit?"

"No, no," I said, sliding open the patio door and laughing. "Besides, you don't even own a suit. This'll just be a quickie, then you two can go play. Come on out to the playset." I led them across the grass and pointed at the slide. "Why don't the two of you climb up on the bottom there? Em, you can sit behind and Tim can sit in front of you."

"Uh-uh! No way!" Tim's voice went up in complaint. "I'm not sitting between her legs. That's for babies."

"Yeah, like you're no baby!" Em said, sticking her tongue out at her brother. She was already sitting part way up the slide, knees up and tennies tucked tight against the metal to hold her in place.

He shrieked in reply. "Mom! Make her stop!"

Good Lord, how difficult can a photo be? "All right, all right. Em, you move on down a bit. Yes, right there. No, keep your knees up and your feet just like that." I knew better than to say, Oh, how cute you look. "Tim, just stand next to the slide, will you? You don't have to touch her. Yeah, right there. Now, turn a little and put your hands on the edge of the slide."

Tim turned and grabbed it, as if trying to pull it out of the ground. "Like this?" he said, then made a face at his sister.

"Don't hold on so tight," I said, reaching over to twist him away from his sister a bit. "Look, we'll be done in a minute. Just cool it." I stepped back and checked the setup. "Can you manage to smile?" I asked. "Say cheese!" I snapped off a photo and they started to move. "Oh, no, you don't! Just stay there for a minute. I'm not taking any chances. We don't want to have to do this whole thing all over again." I snapped another. "One more," I said.

Tim took off for the house the minute he heard the shutter click, but I held up a hand for Em to stick around. "Can you take one of me too?" I asked.

"What are these for?" she said, as she lifted her feet and slid down to the end of the slide.

"I'm doing something special for Daddy for our anniversary. Now, here's the button to push. Just stand right here, where I am, and it should be about right."

"Don't you want me to stand where you were for us?" Em asked.

"No, I'm just one person and I want you to get closer. Here, see through this? Fill this up all the way. Move close enough so there's not a lot of yard and sky around me. See?" I watched as she looked through the viewfinder.

"Okay," she said.

I moved to the slide and leaned against it. "How's this?"

She took a half-step closer. "Okay, smile!"

"Take a couple more," I said. "Try backing up a little, then moving in closer too."

She followed instructions, taking three more shots, then handed off the camera to me. "There you go, Mom. I hope they turn out."

So do I, I thought. "I'm sure they will," I said. "Now, you have time before supper if you want to go over to the neighbor's."

Off she went. I pushed the rewind button and hoped my brainstorm would work out.

●　　●　　●　　●　　●

I hid the small package in the dining room hutch and it took me no time at all to retrieve it. "Here," I said, as I handed it to him. "Just for you, from me. Although, this is kind of from all three of us. You'll see once you open it."

He already had the wrapping off. "What is this? A leather book? No, wait. I see." He opened the hinges on the double photo frame, exposing the two pictures.

"Aw! This is cool! A picture of the kids." He laughed. "They're kind of big for the slide, aren't they? Great picture of you. This is really neat. I'm going to keep it on my nightstand where I can see all of you every morning."

"Em took that picture of me. She did a pretty good job for a twelve-year old, didn't she?" I said. "And the sentiment." I put my finger on what I'd written on my photo: For King Tom, from Your Queen, Regina Marie. "You're always royalty to me."

Tom slid his arms around me. "You're the one with the grand name, Queen Regina." He kissed me softly.

"Where are the kids?" I asked.

"Remember? We made arrangements a week ago. Betty took them home with her."

"That's right." I did remember. "So, you want to see how your photos look next to the bed?" I smiled up at him.

Chapter 33
Reggie

1992

Mother's eightieth birthday party wasn't my idea originally, although I was ready to go along. It was Tom's idea. He hatched this over coffee one morning, telling me Mother deserved some kind of celebration. I admitted that eighty was one of those benchmarks that should be acknowledged. How on earth did the years zip by so quickly? I wondered if I myself would make it that far. After all, Dad died fairly young. When they left for Mexico, I pictured him clambering over various ruins and strolling down covered walkways, looking at turquoise jewelry with Mother. I certainly never expected him to come home in a coffin. After things settled down somewhat once the funeral was over, what hit me the hardest was I said goodbye as if I'd have a chance to say hello. But I didn't. No more hugs and kisses. No more teasing frowns, faked for some put-on exasperation. I should've paid more attention. But I didn't do that either. Maybe that was why I was ready to agree with Tom's idea of a party. Mother was the only one left for all of us.

We began to scheme. Surprisingly, it was fun. We contacted Bill and Margaret and she offered to come over early and help us set up everything. The ideal place to have the party would be the community building at Mother's condo complex.

"Tom, I don't see how we can trick your mother into reserving the place without tipping her off," I said.

"Leave it to me. She made a flock of friends there. I'm sure one of them would be happy to do it. And the manager's been on her side from the beginning. She charms them all."

"That's right. She does watercolor classes there, doesn't she?" I said. "Then we should have no problem." And we didn't have a problem. We didn't even have a problem finding an excuse to get her into the community center. One of the couples in a neighboring unit, friends of both of us, was expecting a baby and we just told her it was a baby shower.

We decorated the place with yellow daffodils—one of her favorite flowers—and tulips in various shades of pink—one of my favorites. I got ambitious and draped pastel crepe paper in loose braids and twists from chandelier to corners and back again. I surprised myself with honest-to-goodness enthusiasm. She'd enjoy it all, I knew, though I might see only a secret little smile, sweet in its own way, I guess. I was getting soft in the head. Would she really enjoy it? Over the past few years, in particular, I caught her commiserating with Em or Tim, or sometimes both of them at once. When they were little, she cuddled and hugged, doing all the grandmother things. But she never got in the way. In fact, she always deliberately stepped out of the way when someone else was around. That changed a little with Dad's death. Maybe she realized, just as I did, that sometimes you don't get a chance to give homecoming parties, only bon voyage parties.

Once we had all the food and decorations in place, Tom sent me off to fetch her. I thought it was a little too early, but he insisted. "Everything's in place and all our guests are here, so why not go get her? She's probably sitting and waiting anyway. You know she's always ready ahead of time."

When I got to her condo, she wasn't ready.

"You aren't even dressed yet!" I said, as I closed her door behind me. She still had on her housecoat, as she called it. "Come on, get with it, the party won't wait forever."

"I'll just slip on my dress and I'll be ready to go. It won't take but a minute," she said. "Why don't you get yourself a quick cup of coffee? There's still a little left, hot in the pot, if you want some."

"If I start drinking now, I'll never sleep tonight," I said.

"It's the nice hazelnut flavor. And it's decaf. Help yourself."

I found it hard to resist. Tom and I had spent quite a bit of time planning and decorating, picking up food and sneaking around like a couple of thieves. A cup of coffee sounded really good right then. I headed for the kitchen. "Let me know when you're ready. I surrendered." I could hear her rummaging around in her closet as I poured out the last of the coffee. "Still 'a little' left in the pot?" I called out. "There's barely enough here for one cup. But that's okay. We need to get going. Are you ready yet?"

"I'm all dolled up and ready to go."

I didn't even hear her come into the kitchen. I nearly dropped my cup. She *was* dolled up. With her white hair like a halo, she wore a green dress, which seemed to float on her shoulders. "I— You look great. Love the dress. I'll be right with you." I turned to the sink.

She blushed a little. "Oh, Reg, don't rush. Finish your coffee. I'll just check to make sure I have my keys, and turn a little light on in the living room."

"No, really. I'm all set," I said, rinsing the cup and setting it with a porcelain clink in the bottom of the sink.

We slid into our coats, she locked her door and we set off down the sidewalk for the community center. The lights were blazing and I could see the decorations gently swaying from the movement of people inside. The room looked far more crowded than I imagined it would be. At eighty, Mother still had a significant number of friends, but many were not mobile and there seemed to be a far greater number of guests than I remembered inviting.

"Hurry up. It's cold out here." Mother's voice broke into my thoughts.

"Okay, okay. I'm coming." I reached to open the outside door. I heard it suddenly go quiet in the community room to our right. Someone stepped out and swung open the large double door. Mother and I stepped into the room together, side by side.

"Surprise!" everyone called out together and began to sing Happy Birthday, but something was wrong. Well, not wrong exactly, but there were indeed far more people than we invited. The room was packed. Among Mother's friends, old and new, including Margaret and her husband, were a lot of familiar younger faces. Mother and I turned to each other and, upon hearing, "…birthday, Reg and Betty! Happy birthday to you!", it dawned on me that someone pulled off a very neat coup—a surprise birthday party for both of us! Mother burst into laughter. I felt her briefly weaken against me, perhaps with surprise and delight.

I slid away from her. Mother put her hands up to her mouth, not even attempting to move them to hide the tears in her eyes. I never saw such delight in her. She simply glowed. For myself, I looked to Tom. He stood beaming and applauding in the front of the crowd. When I caught his eye, he came over, gathered me up and laughed into my hair.

"You should see your face!" he said.

"How in heaven's name did you arrange all of this?" He was competent, certainly, but never very good at keeping a secret.

"*You* arranged all of it. Along with Betty, that is. She thought she was planning your fiftieth. You thought you were planning her eightieth." He was enjoying this. "You were both right."

"I can't believe you actually pulled this off. This is wonderful! Look, flowers and everything. What's this? A cake! You really outdid yourself. How can I thank you?" I ran off at the mouth.

"Oh," he said, "I'll think of something. Come on, let's go clear everything up with your mother. I had you both going, didn't I?" He gloated.

We were surrounded by friends by then, all giggling and patting me on the back. Fragments of birthday wishes greeted me, as Tom and I wound our way toward Mother and her friends. She stood with Margaret, wrapped in an embrace. Bill patted her on the back.

"Mother!" I called, at the exact time Tom said, "Betty!"

She turned at the sound of our voices over everyone else's. "Look at you, Reggie! You never suspected a thing, did you? Tom and I really managed to fool you! Happy birthday, my dear." Letting go of Margaret entirely, she came to me and reached up to touch my cheek. "May you have many, many more."

Her touch surprised me, but it dawned on me that at her age, perhaps she was getting sentimental. I felt like the smile I gave her was a bit crooked, but I don't think she noticed. She was my mother, after all. I did love her.

"Likewise," I said. "Many more for you, too." I reached out and gave her a hug.

"Come on, you two." Tom's voice cracked for a moment. "Come and cut your cake. The bakery helped me figure out how to get the both of you onto one cake." He guided us to the buffet table, crowned with what looked more like a wedding cake than a birthday cake.

"Good heavens!" I said. "It's gorgeous. I hope it tastes half as good as it looks."

Mother was speechless.

"Look." Tom pointed. "It's got two layers, one for each of you. Betty's is on the bottom, because she's older. Reggie, yours is chocolate. See? The third layer on top, that little one? That's for the two of you to share. If you can't eat it all today, you can take it home."

"Tom." Mother took his hand. "I am so touched by what you've done. This is a wonderful celebration, one I certainly will never forget. It's such a privilege to share this day with my daughter. What a perfect idea."

Her outburst of unexpected emotion made me uncomfortable. "Well," I said, to break the moment, "the cake is gorgeous. I'm going to cut myself the biggest piece, with lots of frosting. No diet today." I grabbed the knife and cake server. "Who else wants a piece?"

Chapter 34
Reggie

1995

I sipped my coffee and settled back on the terrace of the coffee shop, surrounded by all the morning bustlers headed to work. Not me. I was still off for the summer. Not for much longer, but still. Movement and motion were all around me and I was glad I had nowhere to go just yet.

I always chose a table close to the railing so I could look out over the lake. During the school year, I never had time for a leisurely cup of coffee anywhere, and drank my requisite two cups standing at my own kitchen counter, usually in the midst of the turmoil of getting ready to go to work. I figured I stored up enough credits for more cups of coffee to use over the summer.

The treat was not the coffee, although this morning it was the iced kind and very tasty, and the aromas floating on the terrace were enticing. The treat was being able to sit down and savor, sharing a little time with a gaggle of strangers, most of whom didn't know each other's names. Yet, we were mellow enough in the morning to give a little hand wave or head nod to the others who were regulars. The clerk knew I was a teacher. He often teased me, the way strangers do, about "How many days left of freedom?" and "Are you ready to go back? Counting the days, I betcha." The two hours twice a week on that terrace without any responsibility to anyone or anything were my gift to myself for having survived the year. It recharged my batteries.

I saw the woman coming, but didn't know her. People were always coming and going, excusing themselves as they skated between the tables. She caught my eye only because she was far better dressed than any of the rest on the terrace, even though there were clusters of professional women who dressed the role: lawyers, secretaries, saleswomen with briefcases. The rest of us were simply either on vacation or late starters. I looked around and saw decent shorts and tee shirts, or jeans and embroidered denims. This woman, on the other hand, stood out dramatically. Yes, she had the requisite shoes, purse and dress of a professional. Yes, she had a great makeup job. But unlike anyone else, she wore a hat. A big, navy blue, floppy brimmed thing that matched her dress.

I turned my attention up a notch.

The woman's dress was obviously not for any office or meeting. It dropped off her shoulders stylishly, and slithered on down to smooth against her waist and hips. Waist and hips with dimensions that I myself would never see again.

Not that I had grown fat, but when my children were born, they did leave behind a good deal more than they took with them. I became a nice maternal size. Rubens, who loved voluptuous women, would love to paint me. Actually, I might even be a bit too thin for him. I took care of myself in the way that made it clear I was not letting myself slide, but that, nonetheless, I was a woman with a family. Not matronly yet, but perhaps someday.

My mind returned from musing on my shape as the woman moved closer to my table. I watched with interest, but detachment.

Nothing was open around my table, and the woman was not carrying a cup of coffee.

Now I was curious. Where did this woman come from? She was not one of the regulars, I was sure of that.

Between the dress with slithery shoulders and the hat, people were taking notice. The woman smiled her pardons as she moved between the tables, apparently oblivious to the wake she was creating. Oblivious, ha! Someone that gorgeous and all dolled up is not unaware of the ripples she creates. In spite of the interest, perhaps because of it, I went back to gazing out over the lake.

A shadow fell across my table and remained. I swiveled my eyes a bit. The woman stopped in front of me. I looked up, but the backlight of the early sun created an aureole of such bright light that it blacked out the form in the middle. The woman's shape hovered in that shimmer of early morning sun. Automatically, I shaded my eyes and raised my chin higher.

"Can I help you?" I could see just enough to tell that, yes, it was the woman in the hat, but I was sure she was no one I knew.

"May I sit down?" she asked.

Though her voice was low, I could hear the crispness and the warmth.

"Of course," I responded immediately. No other seats were apparently available on the terrace, and I shared a table now and then with strangers, sometimes being the one to wave someone over when they were clearly searching. But this was different. It seemed this woman picked me out of the pond of people out there, and I had no idea why. Curiosity, propelled by good manners, got the best of me.

"Can I help you?" I repeated as the woman sank gracefully into the chair across the wrought iron table from me, moving out of alignment with the sun. Her face fell into the shadow of her hat, while her shoulders still gleamed with light. "Do I know you?"

"No. Not yet." She clasped her hands in her lap and leaned back, turning to look over the lake. Her hat brim shielded most of her face from view. I could see the woman open and close her lips, but she didn't turn or say anything.

"Who are you?" I realized my question was downright impolite, but though she approached with the determination of someone doing more than just looking for a place to sit, she remained silent, across the table from me. Apparently, she was looking for me. Well, you found me, lady, now what do you want?

The woman finally turned toward me, unclasped her hands and placed her beautifully manicured fingertips, just her fingertips, along the edge of the white table. Her face was like a small, far-away full moon in spring, clear and very young.

"It doesn't matter, really," she said, still shaded by her hat brim. "I just wanted to meet you once. To see what you are. To see what took him away."

Alarm bells went off somewhere in the far recesses of my head. I convinced myself they might not be there at all. When I listened, they really didn't seem to be fully formed. In a suddenly protective, reflex reaction, my elbows went up on the chair arms, and I gripped my hands together and rested my chin on my fists. I waited.

"I've been calling him for two weeks now, and he just won't respond." The woman's voice was still low and sweet.

"How old are you?" I asked.

She looked up, startled, not expecting something to come out of nowhere like that. "Twenty-seven." She crinkled her forehead, apparently trying to make sense out of my sudden question.

I created distance. On purpose, of course. Who was this young thing? She was half my age. My resentment rose. But I knew who she was. Part of me way back in my brain knew who she was. The rest of me just willed itself not to hear.

"I wanted you to know. I wanted you to know about us. About…"

The woman clearly didn't do this often, probably not ever before. But it was also just as clear she was determined to see it through to the end.

I was not about to help her. My alarm bells were getting louder. But I stayed back in my chair, chin on my hands, like a carved household god. If this woman came to make any kind of petition, I didn't want to make the first move. But I did anyway.

"Go away," I said, raising my eyes again to meet the other woman's.

I got my first clear view of a young woman with polished makeup to go with her polished fashion, a face young, but not innocent, a stylish, self-assured face. Quickly following that, I heard more than a low voice, saw more than a sweet face, or manicured hands, or impeccable styling. I saw unadulterated anger.

"No, I will not go away." On that, she sounded firm. "You need to know what your husband—"

Ah! She names him at last, or at least his title. Maybe she has the wrong wife. I knew that was unlikely.

"—has done."

I carried on a conversation in my head. No, I don't need to know. I seemed to already know, but I didn't want it acknowledged out loud. Out loud for my public self to hear. But it couldn't be true, it couldn't.

Oblivious to my silent denial, the woman went on.

Though I opened my mouth to stop these stones creating waves in my own personal pond, I couldn't hear anything come out.

"We met at a business conference in Chicago two weeks ago—" the woman continued.

I remembered that conference. Tom called every night, as he always did. Couldn't have been him, I continued to respond silently.

"—even though it turns out we both work here. We were on a team the first day and went out to dinner—"

"That does not—" I began, but the woman cut me off, her hand forming a small, insistent crescent in the air.

"There is not much to tell, Regina Marie—"

I was alert and incredulous. My name? How does she know my name? Tom never calls me Regina. Certainly not Regina Marie.

"—except I fell in love. In love, can you believe that? I wanted him. Yes, I knew he was married, but I didn't care."

She was rushing now, as if I would cut her off and leave her bleeding on the terrace. To be truthful, I would drain every drop if I could, but I was frozen in place. "It's not my husband," I blurted.

"Tom Mackenzie. Tom is your husband. And you have two children, a boy and a girl. He calls you Reg."

My knuckles were white, but I didn't move a muscle. A public scene was not what I wanted right then. Not yet. "Wrong man, I'm afraid," I said.

"How are your kids? That Tim's a handsome young man and your daughter's gorgeous. Cute photo of them sitting on the slide."

Tom's photo display. The one hinged in the middle and bound in leather. The one he kept on his bedside table and packed to take with him on business trips. The photo of the kids we took ten years before. The facing picture was me, hamming it up for the camera and autographed "To King Tom, from Your Queen, Regina Marie." He never wanted to update the photos.

This could not be happening.

"Look." The woman's voice took on a different tone. "I want him back. I want you to know what he did to you. On those nights—"

More than once? What does she want? Telling me isn't—

"—he came into my bed—" Her voice dropped to a whisper, a venomous whisper, but I heard every syllable. "—do you know what he did? He called you." Momentum carried her along, like a pebble scraping along a creek bottom. "He called you and then he made love to me."

"Go away." It was the only thing my lips would form. "Go away now." I moved my gaze out across the lake. I felt the woman's eyes boring into me. "I don't believe you. Tom would never do that."

"Oh, really?" she said. Her smile was sweet, but her eyes were hard. "Take a look at this." She slid a folded paper across the table toward me. "Go ahead. Read it."

I snatched it up and unfolded it, all without looking away from her. I held it up between us. *Meet me in my suite, 9 p.m. We've got some unfinished business. Bring wine. Tom.* It was his handwriting, no doubt about it. I closed my eyes and crumpled the paper in my hand. I stuffed it in my pocket. My fingers clutched each other in terror.

"Your husband, your sweet Tom, makes love better than any man I have ever known, wine or no wine. Your sweet man betrayed you," she hissed.

I opened my eyes. My hands unclenched and dropped to the arms of the chair and I leaned, locking eyes with her, bending forward like a vulture over a stinking carcass. "No, honey, he betrayed you." I made it up as I went along. "That's why you're here, isn't it? Because he hurt you too."

That "too" was enough for the woman and she slid forward, checking my face closely. I unwittingly consumed her poisoned apple.

The woman rose, apparently satisfied her mission was accomplished. "Thanks for your time, Regina Marie." She leaned at a seductive angle and added conspiratorially from under her hat brim, "He fell right into my arms, and oh, was it sweet. That passion—"

My aim was so perfect that one ice cube went right down her cleavage when I flung the iced coffee, cup and all. The clang of my chair as it bounced off the bricks caused nearby customers to grab their cups in anticipation. Before the woman had a chance to even straighten up, I was gone.

•   •   •

I forced myself to move smoothly as I walked into the kitchen, though I felt like a robot under someone else's control. Thank God, the kids weren't here. Em was at college, training to be a Resident Assistant, and Tim was working and wouldn't be home until late. I had a whole day to stitch myself back together.

The first thing I did was grab some matches and pull the note out of my pocket. I didn't ever want to see it again. Dropping it into the sink, I lit a match and touched it to the paper. When the flames went out, I nudged the detritus into the disposal, turned on the water and flushed it all away. I felt like I ran the gauntlet of a knife-wielding gang, and lost. The cuts were deep and I needed more than just simple bandages. I needed surgery. My operating room was always the house. I poured myself into cleaning. Cleaning and convincing myself it just could not be. It was the wrong conference, so it couldn't be Tom. It was the wrong wife, so it couldn't be Tom. It was the wrong coffee shop, so it couldn't be Tom. So, so, so. None of it worked.

I was convinced it should. Plenty of people knew my husband's name. Plenty of people heard him call me Reggie or Reg.

Not plenty of people knew my full name was Regina Marie. No one knew about the photos. And that note. I knew it wasn't forged.

That clinched it for me. She went to him. At his request. She saw the photos as they... I didn't want to believe it, but how could

I not believe? He *asked* her to meet him. I racked my brain for more explanations, but came up empty. Of course, there were other solutions. So, what were they? He had the photos in his briefcase and showed them around. No, that was our private cache, especially that picture of me. Our own private joke. King Tom and Queen Regina, indeed. He had other photos in his wallet; he'd never show our private cache. My mind kept coming back to the note. *His* handwriting, *his* request. There was no other explanation for her accusations. She was telling the truth. She'd been with him. Could I hear muffled laughter behind his phone calls to me from that conference? Was I imagining some tightening in his voice as her hands explored—? No, I couldn't go there. But the nagging voice in my head told me to watch carefully. He would betray himself, if it were true. And if it were, I was gone. Infidelity was the one thing I could never stand for. I watched it happen to too many others. Now I knew the monster came home to roost in my own house.

"Reg? Where are you? I'm home!"

Tom was calling from the kitchen. I was in the living room by that time. Unheard of for me. I was always in the kitchen in the summer.

"Hey! Anybody home?"

"In here." I could barely manage that. Don't think now. Don't think too much. It would only mess things up.

"Hey, there she is." Tom leaned to plant a kiss on my forehead, then plopped down next to me on the couch. He ran his hands through his hair and dropped an arm deliberately across my shoulders. "How was your day?" The question was innocent enough.

"Okay. It was okay." I didn't want to know about his. I only wanted to know about the conference.

Tom let his head drop back, then rolled it onto my shoulder, fitting into the curve of my neck, stiff as it was.

My tension was clearly not transmitting to Tom. "Tom?" I made it a question, even though I knew it was not, really.

"Umm?" His eyes were closed and he had pried his shoes off.

"Remember that conference in Chicago a couple of weeks ago?"

"Um-hmm."

My neck muscles strained for relief. That's all? No, "Why are you asking?" No, "Did I lose something?" No, "Did someone call or something?" I began tightly, "Do you remember—" Suddenly my mind flashed back to Michael, stretched over me on the couch. Michael kissing me. Michael pulling on the waistband of my shorts. Michael backing off when I said no. I did say no. I mentally firmed up that part. But now I only said out loud, "Do you remember a young woman you had dinner with?"

Tom rolled his head toward me, eyes open and—did I see it?— guarded.

"I had dinner with a number of people. We were working."

"Yeah, I know. But this one. This woman. You called me every night. You always call me, I know. This time, she was sitting next to you. On the bed."

Tom sat up and his look changed from simply guarded to fully hooded. "What are you talking about?" he said, his arm now withdrawn from my shoulder and his own shoulders hunched as if against the cold, though he was turned toward me.

Unmistakable signs. I knew she told the truth. "I think you must know, Tom." I sat sideways to look straight at him. "Tell me."

"Tell you what? That I probably had dinner with a female colleague, and then worked late? What's with that?"

I heard fear way back behind there, behind his words. But I heard defiance too.

"Look, Tom, she came to see me today. Apparently, she knew my habits. She came to see me at the coffee shop. Right there on the terrace in front of God and everybody. She turned everybody's heads, she did. Lord, she is gorgeous, isn't she? Does she make love as good as I do?" I spat out the last words, "She called me Regina Marie. She gave me the note you wrote her."

From his face, I could see he realized the implications of that. The woman knew my name. My whole name. Tom's face shifted, lowered, aged before my eyes. His hair was speckled with gray. The luster in his eyes went to matte finish. His jaw became heavy, like a ham in a cloth bag. Yes. His face said yes. It was all true.

I couldn't keep the rising anger out of my voice, even though I promised myself I would stay calm. "She saw our private photos."

"Reggie." Even Tom's voice turned ashen. "Please. She—"

"*She*—" The word was a curse.

He interrupted me. "Yes, I wrote her a note. We needed to finish up some business."

"Bring wine?" I quoted and watched his eyes go even darker.

"It was just a joke, Reg. We say stuff like that all the time. You know, work hard, then drown our sorrows. That doesn't mean we go out and get drunk."

"Some business to finish?" I said, ignoring him and making quotation marks with my fingers. "Wine and business. Let's see. What could that possibly mean? Come on, Tom. I'm not stupid. The ladies love you and you've always been a flirt."

"All right, Reg, so she came on to me, but that doesn't mean I did anything. I'd never do that to—"

I lopped him off like a gardener deadheading flowers. "No, I don't want an explanation. I don't want excuses."

"You're not listening to me. I didn't do anything." He stood up. "You need some time to cool off."

Inside my head, I cried, Stop! But that little voice was so weak and so far away, I barely heard it. I shut it down and said, "Maybe you shouldn't come back."

"What?" Tom's voice seemed honestly surprised. "Yes, I was with her, but nothing happened! Think about this. I don't want this to ruin the best thing I've ever had."

"Well, it has ruined it. So just go ahead and get out."

"Reggie, be reasonable. Let me explain."

"I don't want to hear it, Tom. I don't need to hear it."

"Yes, you do. I wasn't unfaithful."

"I've heard it all, big boy. I don't need someone who wanders. If you did it once, you'll do it again. Take what you need now, and we'll arrange for you to come and get the rest when I'm not here. Or I'll send it. Your choice." Where was my mouth taking me? But I would never say something I didn't mean.

"What about the kids, Reg"

"They're both in college, Tom. They're old enough to understand. They're on their own now. They don't need either one of us the same way they did before. Probably good it happened now, and not earlier." I felt vindictive as I saw sadness suffuse his face. I felt a kind of satisfaction in that. Guilty satisfaction, but satisfaction, nonetheless. He sat down next to me again. When his hand crept to my knee, I didn't respond, didn't move.

"Can't we at least talk?"

"I know everything I need to know, Tom. You were unfaithful. Period. We're done."

"Fine, if that's what you think. I'm telling you the truth. I did nothing with her." He took his hand from my knee. "I'll go, but this isn't the end of it. You need time to think this over. When you're ready, we'll talk." He stood up, but I refused to look up at him, instead turning to look out the window.

There was silence for a long moment. Then I heard his footsteps moving away from me. It wasn't until I heard the front door close that I allowed myself to break down.

When Tom left, I felt like a stuck zipper, unable to go up or down and causing nothing but frustration. I wanted to throw something, or scratch something, preferably Tom's face. I wanted to scream. Instead, I ran into the bedroom. I could hardly bear to look at the bed, still rumpled from the morning. I hadn't touched that room yet, but now I couldn't wait to get at it. I tore at the bedclothes, dragging them off, throwing the dirty sheets as hard as I could into a far corner. I didn't care that I stepped on the pillows. When they got in the way, I drop-kicked them into the closet.

I stumbled my way to the laundry room and stuffed the sheets into the washer, punching them down with angry thrusts. The hottest water wasn't hot enough. The cover slammed shut and I crumpled onto the floor. With only the warm rumble of the washing machine to offer comfort, I sat on the tiles. I leaned in, but nothing could take away the chill in my bones.

Chapter 35
Betty

1995

From the far bedroom that was my studio, I recognized Reggie's voice calling for me—and the tone. Anger. But plaintive anger, I thought, hoping for something, maybe.

"Where are you?" Reggie's voice rose in volume as I heard her close the front door behind her, and come down the hallway toward the studio. "Mom, where are you?"

I boxed up my charcoals as Reggie burst into the room. "Hi, sweetie," I said. I saw anguish on Reggie's face, but couldn't come up with anything more than a meaningless, "Come on in."

"How could...," Reggie began, then switched to, "Have you got...," before I cut in with, "I'll go put the coffee on."

Though I saw Reggie's red eyes and trembling lips, I ducked my head as I brushed past her and headed for the kitchen. What happened? A foreboding lump settled in my stomach, but I couldn't bring myself to ask her. Not yet, anyway. I needed to let her tell me in her own time, which apparently was going to be sooner than later. I wondered fleetingly if Reggie was pregnant. At this late age—she was, after all, in her early fifties, right at that change-of-life stage—she would certainly not welcome the news she was pregnant again.

My thoughts raced. The kitchen was warm from the late summer sun flowing in the patio doors, and the few shadows were speckled with prismatic colors from the stained-glass pieces hanging in the windows. I could hear the finches twittering and questioning as they flitted around the birdfeeder outside the window.

Maybe something happened to Em or Tim, or even Tom, but, no, that didn't make sense. It was anger I saw on Reg's face, not fear or panic. The thought passed on through. While I poured out two mugs of coffee and set them in the microwave, my hands automatically reached for plates. Along with my hands, my mind raced on. I reached into the cookie jar and grabbed a handful. Soft oatmeal cookies, one of Reggie's favorites. I released them onto a plate. Maybe that would help, somehow. I glanced over at Reggie, who deposited herself in the chair facing the patio doors, her back to me. I looked closely at the stiff shoulders, the elbows on the table. I couldn't see her face, but I read tension and anger in her back. I busied myself with the small movements of serving, all the time wondering about this apparent crisis. But I kept silent, waiting for her to begin.

She sat at the table, studying the birds. I hoped she could rearrange her anger so as not to direct it at me. Reggie's "Do you know what he did?" came out exactly at the same time as my, "There. Have a cookie, dear." Both seemed terribly inappropriate.

We looked at each other, glances scudding across, but not taking hold. I contemplated taking the seat opposite her, so I could see her face, judge what might be coming, but thought better of it and instead sat down next to her. I wanted to reach out to her, but the set of her shoulders told me I better wait. I cradled my cup of hot coffee and set my elbows on the table. When I did go so far as to reach out and pat the table in front of her, she sat up straighter. I was afraid to touch her.

Reggie began, "I've kicked him out."

For the life of me, I didn't immediately fathom who Reg kicked out. But then she lifted her face and I saw the pools of tears behind my daughter's eyes, stubbornly refusing to be released.

"Oh dear," I said. The name flashed into my mind. "Not Tom." Although I meant it as a question, it didn't come out as one, but as an answer already formed.

"Yes, Tom," Reggie snarled, her voice quiet. She took out her anger on the largest oatmeal cookie, tearing a bite off and squeezing the rest so hard I could see her fingernails turn white.

I waited.

Reggie waited too, apparently not willing to give up any of the pain and anger by just pouring it out. Maybe it had to be drawn out of her. Like pulling out stitches perhaps. No, more painful than that. Like drawing out a deep sliver.

But I waited. Would she condemn me for not probing? I just couldn't probe. She needed to tell me in her own way. Pushing would only make it more painful. But the clear pain on her face forced me. "What happened?"

"He, Tom, just—" She didn't finish. She stopped and washed down the cookie with a gulp of coffee.

I was sure the coffee was not hot enough for her. But this time she didn't complain. I didn't think she even noticed. If the coffee was scalding, the way she liked it, it would burn her throat clear down to her stomach. My mind was wandering and I brought it to task. I asked, "Where is he now?" Hedging the issue, but what else should I say?

"I have no idea. And you know what? I don't even care."

The dam was breached.

"He—*he*—was the one who walked away. He walked right into another woman's bed. Can you believe that?" Her face became blotchy as the blood rose in her cheeks, keeping pace with her anger.

I wasn't sure I could believe it. Tom? But, of course, this was my own daughter. I struggled to suppress my misgivings. "What—" I stopped Reggie in full tilt. Before she could react, I went on. "Well, I—did he tell you this? That he was unfaithful? Oh, my darling, I'm so sorry. You don't deserve that." I realized I might be saying too much. She was the one who needed to get it off her chest, after all. "I'm sorry, I shouldn't pry so." Inside, my stomach began to turn.

"You know who told me? Do you know? I cannot believe this!" she said. The whole story of the woman on the terrace of the coffee shop came sweeping into the kitchen. Just for good measure, she added Tom's denial.

For me, the lover/woman on the coffee house terrace appeared whole, fancy dress and all. But somehow, in the background, back there in the mists, stood a San Francisco hotel lobby, Earl, and the Golden Gate bridge, faint, but still almost palpable. I felt in my heart Tom could not have done this to her, but I knew nothing was impossible. Then, after that first stomach lurch, I grew angry. Angry at Tom—but she said he denied doing anything—angry with anyone who could hurt my daughter as deeply as I was hurt. Angry at myself too, but that anger I couldn't focus very clearly. I grabbed my paper napkin, ducked my head ever so slightly and pretended to dab at my mouth. I swept cookie crumbs around my plate with my little finger until I had a tiny pagoda in the center.

The story out, Reggie crumpled into her chair. She put her head down on the table, just missing her coffee cup, and released the sob that was building.

I reached out to touch her hair, so lightly I didn't think she was aware of it. But no, she stirred a bit when my fingers swept across. I was encouraged. It was the closest physical touch she allowed me in a long time. I restrained myself. Perhaps if I tried to fold her in my arms as I yearned to, she would withdraw forever.

She cried, "What am I supposed to do? What am I supposed to do?" Over and over, as if she were praying to some distant goddess who never answered directly, but only through garbled prophecies and veiled suggestions.

I, the distant goddess, tried to respond, but found I couldn't say anything useful except "I can't believe he hurt you so. How could this happen? Oh, my dear, I'm so sorry." The old bitterness of so many years ago rose in my throat. Finally, it all came together. I wanted to say, to cry out, I know what you're going through! My husband—your father—slipped into another woman's bed, and a lot happened. A lot! And he did it more than once. More than once, mind you! Tom's one fling—I know you don't believe his denial. I wonder if you've come close, as I have, close to the same thing. Tom's a good man. Your father was a good man. They are precious—and human. None of us is immune to hurt. And oh, does it hurt! It still hurts.

But I didn't say anything. At least, nothing of importance. I could get out only, "Oh, Reggie, oh, Reggie..." over and over, matching the rhythms of her mantra and tears. I wanted so much to tell her what I went through so many years ago, the pain, the unspoken words, the veiled looks and, finally, the forgiveness. But I knew it wouldn't help her. She would rearrange her father in her mind and that view would remain in the forefront forever. I didn't want that. Some things should remain sacred.

Reggie's eyes were clouded with wet and her hair came undone when she lifted her face to me and took a deep breath. "You and Daddy were so perfect," she began, ignoring my almost imperceptible head shake. "But I cannot stay with a man who has been in another woman's bed. I simply can't. So, what am I supposed to do? Forgive and forget?" Reg answered her own question. "I could never. So, now what?" She rubbed the heel of her hand across her nose, then picked up her napkin and buried her face in it.

"Oh, Reggie," I said. "I wish I had answers for you. I don't. All I can say is think about this, about everything. If Tom wants to talk, perhaps it's best to listen."

"I did listen," Reg broke in. "If I believed him, I'd take him back in a flash. But I can't do that. I heard too much. She knew too much. He betrayed me. I—"

I interrupted. Did I really interrupt? I hoped it wouldn't make her slide away from me. "Are you being too hasty? Take some time to think about this. Give Tom a chance to really talk with you."

I wanted to go on, but I was afraid I'd say too much, reveal too much, impose too much. Tom *was* a good man. Earl was a good man too. No doubt about that, either one of them. I myself found the courage to forgive, if not totally forget—how could I?—but that was a different time, perhaps. Reggie would have to find her own way. I patted her hand, stroked her hair, remembered what it was like.

"I wish I could think clearly," Reg said.

How little Reggie knew! I touched her cheek. "Reggie, you are loved by a lot of people. Surround yourself with them, and think about—" I wanted to say, what you've done, but could only manage, "everything. I'm here for you."

Reggie stood up, swiped at her eyes and cheeks, and bent to kiss my hair. "I know, Mom, I know. This is going to take awhile to sort out."

I stood up, took a chance—that kiss did it—and folded Reg into my arms, just as I did when she was little. "I'm here for you," I said. I knew I would hold tightly onto the story that might, or might not, help Reggie, a secret I would never share, a secret I would take to my grave. To compensate, I offered, "Just hold on. Be stubborn, and hold on."

Chapter 36
Betty

1996

Although the April sun was low in the sky and there was still a snow cover, my mind flew to spring. This was the spring Em would graduate from college. My, where did the years go? This winter was harsh, not so much in weather as in heartbreak. Reggie refused to talk to Tom. Tom tried to reach her, but came up against a stone wall. In fall, he moved out to a very cute, very small, and, I was sure, very lonely studio apartment and, for his part, refused to talk about divorce. I couldn't bear to turn him away in spite of Reggie being my own daughter. I didn't, after all, know the entire story. I decided it was more prudent to stay on the sidelines and continue to communicate with both of them. Not that it did much good. Reggie seemed to want something from me, but I couldn't fathom what it was exactly. I don't think she knew herself what she wanted. So, I listened on those rare occasions that she vented. At least she talked to me, although the few conversations were of the vanilla pudding variety, white and bland. Sometimes the anger came out, and then I did what I did best, I listened. I thought it helped. On the other hand, it felt like I was I standing by and watching her immolate herself.

But then I did something I never did before. I called Tom. I stood by too many times and let Reggie find her own way. Find her own way? No, that's what I told myself. What really happened was she floundered when she didn't have to. I could've helped her over the rough places in the road. Heaven knows, I had enough rough places of my own. But I refused to open my mouth and help her. A few questions, some small bits of advice, a shoulder to lean on. And now, Tom wasn't there. It was my fault. Why didn't I stop her, or at least help her see spontaneous reaction isn't always the best. I allowed her to come far too close to the cliff's brink. Maybe she stepped over already, I thought. I was afraid I destroyed her life with Tom, and affected her life with Em, by keeping my own counsel. If she never went back to Tom, part of the blame lay with me. I didn't—couldn't—tell her about her own father and how we managed to handle all of that. Even then, with Earl, I didn't say anything. But Earl understood. He knew, and so did I, and with him, nothing needed to be said. Reggie was different. She needed to have windows opened for her occasionally. Apparently, this was one of those times. But who was I kidding? She wouldn't listen to me. She'd just clam up, she was so convinced she was right. Even with the shock of my unheard of interference, she'd probably shut the door in my face, mentally, if not in actuality. Maybe I could get to her through the back door. Up until now, I kept my mouth shut because it was what I always did. Well, no more.

I called Tom. It was Thursday, a work day, and all I got was Tom's voice mail. But by that time, I was *determined* to say something, to help them see more clearly. I left a message. "Hi, Tom? This is Betty. I need to talk to you. Please, come over as soon as you can." I hung up before I could say, "Never mind." I was interfering, but I didn't care. This time, I jumped in with both feet, sink or swim. I couldn't let Reggie and Tom make what would be the worst mistake of their lives.

Now, all I had to do was wait. It scared the—the hell out of me.

On Saturday, I slipped out of bed early to paint. I gave up the potter's wheel years ago, when my hands began to stiffen, and went back to my earlier loves of watercolor and charcoal. Very different media, those. One ascending in life, one descending. Fitting for my age also. Watercolors for memory, charcoal for the end of things. I headed for my studio.

The doorbell chimed and I turned back to see who could be visiting me at this early hour. Could it be Tom? I shook my head. Hope springs eternal. Most people I knew slept late on weekends, although one who didn't was Em. She knew she could call early. But she was away at school and certainly couldn't have made the drive during this busy time in her year. I usually peeked through the front window so I could pretend not to be home if it was one of those petition-signer people. I didn't mind the Mormons or the Jehovah's Witnesses. They were always polite when I told them I was active in my own church. But it wasn't any of these. I saw jeans and the back of a familiar red jacket. I swept open the front door with both hands.

"Tom, I'm so glad you came! Come in, come into the kitchen." I didn't turn to see if he was following. In a way, I was afraid he wouldn't follow if we began this particular conversation at the door. He might flee at the slightest hint of –what? Danger? What kind of danger did I pose to him? Yet, the tension I'd glimpsed around his eyes told me he was skittish. "I've got fresh coffee," I threw back over my shoulder and saw that indeed he was right behind me.

"Good," he said. "I need a warmup. And the company's good."

I liked Tom. He knew how to treat people, warm and respectful. We got along from the first. I thought Reggie might even be a little jealous. Tom and I made each other laugh. Neither one of us was really responsible for the other and that kind of ease was priceless.

Once at my kitchen table with both of us worshipping mugs of dark coffee, Tom stole a look at me. But I was paying attention and he sighed.

I jumped in before he said anything or I lost my nerve. "I'm so glad you came. You got my message?"

He nodded.

"I want you to know I think you and Reggie are making a big mistake," I began, but he interrupted before I could add another word.

"I have to tell you something, Betty." His words emerged from his mouth like nails, hard and pointed.

I thought I knew what was coming.

"I need to tell you."

I didn't ask what. If he was willing to talk, then I needed to listen. I'd take my turn at the appropriate time.

"That affair Reg—" He couldn't go on, but I waited in silence.

He cleared his throat and took another sip of coffee. I discretely looked at the plate of coffee cake I brought out, reaching out to pick up a piece, more to have something to do with my hands and eyes than because I was hungry.

"Betty, nothing really happened in that hotel room." He stopped, hesitated, then went on more slowly. "Look, I want to tell you the whole thing, because Reggie certainly won't listen and I'm not about to tell anyone else. I know I can trust you. I need you to trust me." His voice grew deep and angry as he talked. He stopped, avoiding my eyes, staring instead at his cup. Finally, he raised his eyes to the window and began.

"You remember I was down in Chicago for a two-day conference? The team spent the afternoon together in my suite.

We went out for a late dinner when almost everything was done. One of the assistant managers and I had a few things to polish, but we figured we'd get to it after we ate. We were all laughing it up, having a good time. She—the manager—said, in front of everybody, 'Well, handsome, whaddya say? Time to sneak off together?' I played along and I wrote a crazy little note, just kidding, you know, that said something about some stuff to finish off. Then, stupid me, I wrote, 'Bring a bottle of wine.' Everybody laughed about it." Tom stopped and wiped his hand across his mouth. His eyes were pools of agony. "I thought she threw it away."

I wanted to ask how many others saw this going on? Did the others tease him too? But I kept my mouth shut and waited.

"Damn stupid decision." He spat it out. "At first, everything was fine. The meeting broke up, and the two of us went back to my suite to finish up. It didn't take long to get it all wrapped up, so then, she poured a short drink for each of us. To celebrate, she said." The edge on his voice was sharp, heading toward fury. "Another bad decision. She poured another drink. We laughed, we relaxed. She unbuttoned her jacket and took it off. She…she had nothing on underneath. Man, Betty…" He stopped again, took his hands from around his cup and cradled his head.

I was listening. How could I not? His pain and anger covered his shoulders like a heavy coat of chain mail. I wondered if he really thought I was strong enough to help him shrug it off and throw it out of the way.

He cleared his throat and moved his hands over his face, so I could no longer see his expression. "She…she came to me and dropped…well, everything. You know. From there, it was a short path to the bed. By that time, she had me undressed too. She was gorgeous, there's no denying and I was ready to go. No denying that either. But you've got to believe me, Betty…" His hands went to his lap. He swiveled to me and took my hands in his. For the first time since his confession began, he looked me right in the eye. "That's all that happened. I didn't...I got out of bed, grabbed my clothes and headed for the bathroom. I was almost afraid to come out, afraid I wouldn't be able to say no again. But I did come out and there she was, getting dressed, but looking mad as hell. I don't even remember what she said, only that she shot some profanity back at me and stormed out." He took a deep breath. "Betty, you've got to believe me. Nothing happened. Nothing!"

Tears glistened in his eyes, but he sat unashamed. I remembered the only other time I saw a man cry. Earl, when we lost our first baby. Now it was Tom. His chin began to tremble and he took his hands away from mine and covered his face once again. I reached out, as I reached out with Reggie, and touched his hair. Unlike Reggie, he immediately turned to me and hugged me tightly. Now I was crying too. When we both dried up, I handed him a napkin. I looked him clearly in the eyes and said, "I believe you, Tom." I did too.

He took a deep breath and said, "I wish Reg did." His smile tilted slightly, making it both sad and slightly ironic.

"I think she does, Tom, somewhere in the back of her head. She just needs some help in getting it out." I should be the one to talk! I could rarely get anything out. Suddenly color shot through my mind. That was the only way to describe it, color. Something warm between yellow and red and orange. Like a hot star burning. I needed to talk. It was time.

Through all of that, Tom was muttering, "I sure wish I could get Reg to see it. It was a mistake to let that woman work in the hotel room alone with me in the first place. I never should have left myself so open."

"Tom, you didn't expect it to happen. You had no reason to think she would do anything other than work." I broke in on his self-flagellation. "You know, I have an idea. Em's graduation is in

May. Come up to St. Ingrid's. You know Em wants you there. So do I."

He wiped his nose one last time. "Reg doesn't."

"How do you know? Have you spoken with her about this?"

His head gave one firm shake, side to side.

"Then you must begin the assault now." Assault? A term I never used before.

Tom looked at me with interest. "Assault?" He echoed my word. "I didn't know you had it in you, Betty, this talk of warfare. Well, what do you have in mind?"

I laid out my plans like Eisenhower before D-day. This might work. "First, ask her out to dinner. That's neutral ground and you know how she loves to go out."

He huffed. "Yeah, right. She'll love to go out with me."

"Now, listen, Tom. You've got to keep an open mind." I leaned closer to him. "We have no idea what's going through her mind, but we both know how hard it is for her to change, once she's made up her mind. And she makes it up far too quickly."

He nodded.

"So, you have to assume she wants to reach out, but either can't or doesn't know how. It's very hard for some women to lose face, especially with someone they love. So, you," and I poked him with my finger, "have to make the first move without seeming to threaten."

"I'd never hurt her," Tom said. "How could I seem threatening to her?"

"By being right," I said. "If you didn't do anything, she may already see she was wrong to react so quickly, without letting you explain everything."

"I don't get that either. Why couldn't she give me the chance to tell her what really happened?" Tom asked.

What surfaced from my own memories was the cabin at the lake, John reaching out to me and how I found myself responding to him. All this, while Earl was waiting patiently back home, waiting for me to work through the loss of our baby. "Maybe," I began, my throat dry and my voice cracking. I cleared my throat and said, "Maybe she knows someone who was unfaithful, someone else no one expected to stray. Maybe she's even been tempted herself. Who knows? And women are drawn to you, Tom, because you appreciate them. You listen and know how to treat people, all people, not just women. Perhaps that surfaced in Reggie as jealousy and fear. Honestly, I think, more than anything, she's afraid of losing you."

"But she threw me out!" Tom said. "Hasn't she lost me already?"

"Has she? Does that mean you don't love her?" I asked.

"No, of course not," Tom said. "I'd go back in a heartbeat, if she'd have me."

"Does she answer the phone when you call?" I asked.

"Lately, she answers, but she won't say anything," Tom said.

"Does she listen to what you say?"

"Yeah, all the way up to when I get frustrated and say goodbye."

"All right, then," I said, patting his hand. "Call and tell her you've made reservations at her favorite restaurant. Tell her what day and time you'll pick her up. Don't wait for her to say yes or no. Just say goodbye and hang up. Then send her flowers. The night you've chosen, dress in your best bib and tucker and show up at her door. And don't wait too long between calling her and the dinner date. Then, expect the best and it might happen." I hoped I was right, though I wasn't so sure myself if she'd accept his overtures.

"Do you really think she'll go?" His voice registered skepticism.

"Yes," I said, without allowing myself to hesitate. "Yes, I do." I added it as much to convince myself.

"All right, Herr General," Tom said. "I'll do it." He stood up, grabbed his jacket and headed for the front door. He paused, came back and kissed me on the cheek. "Thanks, Betty. Thanks for believing me." He squeezed my arm gently and left.

I watched Tom leave with a firmer step and fewer tension wrinkles on his face. Then, I went to my studio and rummaged around for a small leather-bound field sketchbook I purchased years before. I never used it because, though it was small enough to slip into a pocket, it was too small to be useful for my charcoal sketches. Ah! There it was, tucked alongside some old art books. This might be painful, but it had to be done. I needed to talk. If I could do it only through writing, then that's what I'd do.

Long ago, when Reggie came home delirious with Tom's marriage proposal, she looked like a bright angel. But now, I wasn't quite so sure we belonged in the heavenly choir. I had too many slips and falls, too many near-mishaps. At the time, she seemed blessed, so maybe she had an in, where I didn't feel I did. Rather than a bright angel, I was an angel at the gate of a garden, protecting whatever was behind me from intruders. Instead of guarding, however, now I felt I was a prisoner. Instead of standing outside the gate, I was within, looking out, and powerless to know how I got there. In wielding a flaming sword, my voice was seared into silence from the heat. What was I protecting? I spent years never turning around to check. When I did, the garden was dark.

The color that sprang so fully-blown into my mind as Tom spoke was light refracting and reflecting within my own locked garden. I saw I was imprisoned, or at least my voice was. I wasn't put on guard by some higher power, nor was I forced to stay. Earl didn't imprison my voice or make my private garden echo with only my own crescendos and diminuendos. Long before, I myself chose the path of Listener. I thought I was the guardian, building my thoughts, keeping my own counsel, making others hear what I wanted them to hear. It was a satisfying position, for much of the time. But gradually, without my notice, the flaming sword went out. Now, it didn't even glow anymore.

But somehow, from somewhere, light entered. Light from some unseen source, but surely coming through a crack, a flaw in the gate, perhaps. I was alone with only silence. Was that enough? It had been. Not anymore. I would be powerless no more. I had a voice. I needed to use it.

I sat down at my kitchen table in the early morning hour after Tom left and began to write in my little leatherbound book.

Chapter 37
Reggie

1996

When Tom called, I was adamant. "I'm not going to listen, so don't even bother." I wasn't about to talk to him now. I was still angry. And afraid.

Tom's voice on the phone sounded hollow, but I attributed that to the lines or the connection, or something else outside of himself. When I hung up, his voice was still coming out the earpiece, sounding far off and tiny, as if from the antique dollhouse in the corner.

I was still in the house we bought together. Tom refused a divorce and I didn't want to air our dirty laundry at a counseling session. Tom didn't even want a legal separation and that was fine with me. While I didn't want him around, neither did I want the ground to shift too much. Besides, crazy as it sounded, I trusted him on household matters. He never let me down in that arena and continued to do all of the things he would have done, were he living here with me. Tom didn't want the split and I couldn't turn down the good fortune of a competent financial advisor. That sounded so harsh, and more than a little crazy, but somewhere behind a door, my heart still tripped slightly when Tom was around. Though I needed him not to be around, I still...wanted him to be there too. Is that crazy?

For far too long now, we were at a stalemate. Money wasn't really a problem for either of us. Tom saw to that. He kept only what he needed to survive in the studio apartment he found. Tom never needed much. Plus, I knew he still hoped, somehow, we would reconcile. I didn't think we could, though I didn't bring myself to take steps that would burn any bridges.

However, I wasn't willing to talk about...the...the...it. It simply hurt too much. We did sit down not too long after Tom left and hashed out some things. We worked out when he could come over and take squatter's rights, as I put it, so he could stay a part of Em's and Tim's lives when they were home from college. I would make myself scarce. Sometimes I waited in the car in front of the house until Tom pulled in the driveway. I was gone quickly, however, before he could get his car door open.

I knew why he kept calling. This started months ago and I never changed the phone number. I really didn't want to go to those extremes. That would upset the applecart even more with the kids. Even at their ages, they still thought Tom sat at God's left hand—Jesus was at God's right—and had a direct pipeline to the Almighty.

If only that were true. If it were, we wouldn't be in this fix now. The Almighty would've said early on, before Tom threw back the sheets on that other bed, "Thomas, oh you of little faith. Your wife loves you dearly. Heed not the call of the temptress. Remember your vows. You made them to me and to her both. Now keep it in your pants!"

I was almost positive of that last part. Right now, I needed something to drink. The kids were gone. Em was at college, of course, doing her Resident Assistant thing for the last time. Another month—six weeks?—and Em would be graduating. Tim too was in college. Neither one of them needed me much. That was satisfying, yet sorrowful. I missed them, even though the bedrooms stayed clean and the refrigerator stayed full.

The refrigerator let out a satisfied sigh when I opened the door. Relief perhaps at having to deliver up only one little can of soda instead of half of its contents, as it had with Tim.

"Yes, it's only me," I said out loud. I devolved to talking with appliances. *To* appliances, I amended before the door shut with a whoosh. I consoled myself with the thought I didn't talk *with* appliances yet, though that might develop soon.

I explained aloud, "I'm entitled to something to drink. It's after three p.m." Though what that had to do with only a can of soda, I didn't know. Not a lot made sense anymore. I pulled a chair around to the one spot of sun coming in the back window, dragging the chair with one hand, its legs bumping lightly over the tiles. I settled close enough to the table so I could put my feet up on Tom's chair.

Tom's chair. Still thinking in terms of us. I shook my head gently, as if to dispel his face. I reached over and unlocked the patio door, slipping it open just a crack. A wet, not-yet-hot smell squeezed its way into the kitchen and expanded, like a genie emerging from the bottle for the first time in a hundred years. Fresh air finally, after another long winter, a winter a lot longer than any other for me. Granted, it was still early, but the sun was hot on the glass and the snow was gone. Daffodils stuck fingertips up above ground to test the breezes. I tilted my chin up, the better to savor the welcome air, and slid my eyes closed.

When I opened my eyes—it was not more than a couple of minutes later—Tom was standing on the other side of the glass, one hand resting on, not even gripping, the handle and the other balanced lightly, like a moth, on the door jamb.

I almost dropped the can balanced on my stomach.

"What are you doing here?" I demanded. "You better—"

Tom started to talk before I got any further. "Wait, Reg. I have to talk to you. Can I come in? I promise not to do anything stupid."

The genie of spring set loose in the open door sensed animosity and was backing off, sliding between Tom's arms and around his ears, retreating to the bottle. The fragrance of spring became wet dirt and nothing more.

"I don't think that's a good idea. We've talked all we need to."
My hands felt suddenly cold.

"Just a few minutes, Reg. For the sake of the kids." His voice
rose, as if he feared that I'd slam the patio door shut on his words,
slicing them into pieces too small to see.

I didn't move, other than to grip the soda can with both hands.

Tom's hand tightened around the handle and the door moved
with a heavy wooden sound. Although the opening was already
wide enough to step through, he hesitated.

I felt impatient, like an Imperial Somebody, waiting for the
peasant working the land to give a report. "You're letting bugs
in," I finally declared, even though there were no bugs. An
unwanted little shiver tried to find its way to the surface of my
back and failed.

He took my comment as an implicit gesture and lifted himself
into the kitchen without touching anything, as if none of this was
his, and perhaps never was, like the peasant awed by the splendor
of the palace appointments.

I held on to my haughty manners. If I didn't move out of his
path, he would stand, flat as a paper doll between the patio door
and my legs stretched out on what had been his chair.

Finally, I lowered my legs, pushed my chair back outside of the
circle of sunlight and pointed—I tried not to be imperious—to the
vacant chair. His vacant chair. I refused to offer him anything else.
Most of all, not an opening.

"Thanks." He slid the patio door shut behind him and sat,
dropped really, into the chair. He raised his hands and plowed his
fingers back through his hair. Not even gray up there yet. Gray at
the temples, yes, extending and emphasizing the crow's feet—
laugh lines, he would insist—that rayed out from his eyes. He still
was one of the best-looking men I ever saw, bar none. That shiver
finally surfaced. If things were different…

"I only…" His voice trailed off. "I wanted…" he tried again. "Hell, I need to hear you talk to me, Reg. Why won't you talk to me?"

For a man who professed to be in anguish over what the two of us were going through, along with our children, his voice was remarkably calm. I preferred to ignore the angry tone of his voice and the obvious pain in his eyes. I held myself to a high formal standard.

"I'm listening," I conceded.

"It's a start." This was said to his knees and I barely heard it. "Reggie, I love you. I need you. Why can't you understand that? You know how miserable I am. I'm trying here, babe. Please talk to me."

"I have nothing to say to you," I said.

"You know that's not true—no, wait. I'm sorry." He backpedaled when he saw me stiffen. "I promised not to make a scene, and I won't start trying to guess what you know and what you don't know. It was a stupid mistake. A stupid, stupid mistake. But I didn't do anything. I remembered you and I walked away from her."

His last sentence was clear and emphatic, though I heard the catch in his throat. It wasn't fractured telephone lines or a poor connection. I knew that all along. His voice was bleak.

Before I could take time to think about what he was saying, I forced myself to answer, "You didn't leave soon enough, babe. Not soon enough." That brought silence. "And you know it," I added, for no apparent reason. Maybe I was getting vindictive. I knew the story. She invited him, he got close. Guilt washed over me as I remembered my own close call with Michael. Before I could process and deal with it, Tom went on. I focused on the now, rather than the past.

"Yes, I know it," Tom conceded glumly. "Of course, I know I never should've suggested working back in the hotel room." Anger shone briefly under his words. "I'll never forget it. Or forgive myself either. What I need now is for you to forgive me. Or at least tell me you'll think about forgiving me." He glanced up at me and added that last part when he saw something in my face, something I hoped he couldn't really define.

"I can't promise anything like that, Tom," I said. His name felt grainy in my mouth, like sand, or salt that wouldn't completely dissolve. What did he see in my expression? Guilt? Guilt over what happened then, or what was happening now? Maybe only what he thought was a softening. Either way, I didn't want whatever he saw in my face to overwhelm my own better judgment.

"All right," he said.

I watched him inhale deeply. He apparently came to a decision. "Then how about the Ten Step Process?" he said.

"Ten Step Process?" Tom had me hooked before I even saw the line drop in the water. I thought I didn't want to get into extensive conversation. I didn't want him to sweet-talk or explain or confess or berate. But right now, my mind was oscillating back and forth too much to think straight. Get a grip, Reg! Tom was answering me before my brain kicked in again.

"Look, AA has Twelve Steps, right? Why can't we just come up with Ten Steps? You know? One a week or something so that we can come to speaking terms about this?" A half-step up in pitch. Tom was betraying his anxiety.

"There's not much in this for us," I said, moving to get up, but his hands reached my knees first and I felt the warm air as he exhaled. He moved to cover my hands with his.

I looked up, intending to hit him with a verbal left jab, and we locked eyes. It was the first time I looked him square in the eyes since that confrontation when I asked him to leave.

I knew immediately I shouldn't have done that, looked him square in the eyes. They were blue, yes, but they were no longer the smiling eyes I lived with so long. I saw honest pain there. That and unspoken pleas. He held himself in, even I could tell that much. He probably knew many of those questions or requests might not be answered. I could almost read every one of them too, but I pretended I didn't know the language, couldn't read the faded ink, couldn't decipher the secret symbols.

Behind my heart there was a surge of understanding, complete and unadulterated as any jolt of electricity screaming down a storm-filled sky. But it was gone, just like the lightning, before I fully comprehended, and I was left only with a sense of distant rumbling and profound darkness, beyond which there must be a substantial world somewhere. But that world was not visible, I realized, and might never be again.

"What?" I whispered, knowing Tom asked me something, but having no idea at all what it was.

"Let me take you out to dinner or something. No strings. Promise."

I re-connected with the real world and his spoken language at least was comprehensible.

"Maybe," Tom continued, "we can start over, one step at a time. Our own Ten Step Program, you know?"

I still could not answer. For the life of me, I couldn't decide where I should be going.

"No strings," he added, releasing my hands and sliding back from the edge of his chair.

"I—" I had no idea what my mouth planned to say.

Tom tipped his chin towards me with visible effort.

I cleared my throat, began again. "I think you better go." I felt I could write an entire book in the space that welled up at that, but I knew it was a mere heartbeat or two.

He didn't seem to hear. "I'll call you."

I saw what every word, though they sounded smooth, was costing him. Like the pain of pulling out a deep sliver. I said nothing as I watched him, as if underwater, pull the door open, step through, pull it back—almost shut.

He said, "Step one?" A short silent pause.

I didn't answer. Mother appeared in my mind, standing in the background of my life. Was I becoming her? I closed my eyes.

When I looked up, Tom was gone.

Chapter 38
Betty

1996

Even though spring was here and I could smell the early lilacs in the neighbor's yard, it was still cool enough in the early morning to wear a lightweight jacket. I shoved my left hand deep into my pocket where my fingers brushed the surface of my little leather book. After Tom came to see me, I couldn't write fast enough. Now, everything I kept locked up for years was down on paper. All the things I might have told Reggie over the years, but didn't, were there, if she wanted them. Maybe she wouldn't, but I was determined to get beyond small talk and really speak with her this time. Our conversations before were amiable, but I didn't support her enough when she was struggling. Most of the time, I felt she needed to come to grips with things; I would just get in the way or be rebuffed. We came to a quiet understanding, I thought, but the key word was quiet. I was far too quiet. This time, I couldn't step back. She was so precious to me and I wanted to support her. She needed to see what I saw, that there was more than one angle. Would she listen? Could I talk?

I opened the front door, called "Yoo-hoo!" and stepped into the house. Reggie always said to just walk in, but it was her home and I didn't want to burst in on her. I usually knocked first, before I opened the door. Today, I didn't knock. It wasn't as difficult as I anticipated.

"Hi!" Reggie said, coming around the corner from the kitchen. "What brings you over so early? Come on in."

I followed her to the kitchen, where the patio door was open a crack. I caught a whiff of lilacs.

"You want tea or coffee, Mother?" Reggie asked.

What I want is to talk to you, woman to woman. But I only said, "Coffee's fine." As I settled into the comfortable kitchen chair, I felt the top of the little leather book in my pocket bump up against my arm.

She reached for her cookie jar. "You haven't been to the nursery for your flowers yet, have you? It's pretty early."

"It is early, and no, I haven't done anything yet. Actually, I don't really need much. The condo association does most of it. But I am going to put out another pot of patio tomatoes this year. There's nothing like home-grown tomatoes in the heat of summer."

"Do you still eat them right off the vine?" Reggie smiled as she piled cookies high on a plate.

"That's the best way. A napkin and a salt shaker and I'm ready to go. The neighbors are all jealous." I really didn't come over to talk tomatoes, but I also had no clear plan of how I was going to approach the real topic—Tom. That and Reggie's stubbornness. No, shortsightedness, not stubbornness. The long-term picture, at least from my stage of life, was far more important. I thought that's what Reggie lacked, that sense of time. It moves so fast, it's too late before we even notice the warning signs.

"Do they spray the lawns? Don't you worry about pesticides?" she asked, breaking my reverie as she set the plate of cookies on the table.

"The association always sends out an alert and I bring my pots into the kitchen the day they spray."

"Watch your tongue," Reggie warned as she added a coffee mug in front of me.

I was startled. Maybe I shouldn't talk to her about this separation.

She continued as she turned to the dishwasher. "It might be too hot for you. You know how I like mine."

I mentally exhaled. She didn't know I invited myself over to talk intimately. "Your coffee has always been hot enough to scare off a jalapeno pepper," I said. That brought a smile to her face. "Come sit with me and relax for a bit. I came over to give us both a break. You can always unload the dishwasher later."

"You're right," she said, sliding the rack back in and shutting the door. "I just can't seem to sit still lately." She grabbed her mug from the counter and came to the table.

There was my opening. "So, what makes you so restless? Spring fever, maybe." I blew on my coffee and took a sip. I hoped she'd head in the right direction.

"I wish it were spring fever," she replied. "I just can't shake the feeling that life's changing somehow, moving along." She lifted her mug. "Maybe passing me by." She drank, cradling the mug with both hands.

"Em graduates this month. Maybe that's why you got the blues. Tim isn't far behind her. Empty nest, do you think?" I could maneuver this conversation to go the way I wanted.

"Maybe. I don't know. I'm feeling a bit—well, I wish—"

She stopped and I couldn't tell what she was about to say. But it was time for me to take a chance. There might not be another. "You wish everyone were here?" I ventured. I was afraid to be more specific. Even that "everyone" might scare her off.

"Everyone?" she asked, setting her mug down. "Well, they all will be here for the summer."

I knew she was covering up. The "all" would be only Tim and Em. Not Tom. But she hesitated. I could almost see Tom right there on top of her thoughts.

"Well, Em at least will be here all summer. Tim got a job at a camp for cancer survivors. He's going to be running the waterfront, so he won't be around," she said.

This was starting to veer off course. Not at all the tack I wanted the conversation to take. "What about Tom?" I lifted my coffee mug to cover myself.

"What about him?"

When I looked up, she was dipping a cookie into her coffee, delicately lowering it using two fingers. She didn't look at me. She frowned slightly.

"Well," I coughed lightly. What should I say next? But I'd better say something, fast. "I saw Tom not too long ago. He sends greetings." I knew he visited Reggie too, but not what happened. Would she tell me? My heart ached for her. She fell head over heels for Tom years ago, and now she was finding it so hard to see him as human. I wanted to reach over and tell her everything could be all right again.

"Mmm," she said, taking a bite out of her cookie and sucking the coffee out of the edge. No commitment there.

"So." I forged ahead. "Have you seen him lately? Tom, I mean?" If that wasn't blatant, I didn't know what was. I resigned myself to having her tell me to leave her alone, she was a big girl and I could just stop sticking my nose into her business. Her answer surprised me.

"Actually, yes. He stopped over and—he wanted—we talked."

"Ah." I waited, though it almost killed me. If I interrupted now, she might shut down. I had to wait.

"He, um, he wanted to take me out to dinner."

"Did you go?" I couldn't help myself. Please, tell me you did.

"Not yet," she said, then turned to give me a quick glance. I didn't know if it was for approval or out of self-defense.

"Are you—" I began and amended it to, "You could—you should go. I think it might be—fun, maybe." We were dancing around each other like two grandmas deciding who gets the last piece of pie. You take it. No, you take it, I really don't want it. No, I think you should take it. Ridiculous. Just cut the thing in half and eat it.

I opened my mouth to say, "Go to dinner, Reggie. Please." But before I had a chance to say anything, she came back with, "Why should I have dinner with him? He was playing around on me."

I heard wistfulness, not anger. Not the bitterness Tom told me about. Perhaps now was the time for my little leather journal. My hand strayed to my pocket.

"Stepping out and I didn't even know it," she mused, taking a sip of her coffee. She shook her head.

"Reggie," I began, but she cut me off.

"Once, he said. Didn't do anything, he said." She puffed air out through her nose. "But the way *she* told it, it was all too real. She saw things that were private. She had his note. She knew more than she would have if he hadn't—" She stopped, stuffed her knuckles in her mouth and set her elbow on the table so hard it rattled both of our mugs.

"Reggie," I tried again, "I think he's telling you the truth."

"The truth?" she came back. "That nothing happened? He wants to tell me the whole story, but I don't need to hear how—when—"

I interrupted her. "Maybe you do, Reggie. Maybe what you think is the truth isn't the truth. He may not be perfect, but I think he's telling you the truth. He knows he's not perfect. No one is." I paused, but not long enough for her to get a word in. "You, my dear, are a wonderful mother and wife. I just hate to see you in such pain. Tom is not the type of person to fail you. I think we've all been tempted at one time or another." John at the lake appeared as a clear vision in my memory. "With all the good-looking men out there, even I like looking." I hoped I wasn't being too flippant.

She smiled a bit crookedly. "Eye candy for the eighty-somethings, eh?" She shifted in her chair. "But window shopping is one thing. Making a purchase is another."

"Perhaps he only went into the store, you know." I continued her metaphor. "Maybe he got so very close, but decided the price was simply too high."

"That's pretty much what he was telling me. He thought of me, of the kids, and backed off. But Tom. He's—well, he's—"

"Passionate," I filled in. "He's passionate."

"Yes," she said. "Passionate. I don't know that he could stop himself, even if he wanted to."

"Trust me," I said, "with someone like you to come home to, he'd stop himself." I sat back in my chair. She did the same. For the first time all morning, she looked directly at me. I was afraid to say another word. I wasn't used to doing this. If I pushed too hard, it could so easily break apart.

"I wonder—" she said. She didn't complete the thought, but I could see by her eyes she was no longer in the kitchen with me, but somewhere far away, somewhere I could not follow. As much as that might upset me, it had the opposite effect. She was thinking and, under the circumstances, I couldn't do anything but wait.

I came to her to get the wheels turning. I promised myself I would tell her everything she needed to know, *if* she needed to know. I would give her my little leather book and let her judge— or better yet, not judge—whether she was doing the right thing. We both faced terrible choices and I wanted her to see there was more than one way out. I lived through a lot more than I ever talked about. What would be the purpose of telling her of my struggles? Earlier, I thought there was no purpose. But now I saw there could be value in those dark pits. I survived. Not only that, I thrived. I still loved Earl and he loved me. We made it past any number of crises. I could help her get past this one.

"Maybe," Reggie pulled me out of my thoughts. She was back in her own kitchen. "Maybe I should agree to have dinner with him. Do you really think that's a good idea?"

At that point, I could have given a ten-minute speech extolling the virtues of saying yes, but even though my heart was full and I was beginning to tremble inside, I simply said, "I do." I slipped my hand into my pocket and touched my little leather book. Then, before I lost my nerve, I said, "I—I brought something for you." Even though I desperately wanted her to read it, I didn't want to be around to see her reaction. I'd hand her the book on my way out the door. "Walk me to the door?" I stood up and shoved the chair in.

"Sure," Reggie said, but her face showed a mixture of surprise and confusion. "What did you bring me?"

When we got to the front door, I pulled it open before reaching into my pocket. I drew my little leather book out. "This," I said. It lay flat and comfortable in my hand. The book was heavy with my essence.

"What is it? It looks like a journal," Reggie said, extending her fingers to take it.

But I covered it with my free hand. "Wait. This is not just any journal." I forced myself to go on without thinking ahead too much. "Reggie, you and I have never been ones to share pain or glory. To a certain point, of course we do. But," I glanced down at the book in my hands, "when tough times come along, we tend to keep our own counsel. No, let me amend that. *I* keep my own counsel."

She nodded, but her forehead was furrowed and she still looked confused.

"I'm afraid I should have done more, said more, maybe asked more questions. But..." I indicated the book. "I did this for you. Maybe it will fill a few holes." I raised my hands. "After you read it, promise me you'll..." I had no idea what I wanted her to promise me, but then it came to me. "Promise me you'll not judge too harshly." I removed the hand which covered the book, offering the little volume to her like a visible prayer.

"I promise." Her voice was full of questions, but she only crossed her heart in the age-old children's oath and stretched her hands to mine. Her grasp clasped both the book and my hand underneath.

Sliding my hand out from under hers, I relinquished control of the book. I gave her a quick smile and slipped through the door, throwing, "Bye-bye, we'll talk later," over my shoulder. I left her standing with the book nestled between her hands.

Chapter 39
Reggie

1996

"Bye, Mom." I went back to the kitchen, still holding the book my mother handed to me. What was this, anyway? She acted so strange about it, giving it to me and then bolting, like a frightened deer. I sat down in the chair she just vacated. It was still warm. I curled one leg under me and let my curiosity take over. Opening the book, I recognized my mother's handwriting, page after page. Only the last three were blank.

I wanted to sit down and consume whatever it was she wrote, but the book deserved more than that. I had to slow myself down, somehow, or I was afraid I'd miss the whole point. *All right*, I thought, *let's just pick a place. Not the first page, or I'd be hooked.* I opened to a random spot.

"I knew what I would give them for their anniversary. The juice glass in the photo."

That's what she gave us for our fifteenth anniversary, the special juice glasses. I smiled, remembering. I flipped through more pages, just letting my eyes rest on a phrase or two as the leaves fanned by. I couldn't believe it. This was her journal. I let my hands fall into my lap and gazed out the window, though I was seeing my mother, not the backyard. Her journal? I never thought she had much of a story to tell, but here it was, crammed into all but three pages of this thick little book. Amazing. I picked another random spot to stop and read.

Earl walked away from her. Walked toward me. Back to me. I would not allow her to destroy that image of him coming toward me. I placed her behind him, where I couldn't see her for his bulk coming closer and closer toward me. Towards me.

What? "Her"? What was that all about? I backtracked to the beginning of the entry. By the time I reached the part I originally read, I stopped breathing and I could hardly see through my tears. I needed to stop and process. I set the book on the table, watching my hand perform that simple movement, but wondering, in shock, how my body could act so normal when my mind was in turmoil. I stood up and stacked the dishes.

I told myself I was going to clean up, but what I really wanted was to get my head around what was happening to me. And what happened to my mother.

I filled the sink with hot water and soap and plunged my hands in. Even though I had a dishwasher, sometimes the rhythm of doing dishes by hand helped calm me. I was forced to stand in one place and I could watch the dishes accumulate, all stacked up neatly, rinsed and squeaky clean. Kind of like scrubbing my troubles and then washing them down the drain. It was cheap therapy.

Now that my wrists were invisible under the suds, where was I going from here?

Was it true my own father...? An affair? Oh, God! How she must have suffered!

It couldn't be true.

Of course it could. Mother would never—never—create a story about such a thing. She'd think everyone would blame her for his transgressions. Wouldn't she? At the very least, it would embarrass her. She didn't have any reason to create something like that. But they were happily married, I know that. I watched them over the years. I couldn't see my own father... She must have gone crazy when she found out. I can just picture her yelling and throwing things at him.

No, I can't. She wouldn't do any of that. She'd keep it to herself. How on earth did she cope? Her pain must've been massive. Like mine. She never talked about it. Nothing, no sign. She didn't leave him. She probably didn't even threaten to leave him. But she did do one thing. She forgave him.

Was Mother right? Maybe I should meet with Tom. Was he really telling me the truth, that nothing happened? The Tom I knew was so straightforward and passionate—Mother's word fit—I couldn't picture him stopping himself if she, that other woman, got him going. But that's the way he was with me. Maybe with a woman who wasn't his wife, maybe he wasn't that way. I never thought about it before, never figured I needed to. When he touched me, we didn't slow down. Even when the kids were babies, we found time and a place. Sometimes even the way he looked at me across a room at a party could make me flame and I could hardly wait to get home. But was he that way with any other woman? I never saw any evidence of that. Never.

Tom used to bend down and kiss me right below my earlobe.

My breath stopped, on a sudden inhalation, at a picture of Michael at the workshop so many years ago. Michael, pressed to me and kissing my neck. I could almost feel his mouth move from there to—

I leaned forward, spreading my fingers flat against the bottom of the sink. My eyes were closed, but I could see Michael still. I could feel everything I felt then too. The rise in me, unbidden and strong, urging me forward, wanting him. I thought I was trapped in a way, because he held me down, lying full-length on me, fondling me. But I saw now I wanted it as much as Michael. I responded to him, and not just in a physical way either. I replayed it all in my head, dredging it out and slowing it all down. The edges were fuzzy, but it was all there.

Michael had filled a small emptiness, the spot we all have that asks, "Is this the whole thing? Is there more?" Why do we even have to ask that? No, why do I have to ask that? I have everything

I need. I can't have everything I want. No one gets everything they want. Somewhere along the line, we—I—have to come to terms with that. I thought I came to terms when I backed off from Michael. I had everything I needed. More.

I could trust myself, but I couldn't trust Tom? How crazy was that?

I exhaled, slid my hand over to the sink drain and let out the water. I rinsed the soap off my hands and reached for the towel. As the last of the water slurped noisily down the drain, I picked up the phone. I didn't need to look up the number. It didn't ring more than twice before he picked up.

"Tom? It's me. When did you want to go out for dinner?"

Chapter 40
Betty

1996

When I was a coed at this college, St. Ingrid's, I had flaming red hair. I wore frocks, gloves and hats and never went out without hose. Except when I was golfing. Understand, one could not wear just anything. Skirts were not *de rigeur*, but were still favored by most. I adopted pants whenever I could, to the everlasting consternation of Sister Joan.

But now, I see Em graduating from my college and she takes me back in time. I am outside of my skin, looking at the me of sixty-odd years ago. The milling graduates no longer look like a herd of sheep with their white graduation gowns. The college went to black academic robes about the same time they merged with the Jesuit college over the rise.

Hemlines go up and down like the economy, hairstyles go from frouzy to beehive and back again, but some things never change. The quad is still there, faced by the dining hall and dorms and sundry other small buildings like a gaggle of nieces gathering behind and around their favorite aunt. Some buildings house other things than when I walked these paths. My dorm, with the wide sweeping steps, was turned into administrative offices. The entrance is both imposing and welcoming, perfect for the registrar's offices. Most of the trees in the quad grew so much larger, but there are holes where lightning strikes or chainsaws have thinned the ranks. Flowerbeds ooze like honey gone astray around the few largest trees. My particular favorite, a queenly sugar maple, is still there reigning over all the rest. In fall, it blazes with uncommon heat, as if the leaves in full color will burst into real flame at the smallest hint of bellows in the wind.

Graduates continue filling the quad, getting ready for the ceremony in the stadium, not necessary in my years there. Our sports were not for public consumption, but took place on The Field, which still retains its athletic name, though few remember the real battles of field hockey and archery that took place there. As for me, I maintained what minimal decorum I had by playing intramural basketball in the required uniform of tea-length skirt and sleeves that modestly hid my shoulders. I look at my participation medals now and laugh outright at the girl in bas-relief, reaching gracefully for what appears to be the rise to a slam-dunk, but most certainly would not have been called that by any of our coaches, all of whom were nuns. However, underneath a few of those veils and wimples beat the hearts of women athletes, ahead of their time in their joy, hampered still by some form of religious guilt because they were training young women to aspire for more, both on the field and in the classrooms. For the greater glory of God and men. Appropriate that we merged with the Jesuits next door. I don't think the sisters knew how far-reaching their efforts would be. What they hoped to sweat out on the basketball and volleyball courts in order to produce women who knew their places, and the manners to go with those places, turned out to be assertiveness for some and, eventually, a strong sense of self-worth in most.

Changes that flowed across the years could not have been easy. Money shortages and diminishing numbers forced those grand women into compromise of sorts, that merger with the Jesuits. I imagine Mother Superior saying, "Now, Fathers, we need to work as a team here. Our girls are precious to us." She made that clear to all of us then, and would not have made the move without a firm assurance that "her girls" would command the same respect as the Jesuits' men.

Men. Sister Joan must be turning in her grave. Her obituary was published in one of the alumni newsletters years ago, I don't remember how long. As troublesome as she was, I can look back now, retired teacher that I am, and see that she was trying to do the very best for us. We were independent women in a women's college where the teachers and administrators trained and questioned and demanded our best. We were to be women who could hold our own in a conversation with our husbands' associates and their wives.

Sometimes, the more things change, the more they stay the same. Listening to the talk around me, young women are still going to college to troll for men, although that is certainly not the only reason, and many are adamant this is not a factor at all. I doubt that. Overall, the desire that drives us the hardest is biology. None of us saw that. I think the young women milling around the quad today—my own granddaughter included—still don't see that so clearly.

This might sound like grand digression, but somehow I've come full circle, preparing to stand here watching my own granddaughter, as if I am outside of myself, watching both of us bridge the years.

How late we come to clarity! What was I seeing in those early years, gazing placidly through rose colored glasses? I thought the fog was merely lovely clouds. I saw myself as an angel at the gate, protecting and allowing passage. Only recently have I realized, with a small shock, I was not at the threshold, but inside, oftentimes locked in and unable to see who was waiting outside. I trained to hold myself as a useful and fragile vessel to be guarded by myself alone, even while providing service. I was that for many years, the useful vessel, content to fill myself with others' needs. But I spent more years only listening from within my own confines than I care to admit.

I'm surrounded by milling families. Even though St. Ingrid women graduates all seem to look alike, we can pick out our own lamb from the flock without error. They're not sheep anymore, unless they count as black sheep in those black gowns. I chuckle at the sudden vision of Em's cigarettes, finally tossed away without her mother—Reggie, my daughter—knowing anything about that particular nasty habit. I wonder how much of my little book Reggie has read, how many of my habits and foibles she discovered. On the ride up to the college, we talked about everything but that. I was relieved at the time. After all, one can't just step out of a moving car. But now, I wonder...

"Gram! Over here!" Em spotted me through the crowd, and I turn to her voice. She reaches me and encircles me in her arms, monk-like sleeves engulfing me. I can feel the strand of pearls around her neck pressing between us. Reggie's pearls. My pearls. Her arms rest lightly on my shoulders, not with the exuberant abandon of years past. She is attentive to my increasing fragility. My shoulder is chronically painful, and I have slowed a great deal, though I can still walk nicely. No walker, no wheelchair. Even at eighty-four, I don't really stoop.

I could just be fooling myself. We all look in the mirror and see "too fat" when we are blooming in our prime. In middle age, we lie on our backs in bed and stroke our flat bellies, knowing in our hearts that once we stand upright, our bellies are not flat at all. So maybe I do stoop, but I don't feel like it. Isn't that what counts?

"How was *your* graduation here?" Em asks. Her voice is muffled against my neck before she pulls back, pecks me on the cheek and slides her arm across my shoulder, my good shoulder.

"We didn't have nearly as many graduates as you have, of course. We were just the women then. The Jesuits stayed on their own side of the hill."

Her laugh bubbles. "The Invasion of the Men in Black! Must've given your nuns heart failure."

"Some of them. I know a few welcomed it though. The Jezzies had better science labs, and that was a real plus. Secretly though, I think some of those sisters were figuring they would finally have a chance to domesticate the wild males who were always prowling the edges of our campus."

"Didn't work, did it?" She nuzzles my hair.

"Of course not. But it was fun to try, I'm sure," I answer. "Apparently, they all came to some kind of understanding." I pull her closer to me with an arm around her waist. "The place seems to be thriving."

"It is. I love it. Thanks for planting the idea of coming here."

I pull back a bit in mock horror. "I did no such thing, and you know it."

"Well, I love it either way. Oh, look!" She points at the sky above the quad. "Mares' tails. That means the weather is about to change."

The long, filmy clouds move like fine veils across the blue. "In my day," I say, "Sister Joan called them angels' wings. She said the angels were protecting us and the clouds were a sure sign of that."

"Angels' wings," she says. "I like that. Whenever I see them, I'll think of you. You'll be my protecting angel, just like the clouds." She slips her arm off my shoulder and links her arm with mine. "Come on, let's go find Mom."

"She's right there." I point toward the wide green sward before the big sugar maple. "With your father."

"Together?" Her voice rises to her childhood register, betraying her adult body.

"I asked her to invite him, but I didn't know if she actually did," I admit. "But *I* did."

She gives me a conspiratorial look. "Looks like we're lobbying them from all sides."

We both giggle.

She turns to watch her mother and father, a large gap between them, trying to stroll naturally across the quad toward the big maple. I see some tension in Reggie's back, the lack of rhythm in her shoulders. Tom's hands slide into his pockets. I see the tip of his nose appear and disappear in the sunlight as he turns to her and away again. I see clearly, but I can't hear anything. Are their lips even moving? Are they communicating at all? Of course they are. It just may not be with words.

A protecting angel, Em says. But who was I protecting? Myself? My daughter? I thought both. But now I look up at the clouds and decide I've not done either, but only sealed the entrance, melting it shut with my flaming sword. Did I seal Reggie in—or out—too? I sincerely hope not. It's all in my little leather book. If she reads it. No, I know she'll be curious enough to read it. I hope she believes it. It's the only thing that'll free the lock.

Reggie and Tom stop at the tree and finally turn toward each other, Reggie twisting, Tom moving smoothly.

"What do you think they are saying?" Em, like a small puppy, sidles up close.

"Mmm." My brow crinkles. I don't want to say; I'm not sure.

"Maybe," she hears only her own hopes, "maybe they're talking about seeing each other more. You know they had dinner together last week."

Did that work? Words I never dream of saying out loud. Words spoken only in my own heart. Is this too much silence again? "It's a good sign," is what I really say.

Tom's hands are out of his pockets and Reggie holds her shoulders a bit forward.

"They really do love each other, you know," she adds in my ear.

"I know they do. I hope they're able to tell each other that."

We squeeze one another, as if our combined hopes and thoughts will become even stronger and somehow, like a Flash Gordon ray gun, shoot out all our hopes to the couple under the tree.

"Here they come." In a quick glance, I see movement under the tree. We turn toward Tom and Reg. They moved closer together, though we both missed who moved first. Tom moves slightly and offers his arm to Reggie. There is a moment. An almost audible click. Then, Reggie slips her hand slowly yet deliberately into the crook of his arm. His hand covers hers and they walk toward us, this time clearly engaged in conversation.

"Well, I'll be..." Em says, her voice hardly moving the air between us. She comes back to me like a swimmer surfacing. She glances quickly at Tom and Reggie matching steps, then looks back at me, raising her eyebrows. We trade smiles.

"Hey, ladies!" Tom's voice reaches us before he does. "Who are these two gorgeous St. Ingrid grads?"

"Almost," Em corrects her father as he slings his free arm across her shoulder and plants a kiss on her hair. "Almost grad, for me."

"Okay, almost grad, you win. But you're still both gorgeous." Then he turns to Reggie and flashes that special smile of his. "Not as beautiful as this one, however."

Reggie ducks her chin for a moment. When she looks up at him, her eyes glimmer. She touches his arm ever so lightly and raises an eyebrow.

"Well," he says, taking whatever hint she's dropping. He loosens himself from Reggie and Em, "I'm off to stake out places for us. Look for me midfield." He snaps off a smart salute and heads toward the stadium.

Reggie draws both Em and me into her embrace. "So, here we are. Come full circle, at last. You've done very well for yourself." She hugs Em and gives her a brush of a kiss on her cheek. She turns to me. "And so have you."

I'm taken by surprise. What on earth is she talking about? But my good manners take over and I answer, without thought, "Thank you." I open my mouth to ask more, but she removes her arms from us and holds up a finger for quiet.

Reggie swivels to Em, then reaches into her purse. Before she withdraws her hand, she locks eyes with her daughter. "I have one very important gift for you today."

I see it coming before it happens.

"This," she says, "is the most precious legacy you'll get." She pulls my little leather-bound book from her purse and holds it out in front of Em. "We three women hold a bond among us and this—" She taps the cover. "—is the proof. Pearls of wisdom, Em."

I know she's talking to me, though she's looking at Em. *Well, perhaps a handful of pearls*, I think.

"Never forget the stories, Em. They will help you through all the good times and bad. They helped me through mine." She extends the book.

"Remember," I begin. Reggie and Em both pause in midmotion. "Read the words, but pay just as much attention to the spaces between. Sometimes the silences say as much, if not more, than the sentences."

I have exhausted my supply of both words and silences.

Reggie says, "Thanks, Mom" and, before she sees the tears in my eyes, again proffers the book to Em, who lifts it, like a princess accepting a jeweled corona, caught in the depth of the moment.

Reggie shifts to stand next to me, slipping her arm around my waist. I return the favor, feeling the warmth of her back along my arm.

Em opens the little leather book. Seeing the scroll of my name on the first page, her eyes sparkle. She leans over and kisses both of us. "Let's see what wisdom you have for me," she whispers and begins to read.

"I learned to play golf so I could smoke..."

THE END

About the Author

After earning her Bachelor and Master degrees, Mary Ann Noe taught 7th grade, followed by high school English and Psychology. Retired, she now spends time gardening, reading, writing, and communing with nature. Eons ago, at age nine, her first short story was one of those Buler-Lytton prize-winning gems, starting, "The midnight clock struck in the billage. Bong! Bong! B—" So much for the Pulitzer Prize in literature. Much of her early poetry probably lined the bottom of birdcages. Eventually, however, she learned the slash and burn of editing and rewriting doesn't leave scars. Since then, Mary Ann continues to publish short stories, poetry, nonfiction, photography, and the novel *To Know Her*, 2021.

Visit www.maryannnoe.com for her blog, photos, contact link and more.

Note from the Author

Word-of-mouth is crucial for any author to succeed. If you enjoyed *A Handful of Pearls*, please leave a review online—anywhere you are able. Even if it's just a sentence or two. It would make all the difference and would be very much appreciated.

Thanks!
Mary Ann Noe

We hope you enjoyed reading this title from:

BLACK ROSE
writing™

Subscribe to our mailing list – *The Rosevine* – and receive **FREE** books, daily deals, and stay current with news about upcoming releases and our hottest authors.
Scan the QR code below to sign up.

Already a subscriber? Please accept a sincere thank you for being a fan of Black Rose Writing authors.

View other Black Rose Writing titles at
and use promo code
PRINT to receive a **20% discount** when purchasing.

CPSIA information can be obtained
at www.ICGtesting.com
Printed in the USA
LVHW031519060522
717695LV00004B/19